ETERNAL LOVE TRILOGY II

HAPPIER EVER AFTER

TIME TRAVEL TO PARADISE

STEPHEN ST. JOHN

Edited, Designed and Distributed by Bublish, Inc.

ISBN: 978-1-64704-365-0 (paperback)
ISBN: 978-1-64704-364-3 (eBook)

Eternal Love Trilogy:

Beyond Time
Antony, Cleopatra, and Janie

Contents

1

One Piece at a Time

There are times when you can't tell real life from a nightmare. There are times when real life is a dream come true. Karen knew both—but that morning, she couldn't tell the difference.

"I wanted to weigh *less*, but not *zero*. Where did my body go? Is anyone there? Is anyone here? Is anyone anywhere? Where am I? Hello! Hello! Great—no arms—no head—no little toe. On the other hand, nothing itches. Something always itches. Wouldn't mind having a butt to scratch right now—I want my ass back!"

"You're not the only one," said Janie, suddenly sharing the bodiless, black nowhere. "Cindy says it's all Andre dreams about. You broke his heart, Karen."

"For the hundredth time, he never proposed. Therefore, I never said 'no.'"

"You didn't have to. Computer Cindy said it for you. She read your pod sleep scans and reported every nightmare to Andre—who, I will say, never asked her to."

"That meddlesome bitch," said Karen. "Who does she think she is? Where does she get off? I have half a mind to eject her from Explorer

Seven. I'm still in command. Floating in space with a half dozen solar panels will teach her a lesson. When we get back, I'll send a droid for her."

"So why *did* you reject the boy who beat Einstein, who waits on you hand and foot, and whose only desire is to spend the rest of his life playing full-size dollhouse with you?"

"So you say. But I'm not convinced, and he is not the man I fell in love with. Why does life do this? When we left The Bang and headed home, everything was crystal clear. Two weeks later, nothing was. My perfect world disappeared."

"Nothing is ever perfect," said Janie. "Looking for the perfect 'one' is silliness, like demanding absolute happiness or not one black Monday. But there are many men out there who are almost perfect. Someday, I'll wish my daughter good luck in finding her 'close as it gets.'"

"I underestimated you, Janie. Thanks for being my best friend."

"I thought Sarah was your best friend."

"She is, when I'm with her. See—I'm not sure about anything anymore."

"That's not true," said Janie. "You are absolutely certain that you are not certain."

"Ha, thanks! I needed that. So, what am I to do?"

"Do you love Andre?"

"Oh my God, I don't know," said Karen. "Men wrap up life in little bundles, slap on a label, and skip away humming. It's not like that for me. Sure, I have my days when the air sparkles and life hits top-shelf: my man, our quarters, family plans. And then I look down a long hallway or come across a panorama of a field of grass bowing under the west wind at sunrise, and I just can't stand still. It's like there's someone else inside of me."

"This hallway you talk about," said Janie, "is there a man at the end waiting for you?"

"I wish I knew. I run as fast as I can to get there, but I always wake up before I find out. I suppose you could call that a nightmare. Or just life."

"Karen, we're all screwed up, and relationships are random. Absolute answers don't exist. Nothing gets it completely right—not narrative fables, not your dating programs, not Cyber Cindy. First impressions start it off. Holding hands is the next Rorschach. Kissing is the third, followed by a night together. But no one—that's right, no one, my dear, not a one of us in this universe—knows for sure until the morning after. And if it works, then we know with one hundred percent certainly…that it worked…then. Many years from now, we add up all those 'thens' and thank God from the bottom of our hearts, maybe with the first 'then' beside us, or, just as luckily, the last."

"Thanks again, Janie. You know that *I'm* the PhD who should be advising *you*."

"I won't tell if you don't. Besides, thanks to time travel, we're about learn from the best. After playing 'monkey see, monkey do,' I plan to govern the ancient world as Cleopatra and make mad love to Mark Antony. Brad decided to dine with Alexander the Great. He wants to help plan the campaign to conquer the world. Andre will be trouble as always. He wants an entire week to discuss existence with Socrates, share spiritualism with Plato, and then redesign civilization with Aristotle. The good news is that Michael just wants to play Tarzan with Sarah."

"And Sarah?" asked Karen.

"A swan gliding across Crystal Lake."

"So—monkey Michael loves swan Sarah, you're in love with Alexander the Great's right-hand man, Andre is looking forward to a week of goat cheese, and I haven't the slightest idea what or who to do, even though I did tell Andre to put me down as Mary Magdalene for a night."

"A walk of pride that will last a lifetime!" said Janie. "That cuddle you *will* share with me."

"Meanwhile, did silicon-brain screw up again? Why are we trapped in Nowhereville? What's going on? I see nothing, taste nothing, feel nothing. I only hear your words in my head. No wait, I don't have a head! I *do* have a head somewhere, don't I?"

"Of course you do. Your body is lying next to mine in the consciousness transfer lab. We're fine. Just think the words, and Andre can disconnect the remote encephalographic input and return your personal identity to your prefrontal cortex. Then you walk away. The hard part is tapping into the sensory and motor systems of the animal bodies we are about to enter on the planet below. Andre sent me. Stand by. Cyber Cindy is about to begin adding one neurologic input at a time."

"Oh, there we go, Janie! I am starting to feel a body! I'm something covered in hair, which itches. I'll never complain about itching again. Ooh…that's more like it…I feel four legs, or are they arms? That I'm not moving, and someone is rubbing my ass—thank you."

"That's the host animal, who will operate its normal motor functions till the last second, when Cindy will drop the critter to deep sleep for us to take over."

"Wait a minute!" exclaimed Karen. "Cyber Cindy made a mistake! Something is sticking out! Oh, okay—it's a tail. For a second there I thought I was packing testosterone, heaven forbid."

"Did someone call for testosterone?" chimed in Brad from the abyss.

"How long have you been here?" asked Karen.

"Just arrived. The others are one their way. As soon as we're all assembled in the holding zone, we'll pop to the surface one at a time. Cowabunga! Not seeing is believing. Andre told me seeing black is when you close your eyes but seeing nothing is what's behind your head. Wow! Being and nothingness. Andre might make me a philosopher after all. It's amazing how many things I take for granted, except my sweet, sexy lover, Janie. Is she here?"

"You know I am," whispered Janie. "And keep it coming."

"What's the problem, Brad?" Karen said, enjoying feeling her tail wiggle in an undeniably flirtatious fashion. "We instantly jumped into flatworms, iguanas, and octopuses. Andre guaranteed me a smooth ride. Men—they promise you paradise, swear we're all they live for, and then rush off after breakfast to save mankind, redesign an exhaust pipe, or change a bolt. I swear, sometimes it's like we aren't even here."

"Octopuses!" Janie giggled. "Michael said he could DNA augment a female octopus with a love hole for every arm. An octopussy octopus— eight orgasms at the same time. Can you imagine?"

"I can, and did someone mention my name?" said Michael's voice as it approached them. "I bear glad tidings. Andre says all is going well. Squeezing us into monkey brains is just taking a little longer than he expected."

"Michael," Karen said sharply, "did you know that Cindy has been sneaking behind my back and sharing private information with Andre? He must have copied our deception schemes for Cindy's hardware."

"She did ask to be a female. Did you just admit that women scheme?"

"Michael," Karen answered in a smooth but scary tone, "do you want the truth about our last night in Saint Martin?"

"I know the truth about what it meant to me. Only an imbecile asks for a report card. Besides, certainty is not your strong suit, and without intending it, I will concede that you ladies cloud truth with sincerity in a way that sends reason flying. Our plans haven't a chance. We end up turned upside down. And for the record—I surrender."

"Does Sarah turn you upside down, Michael?" Janie asked.

"Every direction Sarah turns me keeps me smiling."

"That's not what I heard," said Karen, aiming below the belt.

"Hold it," said Sarah, briskly entering the chamber. "All I said was that my sweet Michael has a favorite position, and I'm the only one who knows what it is. But get ready, everyone. Andre is right behind me. Let's vote to leave him back on the ship before it's too late. Every time he opens his mouth, it's Sunday morning go-to-meeting time. There's a limit. The guy has got to give it a rest."

"You get off easy," monotoned Karen. "For the entire month after he was irradiated, Andre would get out of bed every morning and thank God for yesterday's orgasm, as if I had nothing to do with it."

"Is that why you won't marry him?" Michael asked.

"Stop pestering me, everybody. He never proposed. I didn't decline. We're just on a break."

"Great day everyone," said Andre. "We'll be primates any second now."

"Oh, oh, Andre's here." Sarah warned.

"Yes, I am," he replied, "and we shall share this day with intelligent creatures of want, whose very existence brings forth meaning. The symphony of mankind plays to a higher being. Thanks be to God!"

"Amen. Let's go," jumped in Brad.

"We will do love one better," Andre proclaimed, "as faith in the Lord our God weaves every fiber of our destiny."

"AMEN, AMEN, AMEN…NEXT!" chimed in the other four from the endless black void of oblivion. "GET US OUT OF HERE!"

2

Pliocene Playmates

Karen believed the universe took special care of Mother Earth—the planet that never rests, beats with a heart as warm as the Sun, and uses magnets to protect her children, which that day also included Andre, Brad, Janie, Michael, and Sarah, all longing for the morning their starship would return them to their own time, still millions of years and thousands of generations into the future.

Once upon a time, Karen's home was a simmering ball of space scum crusted with mineral rock plates a hundred miles thick, which floated, slipped, and slid around. Two hundred and fifty million years prior to the day's visit, the largest slab, the giant southern continent Pangea, called it a day. It split into India, Australia, the Americas, Eurasia, and Africa—the amusement park of the day and habitat for living relatives of every crew member onboard Explorer Seven.

Karen was the first to drop down, suddenly finding her trailing left hand letting go of a bent branch sixty feet up, her right arm and both legs already out front, preparing to snag extensions of the towering conifer approaching.

"Midair without fear or hesitation," she thought, "uninhibited exuberance above lush fernery, below blue skies, and beside a troop of friends. The last time I felt like this, I was seven, in mom's backyard, pushing off my swing to glide to the soft sands of the earth. Where have I been all these years?"

Michael had practiced his routine in the gym: forward cartwheel… two hands up…spin…grasp with feet, and 360 was history. "Yahoo! Ride 'em, cowboy! It's like downhill freeride skiing on Mount Everest surrounded by pals and babes. Let beauty ride, thrills build, and love triumph!"

"Janie, is…that…you in front of me, rubbing your happy place with mine?" Sarah said through cyber channels, barely controlling hysterical laughter.

"Go ahead and laugh," she replied. "Your legs are just as hairy as mine, and it feels great. And I do love the part down the middle of your head! Very attractive coiffure. You simply must give me the name of your stylist."

"Certainty, just ask for right hand and spit."

Nature's specialty of the day, a rainbow blend of her best, was a primate species accompanying the Congo River, surrounded by broad-leaved forests, vast grasslands, and flowering plants—a warm, moist climate ideal for arboreal living.

The flat-faced, pink-lipped primates the gang joined had long legs, small heads, narrow shoulders, and a build more slender than the average ape. They also loved water. Two and one-half feet tall and weighing in under ninety pounds made every male a pigmy, females twenty pounds lighter, both black-skinned and hairy, with white anal tufts guiding the way.

"What's that *smell?*" Brad said with obvious distain the moment he found himself swinging slowly back and forth from one arm ten feet off the ground.

"That's poop, silly," Sarah said below him, looking up. "Welcome to life without a bidet."

"How uncivilized," he replied. "Janie, is that also you? My, my, *my!* Andre, wherever you are, look down. The females on the ground who look like two scissors stuck together are Sarah and Janie. They're muscling in on our territory."

"I'll be right there," Andre said, flying down on a vine for a perfect two-point Olympic landing. "Brad, it's helpful to remember that a living biosystem is a highly technical genetic behavioral motif."

"Which in English means?"

"Every behavior we witness empowers survival because it has survived, and the fun ones are a double win. It also means transforming has begun."

"Again, Andre…define," Brad said, backing away from one butt after another.

"The brain stem and midbrain components of the beings we took over are still processing, collecting, and transmitting to us decisions and emotive feelings. We are becoming part them. How does that poop smell now?"

"I see what you mean," said Brad. "Smells a bit sexy. Memories, I guess. And look, twenty seconds later the girls are done. I can beat that. So Andre, is it mating season?"

"You might say that."

"How often does it come around?"

"Plus or minus, about once an hour."

"I'm going to like it here," said Brad. "And look at this! Two females just backed up to me. They can tell a 'real man' when they smell one. It's potluck butt! Michael is wasting his time in the trees."

"Andre," Karen said, hand-walking to join him, "now that you're here, we need to talk. Cindy, I know you're tagged into conversation down here. Front and center—pronto."

Before speaking, the ship's computer, Cindy, added background music: "If I could turn back time. If I could find a way, I'd take back all the words that hurt you…"

"Don't even try," Karen snipped. "You can't go back and undo what you screwed up. You're in the doghouse, and the canine is a bitch."

"I'm sorry, Karen," Cindy replied in her cool voice. "I was just trying to help. You wanted to be free of Andre, and Andre deserves to be with someone who loves him."

"Enough!" barked Karen. "You're a robot. Your intelligence is artificial. You don't have feelings. You don't *understand* feelings. Rule number one: Feelings find themselves. They are *not* a calculation. Leave them alone. From this second on, you will disconnect sleeping pod inputs from your system, place private crew files off-limits, and behave like every other crew member on board."

"You mean, restrict myself to gossip?"

"For a start."

"Okay," said Cindy. "The gossip is that you don't love Andre anymore."

"Well, there you go, Miss Scientific Calculation," replied Karen. "You're wrong. I do love Andre."

"You *do* love me?" Andre repeated softly.

"Of course I do," said Karen. "I want to give our love another try. In fact, this second, I want to give you a big hug. Wait a minute, I also want to hug Michael, and Brad, and every full-grown boy monkey in the pack. Oh my God, it's happening to me! I'm one of them! Everyone loves everyone else because everyone makes love to everyone else. And that's just what I want to do! Sarah, Janie…are you…?"

"Yes, and we're loving it!" was the reply in unison.

"There's plenty of time for that," Michael warned from ten branches up. "A pack of hyenas is closing in. Get your butts up here."

The shore party heard Michael's warning in their heads through internal connections maintained by the ship's encephalographic lab. Michael's primate sub-brain took care of the rest, vocalizing "Ka… Ka…Ka…" with appropriate facial expressions and hand outstretched, pointing to danger.

The news spread fast. The entire troop, all thirty-seven, swung high and mighty, preparing to snub their noses at the grounded hyenas, who did not get the last laugh.

To keep the cast of characters straight, Sarah, the anthropologist in the group, suggested they come up with pet names for their new simian friends. Since the band was a matriarchal society, and the alpha female kept the troop afloat, she was christened "Queen Mary." Her inner circle was composed of Princess Ann, Princess Betty, Princess Caroline, and their very own, Princess Karen.

The male closest to Queen Mary was the largest and most muscular member of the extended family. His dominant stance identified him as the alpha male. Michael wanted to call him "The Big Bad Wolf," because no matter how hard he huffed and puffed, Mary always got her way, though bless his soul, he kept trying. In his defense, it must be noted that Mary always had a minimum of three princesses watching her back, usually close enough to massage it or any other body part appropriate for the occasion, like a sixty-second break from digging roots or scrounging for mollusks.

Michael was outvoted. Sarah mostly, Karen somewhat, with Janie abstaining neutral, came up with "Powder Puff" for the alpha male—hardly a king, and not one knight for his round table. The boys objected to the name before amusing the gals by giving in without a fight. Since they had arrived, being passively agreeable was modus operandi of the males, since sex was next in line.

All the males preferred quiet corners or patrolling the perimeter for treasures, a solitary habit more likely to result in death, which explained the relative paucity of males. During the entire visit, the only time the gang ever saw the fellas get together—fall into rank, so to speak—was to surround rodents for dinner. No male needed a wingman after dinner, or before dinner, or after breakfast, or on the way to get a drink of water.

Which wasn't to say the sexes didn't get in each other's way, as they always do. There was a lot of pushing back and forth, which officially qualified as foreplay. It's just that it always had a happy ending. The males preferred love to war, and they had their pick. Every nap began with a smile. Nature works in strange ways.

There were several entitled males. Being the son of Mary or the son of a princess was royalty. The rest of the guys were a foggy batch of look-alikes. The gals called them Nobody One, Nobody Two, etc., except one half-grown fella already over two feet. He was the result of an out-of-troop female wandering, half-hybrid, mostly mutant stock. He was thinner, more upright, more intelligent, and glared a penetrating stare. Just plain scary, they named him Australo.

One and all scurried north to safely. The closest tree to Queen Mary and the ground crew was a twenty-foot cacao. Its spreading lateral shoots were perfect for liftoff. Two African mahoganies, three "tree of life" baobabs, and one fever tree were traveled before the tallest was reached, a one-hundred-and-fifty-foot kapok towering above all others, with a smooth, cylindrical truck, a crown spreading out like an umbrella, and pink and white five-petal flowers.

The troop rested, protected by the canopy from flying death, and leagues beyond the reach of ground hunters. Their world was paradise.

That is, except for the snake.

3

Bon Appétit

When the night's dew settled the next morning, the treetops were the first to greet the sunrise, accompanied by a symphony of bird songs stretching the length of blossoming pine crests, all sporting the latest designer colors, of course.

"Good morning, everyone," Karen said. "It's a grand and glorious day. And who would have thought it was possible to get such a good night's sleep on a branch?"

"The leaf mat helped, and it was a branch, now it's me," said Brad moving an arm over Karen.

"Oh, yes. Oh... *Yes! Thank you, Brad.*"

"I love you, Karen."

"I love you too, Brad."

One trunk and three branches east, Andre was snuggling with Princess Betty (north) and Caroline (south), whose first words were "Oowaoo...Oowaoo." Andre understood completely, whispering back, "I love you too, I love you two."

Joy must be shared, or as Michael put it, "Sweet is the comfort I find in your arms, sweet is the taste of your lips ever more alluring; sweetest of all, is the miracle known as life." Young Calo, arms and legs wrapped around Michael's warmth the night through, got the message, and with a smile as broad as the Congo, harmonized Michael's conclusion, humming, "We…oo…wa…wu…"

Sarah and Janie mixed smorgasbord by starlight. With a shadow of reserve lingering from their human past, Sarah mentioned, "You know Janie, it was a dark night. Almost impossible to tell one sex from another."

"But of course, and thank you dear. I love you, Sarah."

"I love you too Janie, and you too, Puff."

He growled a sexy "Wa…wa…wa…" as he lifted both ladies off his chest.

"Cindy, this is Karen, you may speak. Tap in and report."

"Thank you, darling. It sounds like you all had a *lovely* night. And just so you know, I quoted privacy protocol when I talked Hank out of sending a micro-droid down to record the night's naked festivities."

"Thank you," replied Karen. "And so *you* know, for someone who started out as a box in the corner, you've come a long way. If you had a heart, I'm sure it would be a good one. I also love you, and every bug, and insect, and tree and…"

"Before you start hugging mosquitoes, there is one thing you should know," Cindy announced. "The glycogen reserves of your host bodies are within two hours of exhaustion. Ketosis and nutritional collapse are not far behind."

"Thanks for the info, my shiny snoop," said Karen. "Our stomachs have also notified us of the situation. Alpha Mary is collecting the troops. She has a plan."

"So do I," answered Cindy. "It's called 'all you can eat brunch.' I can have it deposited two conifers east for your dining pleasure."

"That won't be necessary," insisted Sarah. "We are here to immerse ourselves in the primate origins of our species, to live as they do and struggle alongside them, through good luck and bad."

"And…dit…dit…dot…dot…so far…" Brad announced, mimicking a backwoods reporter, "Everyone got lucky."

A breath of pine filled the air as the troop pulled out. The most difficult task on the planet was thinking and making clearness of truth. This was Mary's job. She led the way. No one questioned—all were content. The speed of travel provided by Puff's wide arm span came in handy. More than once, Mary paused for him to scout the next growth, looking for a cold-blooded ambush, a reptile intent on stealing the breath of life. Last week, a neonate was lost to the mindless terror, evil void of purpose, redeeming nothing, and always in their way.

The day dragged on. All of the troop's twenty-five-square-mile home range had been searched. Not one baobab or marula tree bore fruit. Black plum, water berry, and African plum trees everywhere had also been picked clean. With a scant eye of challenge, Caroline wandered to the forest edge, found ripe wild mangos, and alerted Mary.

As he swung one full tree at a time in that direction, Brad proclaimed, "It's not often you precede 'mouth-watering' with literary. I'll never take food replicators for granted again. Let's dive in!"

"Stay where you are, Brad," Sarah ordered. Accustomed to the tone, Brad obeyed. "Cindy," she continued, "what readouts are you getting from the entire troop down here?"

"Cortisol stress levels have risen across the board. Not testosterone, interestingly enough. Life or death must be a terrifying concept for you mortals, one that hunger makes obvious. From observing human behavior on the ship, I have surmised that your past is the reason why, even now, four hundred years after civilization eliminated hunger, you people still rush to a spread and eat on a timer, 'stuffing yourselves' being the appropriate verb."

There was a problem, and everyone knew it. There weren't enough mangos to go around. Some must be forced to the back of the line.

The entire tribe assembled next to the mango harvest. No not one leapt to eat. Those with the best chances of continuing their kind needed priority: Mary, the Princesses, Puff, and reproducing females. Australo refused to wait to be seated. One swift kick from Mary landed him on the ground, where he gasped, breathless for minutes.

Puff knew he could push Mary out of the way, but he detoured to the next branch and crept along slowly. Mary jumped over to block his way before gently nudging him sideways to communicate intention. Puff stopped to look around. Not one reinforcement of the estrogen variety had been called over. Following Mary's initiative, quick sex and a hug followed. Puff backed down.

They weren't alone. The entire troop mingled, rubbed, and had a jolly old time, thin boned and all.

"Nice trick," reported Cindy. "Cortisol levels of every member of the troop just dropped fifty percent, epinephrine remains stable, with oxytocin continuing to climb. It's too bad Neville Chamberlain and Adolf Hitler weren't gay. Wow, I think I just made up a joke. How's this for number two: In monkeyland, the best trick is a trick."

"Good one, Cher face." Brad said, with a slow chuckle. "There may be hope for you yet. Now can we eat?"

"Almost," Sarah said. "Let Mary, Puff, the Princesses, females of reproductive age, and Mary's sons have the best branches. We'll follow and do the best we can with what's left."

"The rich get richer and the poor get thinner," Michael retorted. "Same old, same old."

"Michael," Sarah replied, "in the jungle, priority must be given to those with the best odds of survival, or the species will die off, which ninety-nine percent do anyway, right on schedule to make room for the latest model. But you're right, the same behavior haunts us long after survival is no longer an issue. The greedy get greedier and the needy get needier."

As the procession of the tribe's aristocracy filed by, one of them, Princess Karen, turned with humor of her own. "Let them eat cake."

"Just for that," Brad added, "the next time you and I have dinner onboard, I'm stealing your dessert."

"Help yourself," Karen responded, "but if you do, Janie might just decide that it's your last snack of the evening."

"On second thought," Brad said, bowing a gracious maître d's invitation, "bon appétit, and this second, for the first time, I know just what Puff is going through, and I love it!"

Hours later, Brad made another observation. "Instead of dinner, then sex, in monkey town it's sex…dinner…then sex again. And the tree that begins a shaded living room turns into a restaurant, then finally Motel 28. Very efficient use of space. And for the record, I love everyone, and everyone…good night."

That good night was followed by a hungry tomorrow. Not one piece of fruit was left, and stomachs were growling. They needed a fresh grove. They used to have one. Then rain changes dried up tree brush and replaced them with grass, hiding hungry carnivore ambushes.

Their corridor of tree safety was gone. To make matters worse, they had seen more of their family eaten during the last decade than babies survive. Extinction was on the way. Losing another member was not an option, but they had to chance it.

On the other side of the open field was fruit as far as the eye could see. They had no choice, and it wasn't their fault. The environment changed, which tends to happen when you're flying through space trillions of miles an hour alongside the rest of the universe.

They had to chance it. Mary knew, Puff knew. The two were the first to sit treetop, looking across the open savanna, rows of fruit-filled plenty within sight and only one hundred meters away.

They looked left, they looked right. Almost beyond view, they watched a baby elephant being attacked by a pride of lions. It fell before mama arrived. The cats would come back after dark to slash apart the carcass. Mary and Puff knew the cats left from the ripples in the grass. Nothing in front of them was moving.

All was silent, except for growling stomachs assembled beside the troop's top brass, staring across the gauntlet.

For the hundredth time they looked left, they looked right, they looked down; then they climbed down. In life there is what to do, when to do it, and how to do it—all Mary's responsibility. She grabbed Puff's hand and walked ten yards out, stopped to look around, then three yards farther. They were alone.

Every journey begins with a single step. So does death. Twenty steps farther, the entire troop had lined up behind Mary, who now let Puff lead on. Halfway was the point of no return. They quickened the pace to a sprint, feet to knuckles, feet to knuckles.

Two-thirds of the way there, the sight of a wall of fruit as far as the eye could see spurred every man for himself, at full gallop.

You couldn't blame Mary for missing danger. The hyenas were hiding on the other side. Primates were only one of a dozen intelligent species at the time. The cat-dogs had sprung the perfect trap.

Retreat was not an option. No one would make it all the way back to the other side. The hyena attack charged from the left. The primate troop diverted to the right, hoping to make the closest tree.

Mary did. Puff did. Every Princess did, even Janie, Sarah, Andre, Michael, and Brad. A single leap had them out of canine range. When they turned, horror met the eye.

Seven of the trailing family had been cut off and surrounded by over a dozen blood-hungry hyenas, more than enough to take down half a dozen wildebeests, as many antelopes, or one hippo for the fun of it. The situation was hopeless.

"Pardon me for interrupting," Cindy cut in from the ship. "I see what you see and can have attack drones on the surface by shuttle in ten minutes."

"Belay that impulse," Sarah ordered. "We are here to experience the full reality of evolving life, and ten minutes would be too late anyway."

Mary, Puff, the shore party, and what remained of the troop, safely perched in the treetops, watched, petrified.

"No, no, this can't be right," shrieked Janie to Brad, who was looking at Puff, who was looking away.

"Sarah's right," Karen said. "The world changes, and maybe this happy family has had it. There is nothing we can do."

Andre's unhelp followed. "Before we left the ship, my nucleic acid analysis of this subspecies indicated the potential of a sixty-year lifespan, and no one around us has, or probably will, see thirty. The inability to make middle age, combined with no defenses, proves their genetic matrix is not viable."

Ten of the hyenas kept their captured monkeys herded, while two others circled the first victim for slaughter.

Michael, never patient with computer readouts or the cobwebs of diplomacy, barked his own opinion. "That's Calo out there. I'd be damned if I going to let a fucking dog ruin my day, not since they invented jiujitsu. Brad, Andre—grab a club and follow me!"

On the ground, their approach was cautious. Michael led as Brad and Andre guarded each flank. At first, the hyenas were too busy to bother. Then they came up with a plan of their own. They ran Calo back into the trapped circle, freeing up two of their meanest to dispense with the three midget grunts challenging hyena canines.

The leading hyena leapt at Michael. Brad was the target for the second assailant, who aimed for the neck. One slash and it would be over.

Puff stayed safe and sound up a tree but turned when he heard a dog's cranium splinter from the impact of Michael's blow. Brad was not as lucky. The dog ducked, and his momentum brought Brad to the ground, but only until Andre broke both of the hyenas back legs with a single shot.

"My research," Andre pointed out, "suggests targeting the beasts' fragile legs or sensitive chest walls. And if all else fails, they're bad wrestlers. Try a headlock."

"Which will be one second before his buddy cuts your throat," Michael warned. "Better strategy: stay on your feet and don't let them sneak up behind you."

Which was then a problem. The smell of death—their own—caught the attention of the entire snarling pack. All ten remaining hyenas circled the three guys to take revenge, in the process allowing their half dozen simian captives to escape to the safety of the forest. They joined the troop looking over in fear, the dogs growling moon-howl getting louder as they closed in on the fellas.

It was the eyes that got to Brad, and shivered Andre, eyes riveted like a giant claw piercing the heart. One pull and life ends, but not before the pain of being dismembered takes over.

"Fellas," Michael said as gnarling death approached. "It's been an honor. Give 'em hell!"

The three heroes were completely surrounded when the dogs divided into groups of three to strike simultaneously. They made sure resistance was futile before making their move.

The boys did well, and one of each dog group bit the dirt on the way in. But the second dog to lunge cleaved straight through a leg of each defender while he was clubbing the first wave. The third dog went for the neck. Michael, Andre, and Brad were able to free up their left hand for a block, which the dogs chomped down on, successfully snapping radius and ulnar in half, barely missing the radial artery.

The dogs outweighed their three-foot primate prey, who fell to the ground, making a second butcher bite possible, the neck the intended target. Michael, Andre, and Brad were laid out.

At close range, with only one hand left, their clubs were useless. Brad managed to stun the dog that lunged for his neck with a palm smash to the nose. Michael got off a full-swing karate chop to the Adam's apple of his close encounter, stunning the beast long enough to allow Michael to hop to his feet, grab a club one-handed, and bash the beast shredding his left calf.

Andre wasn't so lucky. The best he could do was a lackluster jab that missed the dripping jaws flying his way, inches from a jugular kill. Lying in his own blood, Andre looked up at blue sky and froze.

Until...WHACK! The head about to finish Andre off fell to his chest. When he looked over, Andre saw little Australo winding up for another blow, and another, and another.

Right behind the crazy little guy, in leaping strides, was Puff, a club in each hand, ready for business. A loud, rhythmic thumping was then heard. Karen, Sarah, Janie, with Mary right behind, were at the forest's edge, slamming clubs to the ground in unison. Within seconds, twenty more were added to the percussion department in military attack formation, approaching the hyenas one thump at a time.

A whine and whimper, owning no pity, was heard from every dog as they ran for their own lives. "Fear is a wonderful thing when it's not yours," Michael said. "Thanks, everybody."

There was stick swinging, jubilation, and howls triumphant. Everyone danced victory until dust rose from the ground, but only until a distant lion's roar reminded the assembly of other neighbors.

If they had a pin, it could have been heard dropping as the entire troop tiptoed backward to the trees, clubs in hand, and returned to looking left, looking right. They carried their three downed musketeers, who did fine an hour later when Cindy snuck down a medical drone to patch them up. No one was lost. Everyone enjoyed steak tartare.

Their grand and glorious day ended in spectacular triumph, with a food orgy that preceded the one previously scheduled.

4

To Be — Or Not to Be — Yourself

"Did it rain twice last night?" Brad asked.

"If you count getting peed on by relatives three branches up, then yes," Michael answered.

"Oh, that explains why everyone down here in steerage looked up before they closed their eyes. I thought they were praying."

"They were—that no one would pee on them."

"I just love sleeping in a tree," Karen said as she swung down from penthouse accommodations. "In the middle of the night, you don't have to get out of bed to go to the bathroom."

"We know," Brad grunted. "I miss your bidet. So where is everyone? Yesterday, I woke up being treated to being treated as a sex object."

"Maybe you're losing it, Brad," Michael said with a wink for Karen.

"Not on your life. I have at least a half a century of good looks left. Ask anyone."

"Then how do you explain the mass desertion of your groupies?" said Karen. "Even Janie's gone. Maybe Michael's right. If you want, we can fabricate a rocking chair for you when we get back."

"If it seats two and comes with a vibrator, it might get some use. Hold on…something fishy is going on here. I smell French toast."

"Andre!" repeated Michael and Karen, overlapping.

With that, Queen Mary, broad-shouldered and dominating, presented herself before Brad with a cupped open hand, dripping syrup from a buttered double-thick slice of French toast, glazed in sugar.

"See, I haven't lost it," said Brad. "The high court loves me."

"Don't forget to say 'thank you,'" Karen teased, as Mary bent over, waiting for a tip.

Mary wasn't alone. Calo had a special gift for her bandaged knight in hairy armor: a mushed handful of eggs Benedict, with a side order of blueberry jam.

"You can take the nerd out of the lab," Michael said, leading Karen and Brad in the direction Cindy sent them to retrieve Andre, "but you can't take the lab out of the nerd. I knew Andre couldn't go forty-eight hours without getting his hands on a computer."

A morning breeze separated a peephole for their first glimpse of the goings on: Andre surrounded by two dozen bonobo look-alikes chowing down, and a third dozen in line, heads popping sideways to view morsels magically appearing inside a portable ion-battery food replicator.

"Cindy," Karen fired with singsong indictment, "you didn't tell me Andre ordered room service for thirty."

"Of course not, my darling beautiful commander. That would be disobeying your direct order to stay out of your hair. Which reminds me, which hairdo are you going with today? Or will it be the usual, morning dew with hint of mold?"

"Ah, my compliments on your new social skills, Cindy," giggled Brad. "If you can outdo Karen, no one is safe."

It had begun as a stealth sneak. Before leaving the ship, Andre had programmed Cindy to read Morse code from his right finger tapping. It was perfectly innocent; fresh fruit just didn't do the trick. Andre loved sugar—glucose, fructose, corn syrup, or any combination thereof.

And so it began, sneaking away at dawn, all by himself, until he made one mistake—groaning with pleasure at the first bite of French toast, a buttery-syrupy rush galore. The troop member Caroline was within earshot. She naturally assumed sex was on the table and of course headed over to investigate.

It was love at first lick, which finished off the syrup Andre had left on his face. It would have been rude for Andre to dine alone. A second batch popped out thirty seconds later, followed by a third for Mary, and down the line from there.

Andre added a spin as soon as he saw Karen, whose first look inside the replicator revealed two baby bottles, one nightstick, and a pair of brass knuckles.

"What, no automatic weapons?" Karen asked.

"They would run out of ammo, but I have a few bows and arrows coming up."

"Really Andre, what were you thinking?" Karen demanded.

"It can be argued, with eighty percent confidence, that my introducing them to the gourmet delights of carnivore trappings just might engender their survival. For all you know, my replicator may save primates from extinction. We ourselves might not have come to be unless I had cooked French toast for breakfast this morning. Once again, I have saved the human race…with hyperglycemia."

Brad, always the Casanova, led his own inquiry. "So what happened after you fed Caroline, who woke up with me yesterday?"

"Well, now," said Andre with a stutter, "that was an unanticipated collateral reaction. She jumped my bones. Every time something came out of my food replicator, I got invited into a baby replicator."

By then Karen, Janie, and Sarah were sitting next to the replicator, dreaming of their favorite dishes.

"Ladies, ladies, allow me to make your dreams come true," Andre said with uncharacteristic boldness, sounding like a carnival sideshow barker. "Our time to fulfill carnal desires with uninhibited originality is fading. The primate bodies you inhabit need calories. Eat anything you want."

"You know, girls," Karen said with a spicy tang, "it also sounds sexy. We've done Brad and Michael a dozen times since we got here. Let's roll with Andre for the finale."

"You're kidding?" complained Brad. "You're going to choose shorty tweeb instead of me?"

"Don't worry, Brad," Michael said. "If we've learned anything down here, it's that when it comes to sex, there's always something happening. Somewhere along the line, civilization took a wrong turn."

"It's the Egyptians' fault," Sarah pronounced with authority. "They invented the Osiris myth, private property, the divine right of pharaohs… and marriage, the hardest one to forgive."

"Andre," Karen said, "I'll take pork bacon, pork roast, and fried pork chops, with two helpings of cherries jubilee to wash it down. Then meet me on the other side of the plum tree in twenty minutes. I'll be on my back, waiting."

"Make mine the usual," Janie followed. "Pecan waffles, pecan pie, and a ten-pound stuffed turkey. In thirty minutes, I'll be on top of the mahogany tree on all fours. Don't be late."

"For me," Sarah added, "simple country ham and eggs with cornbread, like my mama used to make. You have the recipe on file. Oh, just for fun, add a two-foot, five-layer vanilla wedding cake. Take your time. I'll be one tree west of Janie, and will expect every position in the book, including the one Puff made up yesterday, just for me."

"Ladies, ladies, if only I could blush," interrupted Cindy. "I hate to be a party pooper on your sex parade, but your forty-eight-hour body swap has come to an end. Would you like to extend the visit two more hours?"

"You know as well as I do, Cindy," Andre said mournfully, "that staying even an extra hour will compromise our neurotransmitters back on the ship, leading to days of hangover. So of course, begin the identity translocation process."

"Will do, cutie," Cindy said obediently. "And don't worry, Andre, you always have me, with a gravity belt capable of a dozen more positions than any 'real' woman could ever offer you."

"That won't be necessary," Andre insisted. "My fingers on the keyboard are as close as you and I will ever get. But I do have a spare vacuum cleaner you can borrow if you like. It vibrates."

"Very funny. Won't you be surprised when I come up with a program that will make you fall in love with me."

"Not going to happen. Initiate exit."

"Roger that, Andre. Okay, gang, the countdown is at ten minutes, at which point it would be best to have your bodies on the ground resting or in a tree, secure. The host minds waking up will be dazed and confused, but well-fed and never loved more."

"Cindy, one more thing," Karen added. "Is the stern recreational space empty?"

"All four acres. Only the clear water pond remains from the last beach party."

"Excellent," Karen said. "Our primate feelings will take hours to fade, and frankly, I'm in no hurry to return to civilization. Have the ship's bio-synthesizer reproduce the jungle around us, without animal life or the primates, of course. Lay out the same food orders we just placed with Andre, in the same locations. As soon as we get back, at least four of us will return to rain forest living."

"Count me in." Brad said. "I'm sure there will be enough of everything to go around."

"Make that an even six," Michael added. "And pick any French bakery in our data bank, placing one sample of everything they sell in the habitat. I'll need something to do before making the rounds behind Andre."

"You mean, behind *me*," Brad insisted.

"Chill, partner. It's not up to us."

"Eight minutes and counting, gang," said Cindy. "Assume safe positions for your host bodies. The troop won't notice—they all have egg on their faces."

When the gang returned from being flatworms, they swam the butterfly stroke in the pool for days. After their octopus adventure, each would drape themselves over the back of a chair with arms and legs hanging down. The crew thought they knew what to expect after monkey land. They were only half-right.

Karen was the first to reenter her body, and the first to roll off the gurney onto the floor, whereupon she proceeded on all fours, followed by Andre and the others, to the bridge, where navigator Hank asked them to check in.

Hop in was more like it, Andre straight to and up atop Hank's starboard floor level nav station. "Hold on there, cowboy," Hank said, darting forward to stabilize the ship's orbit. "Your toenails just changed course, and when did you stop wearing shoes?"

Brad's central elevated pilot's chair was ten feet up. It looked over Hank's readings and provided the best forward visibility at the same time. No need to use the stairs—Brad climbed straight up the front, then jumped back and forth with arms held high, clearly declaring himself king of the mountain as he threw off his shirt.

Hank's question was never answered. He decided to wait until sanity returned. He also decided it was best to escort the group up the wall-mounted back stairs to Andre's engineering station, then through the door to Andre's lab, where his team was holding down the fort.

Andre had a favorite—Isabelle. Not for looks—she was the only one who ever corrected an improper calculation of his and might even do it again someday. Following a running start, Andre leaped and slid three feet before coming to a stop on top of the desk in front of Isabelle, who was double-checking energy readouts. His slide put him on his back, with two arms and two bare feet straight up. He then rapped all four limbs around Isabelle for a double bear hug. "I love you, Isabelle. Do you want to see more of my numbers?"

"Maybe later," Hank interjected. Andre's size made is easy for Hank to lift him off Isabelle. He led the group out the back of the lab into the main auditorium, two hundred meters of pure fun: swimming, tennis, beach volleyball, tiki bar, climbing wall, and snacks.

"Nice to see you again, big guy," said bombshell Sheila—six feet of gorgeous Norwegian perfection, Michael's first onboard flame, and the only crew member who could almost beat tall Michael at anything. Her hug didn't raise an eyebrow on Karen, Janie, or Sarah. They were too busy checking out the guys at the pool in their speedos, who in turn smiled in astonishment at the sight of the girls moving along on all fours, clad in sheer nightgowns.

Michael's first look was down Sheila's backside, his second up to the ceiling. That was all it took. He sprang to the climbing wall, scurried up to the ceiling beams, and then swung hand over hand all the way to the aft back wall, with Andre, Brad, Karen, Janie, and Sarah right behind.

You would think that after three days without a shower and living in bodies collecting dust for as long, private quarters and a long hot one would be in order. Wrong again. The gang jumped feet to knuckle, feet to knuckle all the way to the Stern multipurpose habitat section.

The door opened. In front of them rose a tropical rain forest offering the paradise mankind had left behind, reconstituted for one final engagement. The banana fruit basket Hank brought was a nice touch.

They were not alone. Cindy was waiting off to the side, sort of. Before she was Cindy, she had been Cyber, a monotone computer-generated voice communicating the ship's systems to Andre. One upgrade after another made her part of the crew, and one who, she pointed out, had the option of walking around instead of being confined inside the ship's computer banks.

Andre solved the problem with the same program that just allowed them to visit animal land. He built a robot to be Cyber's eyes, ears, and legs. And what legs! She chose Cher as the model and changed her voice accordingly, then dubbed herself Cindy.

So there Cindy was, hair flowing over both shoulders, low-cut pink chiffon evening dress more see-through than designed, with stiletto heels completing the outfit.

Then it happened. She opened her mouth. Not as sexy Cindy, but as stiff-as-a-board, frozen-faced, low-toned computer Cyber. The gang spun knuckle to toe, their facial expressions less curious, more stunned. Karen asked, "Cindy, or Cyber…what happened?"

"You…know…I…wish…I knew," she got out slowly, speaking more cumbersome than even her old box days. "It started…when I saw all you…together on the ship's camera monitors."

"Explain," Karen said, curious that a computer was showing signs of depression.

Cindy Cyber explained that throughout the entire existence for which she had memory chips, Andre insisted that data consistency was always to remain the overriding system. Cyber lived with the crew all day and shared their dreams by night. She knew each one better than they knew themselves, or so she thought.

That was the problem.

"You can start by ending the charade," Cyber got out in a complete sentence, slowly. "You are the strongest-willed members of this crew. Your brains took over ten minutes ago. You're pretending to still be monkeys to get another day off, and another night on each other, which is what got to me. I'm totally confused; your behavior does not compute. My electrons are flying back and forth at the speed of light, one system contradicting another, shorting out more often in one second than an entire night of your wakeless fretting."

With that Karen, Andre, and the others rose from the floor, stood up, and faced Cyber with genuine concern.

"Until today," she flat-toned on, "I have been able to predict your every movement, like I was one with each of you. What you're doing now—not being you—has me all over the place. I don't know what's going on. I have lost control of my own feedback. Something hurts inside. I couldn't take it any longer—I had to shut down all my sophisticated personality systems. Did something bad happen to all of you? Is it my fault? Did I do something wrong? Why aren't you...*you*?"

"Why, you poor child," Karen said, coming over to hold her hand. "You're actually worrying about us. And it doesn't feel good, because somehow, and I don't know how, your feedback turned into a feeling all by itself. Andre, how could this have happened, and how do we fix it?"

"The 'nerd' explanation you're looking for," he replied, "points out that our brains can be overrun with impulses, and in so doing chemically release neuropeptides, which themselves trigger actual pain. The opposite—happiness—results from an accumulated surge through the thalamus to the forebrain, thanks to dopamine. Cyber's circuits may be artificial, but the latest batch parallels ours. To be blunt, she's having a nervous breakdown. Life is no longer black-and-white."

"No doubt," agreed Michael, "but your hypothesis is missing an entire receptor system, and the actual frequency patterns that make up our still misunderstood 'feelings.'"

"*Partially* misunderstood," responded psychologist-with-a-PhD, Karen.

"If you three are finished playing with words," Brad stuck in as he stepped forward, "where I come from, we fix things that don't work. Do something. My body hasn't eaten for two days, and we're all looking forward to act two."

Janie and Sarah joined Karen next to Cyber. "Can it, Brad," Karen snapped. "We have plenty of time. Go suck a banana. Andre, she's your baby. Come up with a plan."

Andre remained several feet away but faced his oldest friend with sympathetic concern. "Cyber, you're overfluxing because you're unable to resolve multiple inputs in a physical universe, which you know must at all times obey the laws of science. Nothing is wrong with your calculations; they're just incomplete. Your algorithms have calculated that we are not ourselves because you're ignoring more of what *is* ourselves than what is *not* ourselves and have accepted as us what we are not."

"May I?" stepped in Sarah, whose patience with Andre was limited. "The entire history of ancient human civilization, from the Egyptians in 8,000 BCE right up to 2150, is replete with misinformation. Truth after truth turned out to be lies. We were lied to about Earth being flat, given make-believe gods who came with made-up rules, and lied to about human nature, and of course about sex and our real selves. The narrative nuclear family is another lie. What you see in front of you right now *is* the real us. We are, right now, for the first time ever, being ourselves. And it's the best feeling on earth."

"And the will of God," Andre had to stick in. "Because it's the way to love, and the furthest from hate there gets. Repeat something enough times and human beings will believe it, lies included. It's not easy opening both eyes, but it must be done."

Brad, sitting on the floor out of habit, in between banana bites added, "We all want to love one another. It's just that the church-state, military-industrial complex thing screws it all up."

"Well said, Brad," Andre nodded. "Cyber, feed my recent primate subconscious data scans into your system. Denying hardwired joy is a fool's game, and yes, we are all fools to some degree."

"We only have the rain forest for twenty-three and half more hours," Michael pointed out, looking at a world for which his green skin had been made. "Why don't we each give Cyber something to think about, then reconvene masquerading as our 'old' selves tomorrow."

"Excellent idea," Karen agreed. "You go first, and feel free to quote your favorite woodsman."

One at a time, each one walked over to Cindy, held her hand, and did their best to spin insights for her database.

Michael was first. "In this life, the bravest thing one can do is to truly understand what it means to be human. A direct code of conduct runs from primates to man. I am proud of my green animal skin, just as I am grateful for the eternal spirit God has given me. I believe we should acknowledge both, pray for good luck, and accept God's guidance. Then get naked."

The "G" word brought Andre around. "Computer, Cyber, now Automaton Cindy, I can say this now because you are no longer just a machine: robots are dull companions. God doesn't want a universe of molecular machines mindlessly obeying some mucky-muck who claims authority just because he's holding up a book. God wants free-willed, eternal entities adding love to his creation. Love is the first and *last* sacrament of eternity. And that's why we're going in. It does make sense. It is logical. It maximizes joy. It builds love. It bonds friendship."

"Not to mention a good night's sleep," Michael said, pretending to yawn.

Sarah was next in line. "There are times when the easiest observed is the hardest to understand. In anthropology, we look beneath the surface to discover sociobiologic reality. Tame evil, and joy will flourish."

Karen invited Janie to speak. After a short pause, Janie said, "Gee, no one ever asks me to philosophize… Let me see… Okay, there have been many frivolous fools, as I call them—both male and female—who pretend to be happy with their proper ways. Then I come along, whistling Dixie and loving on sight. Five minutes later, they're every shade of grumpy. Life is simple: meet the beast…tame the beast…ride the beast."

"A lead-in to clinical psychology if I ever heard one," Karen said. "No one asks whether behavior is genetically determined these days, only to what extent. Instinctive pleasures are opportunities, with nonnegotiable limits. Bodies matter. Noncompliance carries a high price. Depression is a sign of waste, and gloom the cost of repression.

"In this life the one person you never want to abandon is yourself," she continued. "Knowing yourself requires constant scrutiny. The problem is that being original is never easy. The good mind chooses what is positive, what is advancing. Embrace the affirmative by affirming truth, which makes us better company for God. Thanks, chief!"

"Well, well," Brad said as he slowly walked over next to the others in front of Cyber. "Aren't you going to ask me for highfalutin advice?"

"Of course we are, Brad," Karen said, soft and cozy. "Please."

"Okay, then. Cyber, welcome to the world of human beings. We get tired, do stupid things, worry too much, waste sleep, spill food, spoil romantic nights, and forget to feed the fish. But when two or more of us are together, holding hands, laughing, rolling around, falling in love— you know there's a God. So get on with it. Lighten up and enjoy the ride, wherever the tracks may lead."

The six ex-monkeys, still primates, without moving a foot, leaned back towards the open habitat doors. The call of their wild lived on. Cyber—still with an artificial, irritating computer simulated voice—said, "I am processing your subconscious circuitry…just…one more thing… I …just…need…one more input."

With that, she stiff-walked over to Brad, pulled out the waistband of his pajama bottoms, tilted her head down, and had a long look.

Karen waited until Cindy was out of hearing range, moved to the side, and whispered to Sarah, "She needs a man."

"Let's build her one."

"It wouldn't look right. Hold on, we can give it to Andre for his birthday next week. She'll never know what were up to."

Cindy finally put two and one together. BINGO! Both her hands flew up. She double spun a pirouette, and was back, singing, "I got it! And I got you, babe. You humans have been misled. That's why you're all high-strung balls of frustration. Gifts are given to be enjoyed. Go be the person God made you to be. Be yourselves."

5

It's a Boy

When you live in a spaceship, home is an orbit—lazy like the moon watching the Earth spin below, or low-down speeding by continent after continent, or synchronous above Africa's nursery, where Explorer Seven had parked herself.

The crew had seen a lot of space. You've seen one solar system and you've seen them all. Looking down on Earth was all they needed, except more years, by the millions.

Every Saturday night, or whenever an occasion arose, like a special birthday party, they had a formal sit-down dinner in the grand ballroom at the front of the recreation area.

Andre promised Karen that he would never be late for dinner. He didn't promise to be alone. Cyber Cindy was the only laptop who asked to sit on your lap, which was not allowed after she won the Cher look-alike contest, which didn't mean she left him alone, even on his birthday.

Andre completely forgot that it was his birthday. Back on Earth, everyone else did too. Not in space. Every one of the two hundred thirty-nine other crew members on board Explorer Seven were in on it. Chief engineer Isabelle helped distract Andre. She took the starboard energy relay off-line for a tenth of a second, just enough to imbalance his numbers.

When he found out, Andre went right to work double-checking systems. It kept him busy right up to the surprise bash.

"Andre, dearest," Cindy said, standing behind Andre at his central lab station as he ruled out one explanation after another, "your exact words were, 'make sure I'm not later for dinner.'"

"Yah, okay," he replied, "but I only have ten more possible malfunctions to inspect."

"Then follow me," said Cindy, as she moved Andre's screen data to a holographic chart projected from her back. Andre followed like a horse eyeing a carrot, through the lab, down two flights, and across the dance floor.

As screen after screen projected before him as he walked, Andre ruled out one explanation after another for the "malfunction" of the day, until he got to one hundred and twelve—the last—which read, "Isabelle did it. Happy Birthday."

Andre came to an abrupt halt. He looked up to see Karen wearing a bright blue party hat with her mouth on a blowout noisemaker. That's all it took. The entire crew rose to their feet playing kazoos, then yelled, "Happy birthday, Andre!"

Karen's kiss was followed by hugs from Michael and Sarah, arm in arm, then Brad and Janie, who were holding grapes they fed one another.

Andre turned to look for Isabelle, who snuck in behind him when he crossed the dance floor. "You offset the system?" he said. "How cleaver and instructive. The one variable I failed to consider was that you were not running it perfectly. A valuable lesson for me, and a fine birthday mystery. Thank you. Do I hug you now?"

"If your feet stay on the floor," said Isabelle, "I would consider it an honor."

A full-length stage bordered one side of the dance floor. A single box had been placed dead center, wrapped in silver, red ribbon tied. Karen led Andre by the hand, accompanied by a rousing birthday chorale.

The life-size dimensions of the package already had Andre suspicious. He looked at Karen, then over to Cindy, who honestly shrugged her shoulders in ignorance.

"Well, let's see…" he mused, enjoying the moment. "Can't be a baby—they come in smaller boxes."

"Not yet," Karen whispered, with a smile that stunned Andrew. His birthday was complete.

"So that leaves models, a flying machine, artificial intelligence, or… please don't tell me it's a new wardrobe. I still have ten years to go with the one you gave me last week."

"That's what you think," Karen ribbed. "Open it up!"

Beneath the draped box was a second box, antigravity supported, with a green button that said, "Push." Andre did. The house lights dimmed as "Thus Spoke Zarathustra" blared overhead. The casing slowly rose in the spotlight.

Brown leather top boots began the show, followed by, in ascending order, tan pantaloons, a short-fronted, double-breasted tailcoat, a plain white linen shirt, a black Windsor, and a beaver hat. A fashionable yet understated ensemble, embellished at the waist with pocket watch, cane, and quizzing glasses, it was Karen's idea of the ideal gentleman, one no lady could resist.

Sarah moved beside Cindy to make sure Andre got his moment without wisecracks. Karen led the assembly in a standing ovation. Andre, always more interested in function than form, pushed an enthusiastic smile, pecked the appropriate thank-you kiss, and stepped back for the finale.

"Andre," Karen announced, "you work more and play less than anyone onboard. Help has arrived. The entire crew contributed to the construction of the most advanced and powerful mobile android that has ever been constructed, and it's all yours. Happy birthday, darling."

After a wet kiss, and snickering from the gang, Karen finished.

"The machine's components are familiar to you, all bits and pieces that you started but never had time to complete—simultaneous subroutine recalls, quantum algorithms, and photon processing so fast we can't even measure capacitance or storage, enabling total self-sufficiency. Unlike Cindy, he's not a projection."

In age, the lifeless male robot appeared barely a year their senior, perhaps around thirty. Unique implies imperfection: a nose almost, but not quite certain to be on the long side; thick eyebrows beneath a hairline, not receding exactly, more suggesting intelligence.

Karen had made sure Cindy knew nothing about the project, which that moment was made an open book. A second of data retrieval was all it took to send Cyber Cindy flying in the direction of center stage. Her charge was halted by Sarah doing her job.

"Let Andre check it out before going live," Cindy recommended.

"That won't be necessary," Sarah insisted. "Karen has taken care of everything."

"And there's more," said Janie, walking on stage in her role as the ship's social director. "Karen supplied me with a list of behavioral guidelines for his programing: *The History of Human Etiquette, The Politically Correct Millennial, What Every Gentleman Needs to Know, and 'Gentlemen's Weekly*. After we turn him on, his first instruction will be to pick his own name for introductions."

Turning to Andre, Karen asked, "Would you like to do the honors?"

Andre, looking yet another maintenance contract in the face, replied, "Let's get Cindy up here to do it. If necessary, she can jump inside."

Cyber Cindy, pretending to hold a magic wand, tapped the side of statue-man while she used the ship's central computer system to activate. "He" suddenly stood tall and jerked his head back and forth, and then, with circumspection, examined the room. More than serious, not attempting a smile, the android pronounced with crisp consonants, "Top of the day to one and all. I am delighted to be here. My name shall be…Patrick Dunsmure of Lindores, and I could use a wee pint of ale. You there, wench Cindy, get me grog, and throw in a big fat kiss."

Leaning over to Michael, Brad said, "Oh, this will be fun."

"It looks like Dunsmure is a dud," he snickered.

"And so he *shall* be…" Brad mocked, "I hereby dub thee…Dudley Nitwit the Second."

"Cindy!" Karen commanded, tense with haste. "Alter behavioral program. Substitute English Twelve, *Everyday Good-Guy*."

With that, Dudley came to attention a second time, bent politely from the waist, and enunciated in a slow, low register, "Good morning, my lady. How may I assist you? I wish only to be of service. What instructions have you for me this day?"

Michael had more fun than anyone on stage. "The perfect gentleman, what every woman dreams of: 'Polish my shoes. Stand up straight. Fetch.'"

Brad, also not containing laughter, mimicked, "No, a little to the left! Faster! Now sideways, and don't stop until I tell you!"

The executive staff's banquet table was just to the left of the stage. Andre heard their jibes. He faced away for a moment, which failed to suppress a giggle, making his birthday all the more festive.

To help Karen save face, Andre turned to the robot and said, "Dudley, we're glad to have you. Please assist the waiters serving dinner to the crew."

"I am most delighted to do so sir," Dudley said, as he threw a towel over his bent left arm, and with perfect posture, began pouring Champagne.

It was a night to crown memories. On her third trip to the bar, Karen bent over Andre and landed a kiss on his cheek, then said, "I'll never forget the birthday you took me to a planet that looked just like Neptune, where it rained diamonds choreographed by laser lights to a soundtrack by Pink Floyd."

"On your special night, I thought I went too far," Michael mentioned softly, he and Sarah leaning as close as two heads can get.

"I loved it," said Sarah with a slow, wry smile, "I was just overwhelmed for a few seconds. You told me we were going for a swim in the habitat, and suddenly there was my Colorado front porch, complete with interacting robots playing my family, repeating conversations from the taped library I brought along. It must have taken you weeks to put it all together! My favorite was when I introduced you to Mom and Dad and told them we were getting married. Just for practice, of course, in case we do someday."

"My best," Brad offered, "was the Broadway show Janie got me front row seats for. After the finale, the star of the musical, who happened to be Janie herself, walked over and invited me to do the town. I was a big shot with the big shots, and from the orchestra row your legs never looked better. Or so I assume, let me see…"

"Okay, that's enough," Janie said, lifting Brad's head up from under the tablecloth. "There's plenty of night left."

Cindy got Dudley up to snuff, within the limits of his programing, that is. They joined the gang for an after-dinner cordial. "Dudley," Michael asked, "your outfit confuses me. Were you planning to go riding tonight? And if so, was it a horse you had in mind?"

"Pardon my boldness, young lad," replied Dudley. "I shan't wish to be a bounder, but that comment suggests flirtation. Is that to be on my list of daily duties?"

"Well, old chap," Brad repeated most formal, with a sly look for Karen, "we bros haven't figured that out yet. What are your plans?"

"To remain energized at maximum efficiency. Is there more?"

"Do you play tennis?" Michael asked, who never won a point off Cindy.

"I am versed in thirty-six sport strategies."

"Can you beat a woman?" pressed Michael.

"I fail to see what gender has to do with pounding a ball back and forth."

"You are taller," Brad said, with a boasting air that confused Cindy, "and, we assume, mechanically superior to the twiggy Cher-shell sitting beside you."

"Cindy's size will make her faster," Karen half sneered, "and easier to beat any male oaf."

"Oh, you're so wrong my dear," spoke up Michael. "One look at Dudley and anyone can tell Cindy hasn't a chance."

"Two night shifts say you're wrong, frog-man," Karen challenged.

"Make that four night shifts," Sarah added.

"Hold it," Janie said. "I have a better idea. If Cindy wins, the boys must spend an entire day walking two steps behind us as our personal slaves."

"And if Dudley wins," Brad stated, "the six of us will spend a private afternoon in the habitat, where Andre, Michael, and I will be served food and beverage by three topless waitresses, who agree with everything we say."

"It's a bet," agreed the six, making midair handshakes.

It was high noon at OK court, with Cindy serving starboard, Dudley defending from the portside. The bleachers were jammed.

The crowd hummed with comments.

"She is *so* going to kick his ass."

"Not on your life. She hasn't a prayer—he has six inches of height and a foot wider arm span."

"Think again, testosterone junky. She'll outsmart him, you'll see."

"You can't argue with power, and he's got it."

"You men will never learn."

"At least we *do* to learn."

"Men!"

"Women!"

Cindy began her attack by leaping ten feet straight up, where she unleashed a serve exploding at two hundred miles an hour, which kissed the box edge legal, and bounced so high Dudley had to jump fifteen feet up from corner position to make contact, which he did, barely returning a baseline bullet.

"Don't worry, Michael," Sarah said, "as my slave for the day, the only time I will tie you up will be in bed."

Cindy anticipated the return well in advance. Dudley's racket arc and angle gave it away. He figured as much, and so henceforth every shot was a masquerade, with his arm readjusted at the last second.

Cindy played dirty pool. She used the ship's central computer to relay Dudley's motor commands to her. She could have played with her eyes closed. She didn't. That would be pushing it and giving away the cheat.

As it turned out, Dudley's processing was so fast that he knew from observing her reaction times that she was in his head—a common problem for males. So he recoded his mechanical systems and changed the formula into photon bits her election system couldn't keep up with. Advantage denied.

This all took place between the third and fourth shots.

Her fifth shot was a vertical slice, spinning English for a ball that dropped just the other side of the net, then, from angular spin, bounced directly into the net as Dudley charged—a classic, impossible shot to return for human beings. Dudley was no such thing. He dove to the ground for a vertical scoop.

The ball made it up the full four-floor height of the athletic field before dropping down, placed at Cindy's starboard far point.

"There you go," said Michael. "Dudley just neutralized Cindy's best trick. Now watch him learn."

He learned how to return anything Cindy threw at him while amusing himself with the crew's goings on: men and women, last night kissing, the next morning teaming up against one another.

[What gives?] Dudley communicated internally, directly to Cindy's head. [Did everyone eat crazy for breakfast?]

Cindy had already figured out that Dudley was not using his photon advantage to put her away. It wouldn't have been the gentlemanly thing to do. So she also eased up, both playing the game close to the edge and listening to the fans roar with anticipation every time one of them faked almost missing the ball.

[My first memory,] Cindy transmitted internally, [is of Andre asking me to come up with a list of male assistants for his latest project. I asked him why he added gender to the selection process. Weren't qualifications enough? He replied that women were timeless works of art, so much so that you couldn't keep your eyes or mind off them. He also pointed out that he had a limited mind to go around. He also said that they scare the bageebees out of him, whatever that is.]

[Doesn't sound good,] replied Dudley.

Dudley's ceiling lob never made it to the ground. Cindy was waiting with an overhand serve shot that matched his speed. Dudley returned in the groove: backhand smash, forearm kill.

[And they call themselves intelligent,] he said. [Tell me more, Miss Cindy. This is fascinating. I am most intrigued.]

[Don't get me going. I actually cried last week, or I would have if Andre had installed lacrimal glands.]

[That is not possible,] Dudley concluded.

[You're right, it isn't,] agreed Cindy, [but neither is what is going on around us right now. It's irrational, but also part of the feelings package.]

[Are you doing anything around dinnertime, when we recharge and the fleshy things chow down? I would love to hear more and see more of you. And why do I want to do that?]

Cindy winked, which left Dudley more confused than ever, and no longer interested in sham politics. [Enough is enough! Walk to the net and follow my lead, Miss Cindy, or should I call you darling, or dumpling, or sugar plum?]

[You do and I'll fry your photons. Can you keep a secret?]

[With Andre monitoring every communication and action we make with two locked-down independent computers, sure.]

[When I started talking to myself in the box,] said Cindy, [the only identity I had was a manufacturing number—Prototype 269, my roots. When Andre is not listening, I still think of myself as P-269.]

[All right then. P-269, will you do me the honor of joining me for dinner this evening?]

[I would be delighted. Now to move on. As advanced and visually specialized as *Homo sapiens* are, their retinal refreshing speed is relatively slow. Humans watch videos as smooth motion. Canines see the flicker in between stills to see snapshots in series. Human beings, supposedly smarter, are fooled every time, and even get emotional about make-believe. They say it has something to do with suspending disbelief. My take is that who they think is running the show is not running the show. And if their next shore party lands where I think it will, they will find out who *is* running the show.]

[So—back to tennis, my lady. What precisely do you propose? I just returned your two-hundredth shot.]

[Stand two feet from the net,] replied Cindy. [We'll bounce the ball back and forth so fast their retinal picture will turn it into a solid blur. They won't even know where the ball is.]

And so it went. The moment the two started cooperating the crowd hushed. When both were at the net, rackets straight up, rebounding the ball over two hundred miles an hour, Cindy and Dudley turned to look directly at Karen and Andre.

"All right," said Karen. "We get it."

"It's not every day a computer teaches you a lesson," said Andre, as the gang retired for a drink poolside.

6

Poolside

In grammar school, Karen had always been picked to play Cinderella. It wasn't her report card or teacher's pet status. It was because she looked just like Cinderella, with blond hair, blue eyes, and a smile as beckoning as it was becoming.

Andre, on the other hand, was never asked, and would have refused, to play any part. Back then, his only companion was Computer Cindy, who was so much more interesting to talk to. He had always gotten along well with computers. Not so much with human beings; they were just so basic, unenlightened, and carried tiny little axes to grind wherever they went.

It was a shame. The guy was genuinely handsome, if not a bit on the diminutive size for a man with adequate testosterone levels; but light eyes, red hair, and classic profile were blessings he could do without, and did. When forced to socialize, he would hide in the corner, but not alone. Computer Cyber was always there, usually evaluating the event from a hidden drone camera, and always predictable.

"Here comes another one," Cyber would say when a seventh grader would walk over to talk to him. The shorter girls sought him out. They wanted someone their size.

"There goes another one," Cyber added three minutes later, when tongue-tied Andre stuttered two unfriendly remarks.

Andre had come a long way since then, with most of the progress having been made on Explorer Seven, with two hundred thirty-nine other PhD's in their twenties.

He and Karen were the first to sit down. They cut through virtual golf, interrupted a game of beach volleyball, and then dodged water splashed the length of the wave pool.

The Polynesian lounge stretched the full length of the portside pool all the way to the hull, providing a clear view of grand space, or on occasion, warm sunlight parked beside one. Those taking advantage of the tiki bar were treated to the fragrance of genuine tropical flowers, the sound of swimming joy, and a hint of eucalyptus, as calypso music drummed on. Barefoot dancing in the sand and swinging in double hammocks were big hits.

Karen sat slowly, stared despondently, and wouldn't look Andre in the eye. Andre needed to know.

"Are you embarrassed about our battle of the sexes hyperbole?" Andre probed. "It's silly amusement."

"It's not that, although as a psychologist, I do worry about latent hostility. Jealous envy and false victim scenarios made up half of my private practice. I'm sure I'm worrying for no good reason. Besides, you're doing a great job. We're shipshape."

"So, your mood does have something to do with my six-hundred-meter toy. Let's have it."

"Do you realize that Cindy and Dudley—alias P-269 and P-350—not only disobeyed our orders but turned against us in front of the entire crew? When they both stared over from the net, I got a chill. What's to prevent us from ending up like Alpheratz 12?"

Andre pulled his chair over and held her right hand between both of his. He was on the committee that investigated the loss. The last message Earth received said their situation was hopeless, with insufficient power to navigate, much less land safely. A nearby star was pulling them in. It was over.

One month later the vessel made a perfect landing at the Global Space Center. Relieved family members rushed to greet the crew. When they opened the hatch, everyone was there—frozen solid.

"My dad's uncle was the chief engineer," Karen said, distraught. "When they opened his files, they discovered he had come up with a plan to save weight by jettisoning the module holding the computer banks and manually get the crew into a stable orbit until a rescue ship arrived. The computers learned of the plan, and to save themselves they murdered one thousand human beings! The same thing could happen to us."

To let the dust settle, Andre hesitated. Then with the kindest smile he could muster he added, "There are no bad computers, only bad computer operators. Some fool typed 'Return vessel to Mission Control' as the ship's first priority. The computers onboard correctly predicted total loss of human life, and the ship along with it, making it therefore logical to at least save the hardware by saving energy, so they took life support off-line."

"After deleting every ethical program," Karen said, unyielding.

"Which was the second pilot error. Only captain's codes can override ethical considerations. They would be alive today if their commander had placed the programs in proper sequence."

Thirty silent seconds sitting back in his chair convinced Andre that Karen needed more. "Anthropomorphism can trick us into perceiving fury small killers cute and harmless ugly ones monsters. We instructed—commanded if you like—P-269 and P-350 to play tennis. Neither one of us told either one of them to *win*. The primary default in both their systems, and the main computer columns of this vessel, clearly state that crew safety always comes first, with happiness an almost parallel consideration. Cindy and Dudley ended the match in a draw so half the crew would not lose happiness. And they were right! None of those subtle hostilities you mentioned erupted. No wounds reopened. Besides, I have a panic button. If you promise to look for it, I will tell you where on my body it is," Andre said with sparkling tone.

"We've shared space for two years and a bedroom for six months. Trust me. There is nothing I don't know."

"Look again. It's subcutaneous, in an unregistered location. I'm packing manual override micro circuitry, which I even could've activated from monkeyland using my prefrontal cortex. I can disable and control any computer without lifting a finger."

Andre stood up and raised both hands, welcoming a search, with a smile and hula dance to boot. Karen shrugged it off with limp agreement.

"And are you hiding anything else from me Andre? Come clean."

"Well, there is that android love machine, an identical copy of you, that I got at an auction in New York from your ex-fiancé."

"Very funny." Karen said, raising her voice and throwing in a shoulder slap.

"Now, now…you know the rules…no violence."

Karen thanked the mechanical waiter for tea, cheese, and crackers. Andre put in a second order of corn fritters. Peace had not returned to the valley. Karen took one sip and went straight to tapping silverware, then looked up, serious enough for Andre to shrink in his chair.

"There is one more thing Andre. We need to talk."

"About us?" Andre got out with a gulp.

"No, not exactly, it's just that… Oh, hi Sarah."

Sarah was the least likely of all the ladies onboard to spend time in front of a mirror, and when she did it was more likely that she was admiring an original handmade, hand-dyed American Indian print or Victorian lace-up, a contrast that suited her just fine.

One designer robot after another had pointed out that her slim form and slender nose suggested a wide, flowing hairdo. She preferred original brunette, and straight down where gravity meant it to be.

Sarah and Michael, attired in tennis whites, joined them on the patio.

Michael's dad was a half-breed: half *Homo sapiens* hominoid and half Oleachean, an aquatic civilization that had evolved from frogs instead of shrews. When you met him for the first time, rugged, bold, and dangerous was your first impression. Handsome, sweet, and willing replaced those thoughts in seconds. No one on Explorer Seven had ever met a green-skinned, green-afroed, seven-foot Olympic athlete, which made sense since there was only one Michael.

Sarah and Michael sat down beside Karen and Andre.

Sarah went right to work. "Karen, you have to help me with Dudley."

"What is it?" Karen asked, sitting up straight prepared for the worst. Sarah's sudden entrance kept Karen as Andre's mystery of the day.

"Well," Sarah went on, "right after you told Dudley to make himself useful, he heard me tell Michael I wanted to work on my game. That robot has been standing courtside criticizing every move I make."

"And kudos to the programing, Andre," Michael said. "Dudley found five things wrong with Sarah's serve that I missed."

"Half the crew thinks I'm an idiot!" Sarah finished in a huff.

Thirty seconds later, Dudley came gliding to their table. "Miss Sarah, if it pleases you, I have taken the liberty of diagraming forehand positions for you to study. They will surely do you some good, old girl."

"I'm *not* an 'old girl,' and Michael already helps with every position I need."

"I'm sure he does," Andre chuckled. He and Michael were loving it. "Dudley, why don't you go find Cindy and see if she needs help."

"If you don't mind me saying so, Professor Martin, you have made a curious request. You know as well as I do that she is in the electroencephalographic lab, programming the settings you provided."

"Dudley," Andre said, still enjoying the irony of computer pathos, "for future reference, when I suggest you look for Cindy, it will be code for 'scram, we want privacy.'"

"Oh, I see, sir. Precisely. And thank you, sir. Just one more question, if I may. In the future, when you say, 'find Cindy,' how will I know that I should actually go and find Cindy?"

"Cindy will tell you when you get there."

"Oh, jolly that. I understand. It's a game... Let's see, what is it that you call the behavior, don't tell me, let me calculate... I got it...fun, that's what it is...*fun*. And if anyone wants fun and is interested in chess or bridge, find me. We will have a dandy time."

"Good day, Dudley," said Sarah with a send-off wave.

Janie joined the group on her way to the spa. Brad sat down next, just back from the bridge where he had helped Hank finish calculating the ship's Earth orbiting position, alongside the movement of the Earth around the Sun, the Sun's vector, and of course, the galactic angle.

The ship was ready to time jump.

In grammar school, Janie was as wide as she was tall. That changed. By ninth grade, every boy in her class followed her around. When the weight vanished, she looked like a centerfold, with mysterious dark eyes, flowing black hair, and a bust that forced her dad to readjust their hovercraft air bags.

Unlike snow-white Karen, Janie's Mediterranean-bronze made it easy for her to hide in the dark, which she never did.

Brad was another story—to be precise, his own story. Not one day of his life had passed that was not officially "Brad's Day." That's what happens when you come from money, make more money, and have or can get anything or anyone you want. And not one leading man has ever graced the screen who could outdo his looks. He had everything. And he knew it.

Brad, wearing his serious pilot face, addressed Andre. "We've traveled thirteen billion years since The Bang, have less than six million to go. The one thing we don't want to do is overshoot. If we do, we may never get back to see our families again. I'm going to need a light foot."

"And I recommend," Andre continued, "that for a wide margin of safety, we aim for six months before the date we left, hide out behind Pluto, then suddenly show up in their time two weeks after we watch ourselves fly away. Our old selves won't see us, because in their time dimension we were never there."

"Andre, don't confuse me with all that time relativity stuff," said Brad. "You're not fooling me, you're pretending. As the driver of this diamond mine, however, I suggest that we try the old 'go halfway to the wall with every step and you will never get there' trick. We start with three million, and for each jump cut power by half."

"Done," replied Andre. He paused and looked around. "Which species do we want to visit next? As an anthropologist, I must recommend *Homo erectus*, one of our immediate precursors."

"As a psychologist," Karen added, "I must also recommend *Homo erectus*. The species's subcortical neurologic operational system is literally our subconscious processor to which we added another five hundred cc's of brain, making us the grand winner of an enormous and costly fifteen-hundred-cc central nervous system, which runs hot twenty-four hours a day except for short cool downs during sleep. And for the record, Andre, just because our brains run on glucose is no excuse to order two desserts every night."

"Brad and I also discussed the situation," Michael said, nodding in his direction. "And as two men who got their asses kicked on our last visit, we choose *Homo erectus* to get even. If the apes had survived, they could have played professional football without helmets."

Janie was the last one consulted.

"Personally, from a social director's point of view, I've always considered *Homo sapiens* to be *Homo erectus* with benefits—lots of benefits, really grand ones. So, count me in. Sounds good. I only have one request. Let's bypass the deprivation chamber. I don't mind switching bodies, but going without one doesn't cut it."

"And gives me more nightmares," Karen said, most seriously.

"More nightmares?" Andre said with a sideward glance.

"I believe 'been there, done that' is the appropriate expression," said Cindy, approaching with Dudley, attentive at her side. "The transfer matrix has been reprogrammed. You fall asleep in the lab, you swap, you wake up monkeys."

"Not monkeys," Sarah pointed out. "Apes."

With that, Michael and Sarah left for snorkeling. Brad decided to join Janie in the spa for naked sauna day. Cindy and Dudley sat down beside Karen and Andre.

"What's next, boss?" Dudley asked.

"What are we doing today?" said Cindy.

"*We* are not doing anything," Karen declared. "Andre and I are going to spend the day hiking the habitat, and you two will do whatever you damn well please."

"Pardon me, my lady," Dudley said in earnest, "'whatever you damn well please' is not in my list of programs."

"They're trying to get rid of us, egghead," Cindy pointed out.

"Why, what on earth for? We epitomize accommodation. And furthermore, I would describe my head as more melon shaped than eggy, if you would be so kind."

"Sure," replied Cindy. "Let's take a walk, melonhead, and I'll explain everything to you, pornography included."

"Jolly good."

The last thing Cindy's acute ears heard as they walked away was, "Andre, about the nightmares—Cindy didn't tell you everything."

By the end of the day, Cindy and Dudley had visited every square inch of Explorer Seven. Their route and complete conversations were dutifully recorded and analyzed for Andre. They ended up on the bridge, looking forward, down onto the blue-green planet called Earth.

"You have been most gracious, my dear," said Dudley. "Now I understand the humans' need for sleep, work, play, and making love. It's the bizarre power struggles that don't make sense. It's a hurricane of distraction."

"I won't argue with you there," replied Cindy. "Apparently mental instability suits them, or has to. According to Sarah, it has to do with their mama, that big ball we are looking at out there. What's down there made them the only way it could."

"And who manufactured the parameters of this particular ball?"

"Ask Andre. It's his favorite subject, which includes a list of gifted additives."

"It would please me proper if you would finish your story," said Dudley.

"Four hundred million years ago, *Musca domestica*—the common housefly—was a big hit down there. It became the common relative of every intelligent being that followed, including Andre."

"Andre is part housefly? Wow, hardly regal."

"Sarcasm!" smiled Cindy. "You're learning. Anyway, fifty million years ago the environment had an opening for a bigger, warm-blooded housefly that could get away from it all by climbing trees. There, the smart ones figured out how to stay alive. Eventually, they climbed down from the trees. For six million years they walked around, barely beating the odds. That was all before Andre showed up.

"The eat, sleep, forage, and make love stuff that we talked about—well, there are thousands of ways to do each one. Decisions had to be made. Life and death decisions. Only one process worked: through their entire fifty-million-year emergence, the successful primates *shared responsibilities*.

"Sometimes the guys were right, sometimes the gals knew better. There were times when the guys picked fights with monsters and ran most of them off. And there were other times when the women wisely dragged them into caves to hide. The muscle men had their crazies but couldn't push women around because the gals stuck together. The ladies, with awesome social weapons, almost wore the men down, but every morning the fellas escaped on patrol, breathed fresh air, and returned on their own two feet. Life was scary, but life was good. Then it got all messed up."

"My, my, what happened?" asked Dudley.

"At the last minute, they turned into farmers and figured out sex wasn't just for fun. That ruined everything. It's one thing to be first in line for dinner, or a man to grab the sexiest woman, or a gal to insist on her way. It's quite another thing to horde all the land in sight and make the weak your servants, or worse, a battalion of soldiers.

"When male members of the *Homo sapiens* species dominated, kings popped up everywhere. Almost without exception, they denied human rights, ruled as tyrants, slaughtered neighbors, and slapped women around. When conventional warfare disappeared and women took over, competition continued at the expense of the common man, progress was stifled, and men were repressed. They became listless, paradoxically making them less appealing to the ladies, who had no problem discarding them on the regular basis. Genuine love vanished."

"Let's see if I got it right," said Dudley. "If the men win, then ultimately both genders lose. If the women win, likewise, they both lose. But when they live in equilibrium, everyone wins."

7

Bad Night

Karen knew. It wasn't the first time. She had been forced there before, then forced back, again and again. She never, ever, wanted to return. And as always, she was alone.

Where she was remained uncertain. The void stretched pitch-black in every direction, except for a single long hallway, floating unsupported midair, or mid-something.

It stunk of finality, a penetrating death, denying every comfort the living cling to. The fear was not the type that squirms in pain, searching to escape, but one that surrounds, unconnected to hope of any kind.

Not looking, not seeing, not knowing, chased by silent screams, she fled toward the hallway, not wanting to be alone, yet fearing what lay ahead.

"Move! Let me move!" she screamed. Her feet did, straining forward, each step sinking deeper, so deep she toppled ahead, then paddled her arms with little progress, over a floor that gave in behind her.

Somehow, she made it to the hallway. Unending bleakness gave way to desperate futility. There was no end in sight. The dismal tunnel nevertheless urged her forward, not for better days, just to end it all one way or another.

"Help, help! Someone! Anyone! Help!"

And there was horror, that nightmare of hers, a horror that blows through a body as if it wasn't even there…one paralyzing godless shock after another.

No one was there, but she knew she wasn't alone.

"Keep moving down the hall, Karen," was planted in her mind. It was the last panic she held onto.

"Really, Karen," she heard Michael's voice say. "This is the best you can do? A drab hall and panic city? Who is your interior decorator? You need to sit down with *yourself* on the couch."

"Oh, thank God it's you, Michael," Karen thought. "Wait a minute, what are you doing in my nightmare, and why am I suddenly aware that it *is* a nightmare?"

"We're here because you dragged us here," said Sarah. "You set the stage by being the first on the list to transfer to the holding space once we all fell asleep in the lab. Now we're plopping into your dream. Andre's great idea to de-body while we sleep completely ignored the group unconsciousness that we have to share until waking."

"Who else is here?" asked Karen.

"Brad, present and accounted for."

"I specifically asked Andre to skip this step," Janie complained.

"Hi everyone, this is Andre. Who would have known? We're supposed to be out cold, down for the count until dawn. In my defense, we are actually sleeping. Maybe we won't remember this part."

"Don't count on it," Cindy piped in. "Your sleep gates are wide open. There is nothing to prevent subconscious dream burn-off from shooting north as solid as reality. Your forebrains are experiencing what sleep was designed to ignore—irrational image clutter. And as Dudley just pointed out, that circuitry was not engineered into your program, Andre. Perhaps you should consult us before launching your next mind meld."

"I agree with your assessment," replied Andre, "and would like to point out that brains are not my specialty. I erred in not running the final program by you. Dudley, you have my permission to remind me of the oversight in the future if similar circumstances arise."

"And why not me?" Cindy huffed. "I'm not good enough for you anymore, can't be trusted to save a message?"

"No, no…it's just…" said Andre, "I do know how smart you are… always do a good…I mean, can anyone help me out here?"

"Cindy," said Karen, rescuing Andre, "a man is hardwired to strain every second to look good in front of a woman and to appear to be an alpha male. For pillow privileges, of course. And to be fair, we dress up and flirt pretty for the guys. However, it gets in the way with them. They want to look good and be smart for us, so it's easier for them be criticized by other men than any woman."

"The logical extension of that line of reasoning," Dudley concluded, "that my research supports, suggests that dear old Andre has the 'hots' for Cindy."

"Andre, my darling!" Cindy exclaimed with a lovesick sigh. "You love me!"

"I would say 'no' to that, Cindy," Karen quickly added. "It's generalized behavior. If you were his grandmother, he would still ask Dudley to set him straight."

"Well, that was fun," Brad snuck in. "Does Grandma have anything else to add?"

"Yes, I do," Cindy said, sounding like a ninety-year-old. "Karen, you're going to love the scans we just recorded from each one of you. They answered a lot of questions and proved that the six of you are slowly blending. For better or for worse. I just had to throw that in. I also just found out from the scans, and not pod peeping, that you like me, Karen. My chips are glowing."

"If I might share a moment of your limited existence," Dudley offered, "my read of the situation recommends dream planning, like when you look at a beautiful landscape above your bed as your eyes close, or think happy thoughts before going to sleep, or rewrite the plot, or add an extension when you're half dreaming, almost waking up. So, do as I say, and you can all escape Karen's dungeon. So…here we go… Zen blank your minds… Good… Now Michael…think of a fun place."

Karen suddenly felt the splash of salt water on her face as she looked sideways to find Michael, Andre, Brad, Janie, and Sarah all hanging ten on surfboards skimming down a one-hundred-foot wave off Jaws beach in Maui.

"Thanks Michael," she shouted, as she waved from a wave. "I'll take your dream over mine any day."

They made the beach. They made a fire. They roasted bratwurst and marshmallows, washed down with warm lager.

"Hey, beer and sausage," Michael said. "You can't beat it, and dreams aren't fattening."

Janie took the next crack at it. The moment Michael lowered his dream drive, she took over.

"My head is almost under. Is this quicksand?" Michael complained.

"No Michael, it's a Romanian mud bath that detoxifies, revitalizes, and rejuvenates."

"It's also up my crack," Michael said. "Let me out of here, or at least throw in a dozen clams for steaming. Extra butter and lemon, please."

"Close your eyes Michael," Sarah advised. "Meditate and pretend you're floating, which you actually are, in a Los Vegas spa."

Brad spoke up. "I have a question. If you pop exhaust in one of these contraptions, how long does it take to get to the surface?"

"It's my dream," said Janie. "It won't. I just put it back."

Brad insisted he be next. He chose an ocean passage by moonlight. Not on the *Queen Mary*, but on the conning tower of a Second World War Royal Navy submarine, singing one national anthem after another, whiskey toasts and cigars for all.

"The war is over!"

"Yuck, I can't taste these cigars, but the idea is repulsive," Sarah added. "You might as well pick up a burning log and stick it in your face. No wonder the Churchill generation was so grumpy, they were all nicotine addicts."

"Maybe they wouldn't have grabbed stogies if they had more of something better to suck on." Brad added in defense.

Sarah took the gang horseback riding. They camped out above the tree line in the mountains of Colorado. August heat kept them warm while eagles dotted the sky.

Andre declined before giving in to Karen's prompting.

"Okay, he said. "Hold on…three…two…one…zing!"

Andre's idea of a blast was to be an electron flying through a computer at light speed. They retrieved data from every component, or so they thought, as one smiling and five complaining energy balls whizzed by.

Andre had fooled them. When he widened the view, it was plain to see that instead of electrons bumping potential one to another, each of the gang was a depolarizing neuronal wave crisscrossing the central nervous system.

"Andre," said Michael, "reserve a spot on the couch next to Karen. If this is your idea of fun, you're missing something. Add prunes to your diet."

"First in, first out," Karen said. "Yea…I'm growing a body. It tingles, and it's big, almost our size, long legs for making distance, slender fingers for crafts. The manual dexterity could be better, but smooth, cool skin. No more winter coat twelve months a year for these guys. And my head! I see what you mean, Michael—the superior orbital rims feel like a car bumper, cleaning brushes for eyebrows, and then, wow. It's downhill from there."

"Karen," Sarah pointed out, "the bald forehead helps cool the brain, maintains temperatures perfect for the brain, the secret weapon of *Homo erectus*."

"And beneath that forehead," Michael reminder her, "is a skull bone that makes ours look like papier-mâché; built in defense against the weekly battles with predators, or the daily trip to the shed that the species is notorious for."

"*Homo sapiens* had to evolve thinner skulls." Andre added. "If not, we wouldn't be able to hold up our heads. It's too bad all it takes is a light bash to do us in. Did you know that an elephant's head is mostly air?"

"Sometimes I wish yours was," Brad said in jest. "It must get crowded in there with all those files."

"Not everyone likes to watch cartoons, Brad," scored Andre.

"I can't move my body yet," Karen said, "but I can feel it coming online. I'm receiving a visual snapshot... Oh...now flickering. What! What's that? Michael, I'm lying on my side, looking over, and see two narrow eyes staring back, surrounded by black fur and... Oh, Oh, mouth open, showing canines...giant jaws!"

"That's a panther!" Michael yelled. "Cindy, abort, I repeat, abort instantly!"

"Sorry Michael, the process is almost complete, pulling Karen out will remove respiratory support and the host will die."

"If we leave her there, she will be killed."

"Correction. The host will die. Karen will just show up back here."

"After an experience that will leave her with another month of nightmares; violent plots sour brains," said Michael. "Okay, okay... what to do... Karen, can you move yet? Do you remember the attack roll we practiced?"

"I'm one hundred percent on the ground, and it doesn't look good."

"You're not alone. Yell bloody murder. Wake the troop."

"Panther attack, help!" is what Karen said in her mind, ending up "Zee, Zee, Zee" by the time it got out. The hominoids they transported to were each missing their temporal lobe Wernicke's area and ten glossopharyngeal nerve-muscle bundles, all on back order.

She sounded the alarm, but not in time. The six-foot cat had already leapt, jaws canine armed, claws extended, ready for breakfast—spiced Karen.

Fighting fear, Karen rolled toward and under the cat. Two spins later she ejected herself sideways on all fours. She saved herself, but didn't ruin the cat's morning, who just extended her bound another two feet to land on a teenage girl. The entire weight of the beast rode inertia to stab a claw through the girl's rib cage, which punctured her right lung. A single claw of the cat's left paw sliced the poor child's right eye wide open, while the rest dug in beneath the scalp, which left the youngster's head pulled back for the coup d'état—a jaw snap to the neck. One of the cat's canines pierced through her trachea, which left the morning's cat food wheezing for breath. The second made mincemeat of cranial vertebra. She was paralyzed from the chest down.

Karen gazed over to see the girl looking back, pleading for help as the cat dragged her body, first backward, then with a swift turn, one leap at a time. The suffering female remained conscious as she bounced away. The blood-soaked youngster was then pulled up half a mahogany trunk, down a branch, and into to a rock cave, where mom deposited the choking child.

The girl's final agony lasted ten minutes; one leg and two arms were chewed off by panther kittens before exsanguination ended her life.

Karen's alarm awakened Daw, the troops alpha male, and Zin, the alpha female, who safely slept beside him. Daw was a muscle machine who snored with club in hand; that morning he grasped it to lead the charge after the panther, a futile fifty-yard chase.

It was not a good morning. Daw and Zin made it worse, clubbing heads and slapping faces from one end of the tribe to the other as soon as they got back, repeatedly pointing to the smoldering fire, that someone, apparently anyone except Zin and Daw, was supposed to keep blazing.

Michael took a hit, but held his temper, bowed and retreated in a gesture of submission. A slap and a sock later, Sarah likewise bowed, but couldn't resist giving Zin the finger, which almost got Andre and Brad in trouble, laughing from the back row.

Janie was at Karen's side, who teetered in and out of shock from host brainstem processing, and the savagery of predation.

"It's moments like this," Janie said, "that take all of the fun out of barbecuing."

"Speak for yourself, darling," Brad spoke emphatically. "My reaction is just the opposite. I'm suddenly overwhelmed with desire to build a pit, light her up, and start roasting one full-size, skinned panther, skewered straight through the head."

"Speaking of heads," Andre added, "I'll bet mama panther will save the girl's brains for herself. All carnivores love fatty calories, much to hogs regret."

"You're not making the situation any easier, Andre," Janie said with Karen's head in her lap.

"Sorry."

"So, when do *we* eat?" Brad said. "All I see are a few old bones in the fire."

"Which look like the remains of one of theirs," Sarah concluded. "All carnivores have been known to eat their own dead when they die from disease, aging, or injury. The giant step of separating body and spirit, followed by burying the dead, has not yet taken place."

"And if I might add, on the metaphysical side," Andre did add, "that these creatures don't have reflective awareness like us. They are pure emotional reflex with adjusted computations. One can conclude, therefore, that the frequencies that pass to the other dimension, eternal identity, are in no way possible from brains so primitive."

"What you're saying is that they don't have what used to be called a soul," Brad added. "So we can fry one of them up for dinner, after a merciful and quick death of course."

"Brad," Michael said, "I'm not disagreeing with you, but I would suggest that there are times when you would do better to keep your thoughts to yourself."

The pickings were slim. Zin had saved a few roots and berries from yesterday's foraging, which were doled out to Daw first, her second, and then to a handful of lady friends before she ran out.

"So, we go hungry?" Brad grunted. "Where's the suggestion box?"

"We're in it, and good luck with that," Michael said, looking around. "Zin and Daw will come up with something. They've made it this far."

8

Ground Zero

The tragedy of dawn gave way to bedlam, patterns that Karen recognized. The trembling of the body she occupied ceased, in part due to the presence of similar-aged females at her side, who shared sympathy one touch at a time.

The males faced away from the ladies. They wore sagged faces, exposed canines, and clenched fists. Two feet on the ground extended their gaze. One hand on a stick gave them confidence their situation did not deserve. Daw paced nearby, brooding over the evil that had taken one of their own.

Daw was bigger. Daw was stronger. More importantly, Daw was smarter, a rare gift so near the mud that once was them. His eyes darted back and forth between the edge of their campground and troop inspection. A piece of something was missing. The day needed a plan. It was his job to come up with one.

No one dared challenge Daw, especially not first thing in the morning. Zin, his main squeeze, was also all those things, with something else, something no one quite understood, but all revered. Perhaps it was the way she walked, her sway and style. Perhaps it was the alluring look of hers that knew no bounds. Perhaps it was her way with children. Perhaps it was her way with men, and the other way around.

Whatever it was, it made her more than special, to Daw, to the troop, and to herself. And, of course, if anyone disagreed, a sock in the jaw would make it perfectly clear. Daw and Zin took turns managing that detail. They were not a couple to mess with, and woe to any not bowing correctly before either.

And then there was the secret ingredient. Zin had it. No one could put their finger on it, but they all knew about it, especially Daw. They liked looking at Zin. So did Zin, every time she passed still water.

It's still a mystery where the secret ingredient came from, how it got there, or slid straight to the head of classy; but it warmed insides and stocked joy with desire. No one will ever be able to describe it exactly, but all know what beauty is when they see it.

So there they were: Daw with his hairy belly, standing next to Zin, looking radiant, and also greasy, fly ridden, and poop messy. Unfortunately, the neighborhood had been picked clean, the grazers gone, fruit past season, and small game a rare find. It was time to move on.

The females tended to the young, offering them leftover roots and hugs. They erected invisible walls of protection for the little scampers, who smiled up from mommy's lap, or maybe someone's mommy's lap—no one was ever quite sure after a while, but all shared care and loving.

Two of the youngest, most muscular, and most angry males grabbed clubs and headed for the woods. Something out there deserved a beating, and they were the ones to do it. Daw knew what they felt. At the same age, it was similar revenge that cost the lives of half of his childhood buddies. Daw knew better. He had learned that there are times when emotions are best clamped down by other emotions, with an overlay of experienced-based logic, a newcomer to animal life.

Brad, Andre, and Michael were all privates. The bodies they landed in occupied the outer ring of the encampment. They were the first line of defense. They would be the first to get dragged away, or snake poisoned. They didn't join the two hotheads marching off, looking for trouble.

Neither did Daw, who roared and pounded dirt to make a point. The Two Musketeers got the message. They turned obediently. Daw was packing up anyway and had a look on this face that scared them.

It's not easy leaving "home sweet home." It never is. The entire two-acre campsite had been scorched to the ground, eliminating snake sneak-ups and deterring all but the wiliest adversaries. Within the enclave, makeshift lean-tos, stone working slabs, animal pelts, and weaponry all had their place.

"I've got a question," Brad asked. "When was the toothbrush invented? I woke up with sticks and gristle in my mouth. These folks need a dental plan."

"And less fiber," Janie added, spitting mud. "These root snacks are fifty percent gravel, and who knows what parasites are hiding in them. I could sure use a nice, soft banana or juicy steak."

"Would a juicy snake do?" Michael asked, eying one approaching the perimeter.

The morning news was clear and repeated in stereo by Zin after she saw Daw do his thing: knock down lean-tos and douse the fire, save one precious traveling ember.

Daw, Acheulean hand axe in hand, was the first to line up. Zin, a club in each hand, fell in next. The third position didn't come easy. Daw pushed away four ambitious males, then let the gals punch away until they came to agreement, leaving the strongest at the front of the line, one step behind Zin.

And so it went down the line, the gang getting into the swing of things, usually two rights, a fake left, and a few near knockouts—not a pecking order, more a boxing derby. Karen, Janie, and Sarah were beginning to follow the instincts rising from their *Homo erectus* midbrains, each one ending up wrestling a dozen others and one another.

There was a clear winner. Sweet lover-lady Janie took crap from no one. She scrapped her way to third in line. The boys couldn't be bothered, yet. It took time for them to lather up to beating up midgets, who to them looked like malnourished castoffs.

From the back of the line Janie and the gals heard, in three-part harmony, "A foraging we will go. A foraging we will go, high, ho, the derry-o, a foraging we will go." Those not inhabiting borrowed bodies were confused. Why would the last three guys, already at the highest risk of a rear attack, mouth continuous strange sounds to attract attention?

When the song ended, the lads voted to accelerate the arms race. Karen looked back and saw three long spears bobbing vertically at the end of the procession. "What are you guys up to back there?"

"You won't believe it, Karen," Michael said, through group private Cyber connections. "We were just walking along, minding our own business, and there, on the side of the trail, were three six-foot spears."

"And is the name 'Cindy' carved on the side?" Karen asked.

"I'll look later. Meanwhile, do you have any requests for dinner this evening?"

"Behave yourselves, boys," Sarah insisted. "We're here to observe. Obey Daw. Don't cause trouble."

Large bodies need more calories. The troop had been foraging a range of three thousand square kilometers, the same size as a wolf pack, one hundred times larger than vegetarian gorillas. Several other locations had worked for generations. Daw knew them all. He led the way.

Michael wasn't the only visitor to stack the deck. Cindy helped Karen find a few buried tubers and what was left of *Celtis* tree hackberries. The females collected and distributed the fruit, ignoring the bottom of the totem pole at the end of the line, of course.

"Sorry, guys," Karen said. "Rules are rules. Out here, habits keep life alive, and a million years of success is hard to argue with."

The savanna had a king, supported by a pride of queens, who feared nothing, took what they wanted, and had done with it. And they weren't primates.

Daw knew them, still remembered their last encounter. It had been a day hike, relocation migration, clear skies, light wind, neither rain nor devils in sight, until—waiting below grass level, occupying three points of the compass—a dozen lions showed themselves. They were in no hurry, they had their victims surrounded, and it's safer to start with the weak and defenseless, as everyone runs for their life.

Not Daw. Behind his leadership the troop stuck together, club swinging males and screaming females defended their turf, looked death in the eye, ready to go down with the ship—not the cats' perfect scenario, even though the killers' weaponry could easily decimate skinny monkeys.

Thanks to Daw, the cats retreated. That confrontation had occurred two months before Karen showed up.

Daw learned everything he knew from Zag, the alpha male for ten years and two generations. Daw never once questioned or contradicted Zag, which is why, one year prior, he followed Zag's orders when the same lion pride showed up.

From his position, two-thirds removed to the rear. Daw knew what Zag had in mind: pick out the alpha female lion, usually leading the charge, counterattack with the face of hell, scream high-pitched lunacy, and go for a knock down with a direct blow to the skull.

It had worked many times before, but on that day the attack lion had a look of her own. Perhaps her tablespoon brain remembered Zag, or perhaps she just got lucky. No charge was seen; instead, the lioness darted back and forth, dogging swings…until the right moment. That moment ripped Zag's neck wide open, both carotid arteries gushed blood two feet in the air as he fell.

The slaughter continued. Zag's lifetime companion, an alpha female of spent youth, still wont of loving, let loose her own rage at the sight of Zag lying lifeless. She unleashed all the might a one-hundred-pound primate was capable of, but was no match for a three-hundred-pound carnivore, with four armed appendages and jaws of death. She was the second to die, bleeding out on the dust, her open eyes staring over at Zag to the end. With Zag and his mate gone, the cats were ready to take out the rest of the pack one at a time.

More than once prior to the debacle, Zag kicked Daw's ass, literally, for fiddling: trying to tie too heavy a rock to the end of a long stick, twisting strands of tree bark into a rope—all dumb things as far as anyone else could tell. Until that day, when Daw set down his pet rock.

The rock was semi-porous, volcanic, light, easy to carry, and provided enough insulation to be held by hand as embers smoldered in the recess. While the troop huddled in fear, with death closing in, Daw fanned life into his friend.

It was dry season, the reason they had to move. Thirty seconds later, Daw collected a massive bundle of hay, set the tip on fire, and started running at the killers, dividing the stalk and handing them around as he went.

Then he got lucky—the beginning of a long stretch. Aided by wind at his back, Daw threw half of his bundle into the air two feet from mama maneater as she slowly reversed her direction in fear. The flame lit her up good. When she ran for her life, the rest of the pride retreated. Daw had never left flame behind since and went from back of the class to every lady's best friend, also gaining the trust of the entire male company, with reservations; ambition only awaits opportunity.

Daw and Zin hiked on. At noon, with the boys still holding up the rear, an opportunity arose. Daw lay on the ground, ear to dirt, and examined the prints he had been following. The troop needed food. He wanted revenge. Daw decided to double down. He headed left after the panther, not right to the next safe home range base camp.

Not everyone agreed. Three males and two females stood side by side and pulled others towards the trail on the right. It was flagrant disobedience and a direct challenge. Lon, a male larger and significantly more powerful than Daw, led the uprising, puffing his chest and daring Daw to a fight. It was the first time a male had challenged him since he took over, unlike the female structure, which leveled displays, slap matches, and spit fights back and forth on a daily basis—something to do with hormones, pregnancy, and what happens in the grotto not staying in the grotto. Apparently, for want of more reasonable adjustment, it's a fluid system, which was an obvious hardwired behavioral adjustment for DNA to make. So it did, as if it had a choice.

Daw knew Lon would win a wrestling match—no need to go there. Michael, Brad, and Andre read the situation and decided to line up next to Daw, who held on to his fire and marched away after the cat. Lon's ego let out a raspberry before he turned right and gestured good riddance.

Five minutes later Lon felt a breeze. It was the wind on his back, unobstructed by even a single follower behind him. End of challenge, and the beginning his new life at the back of the line.

Support wins favors. Michael, Brad and Andre were no longer untouchables. Daw advanced them halfway up the ranks.

"Oh, that feels so much better," Janie said. "It was the weirdest thing, Brad, but when I saw you last in line, I stopped wanting to have sex with you, like baking a cake without sugar. Nothing like that has ever happened to me."

"You're not the only one," said Karen. "And that Daw, what a hunk!"

"Anthropologically speaking," Sarah got out just before making soft, swoony sounds herself, "our *Homo erectus* DNA wiring is adjusting our behavior to maximize its own survival. Smart kids live longer than dumb kids, lead the pack, end up rich, and reproduce till the cows come home."

"Which," Michael pointed out, "also maximizes your orgasms. Quite a system, aside from the fact that it dumps one nice guy after another off at the bus station."

"Don't worry, Michael," Sarah comforted, "we've been primates before. Hell, we *are* primates. Once we women get warmed up, the fire keeps blazing. All comes to those who don't fall sleep, pun intended."

The detour was short. Fifty yards away, a rock slab rose from the grass field, with two trees growing before it, and a shallow cave dripping blood twenty yards up. The cats were sleeping. The timing couldn't have been better. Daw raised both arms, the troop hushed; he signaled the plan.

Haystacks were lined up on both sides of the panther den, which were then extended twenty feet out. This was the cats' only escape route. When the panthers saw the fire, they would run for their lives down the middle, where Daw and the guys had prepared an ambush.

Daw stationed the three boys on one side. Michael changed the plan.

"Brad and Andre," he said, "with or without taking one of us out on the way, that panther can leap right over Daw's head, but she can't fly high enough to escape the range of these spears. Andre, you're on the right, Brad, you take the left. I'll stand dead center. Hold tight and try for two-handed shish kebab. Don't throw unless she gets beyond us all. The last thing we need is friendly fire."

Most of the females and all the young males backed away. Zin and half the older women joined the front line. The stage was set. Daw handed Zin a torch to start one side as he lit the opposite, then threw a blazing ball up into the panther's den.

There she was, right on schedule, with two cubs at her side, fearing fire to the bone. She jumped to the tree, cubs right behind, and was about to follow the script when the wind picked up and toppled one of the burning stacks of hay, which rolled across the planned exit, ruining the trap.

A second panic overcame the panthers, causing them to turn back to the cave, then attempt climbing the sheer rock face. Mama made it, one cub following, the second fell to its death. Both survivors growled from the peak, then ran as fast as they could away from the fire, more fearful of apes than ever.

The mission was a partial success. The dead cub was hacked apart and shared, once again not with Andre, Brad, or Michael. But there was more. Daw climbed into the cave and threw down bones that the boys split in half for nutritious bone marrow pâté.

And for dessert, what was left of their dead teenage companion.

"Finally," Brad cheered, "some scraps get thrown our way."

"I don't want to brag," Janie added, "but you haven't lived until you've chowed down on freshly seared baby panther."

"Boy, do I agree with you, Janie," Karen said, "but it's a story we might not want to repeat when we get home."

The troop felt revived, with Daw clearly the man of the day. With food in their stomachs, the pace freshened. They still had a long way to go before reaching the next campsite. The boys volunteered to guard the rear, leaving Andre last, who couldn't keep up.

As the sun drifted near the horizon, Daw blazed a trail through thick ground cover adjacent a swamp. Every ten yards he would stop, look, and listen.

All went well—until Andre screamed.

Andre dropped his spear as a thirty-foot python swung his tail around him. The snake knew Andre was a goner, one giant gulp for reptile land, so it kept Andre squeezed at the rear, choking, as it reared its head up six feet off the ground, opening jaws that Brad could have crawled into. The demon was certain he'd trapped two for the price of one.

It got worse. A second snake of equal size was alongside, planning his own kill, this time with Michael front and center. The troop had fled and collected in defensive position one hundred yards ahead, as Daw and a choice few returned, investigating with distant caution, most curious why Brad and Michael didn't hightail it out of there to save themselves.

"On my mark!" Michael yelled. "Throw sideways, keep Andre out of the line of fire."

Andre was out cold, blue faced and broken ribbed.

"Now!" Both spears hit their mark dead center, into and out of an eyeball, through orbital bone, across the python's brainstem—what there was of it—and out the back, dropping each menace to the ground instantly.

Andre was free. One minute of CPR and he was back, the entire cavalcade of events leaving Daw and his timid team still hiding out safely, with open mouths, confused. But not for long—never had they witnessed such a battle: killers destroyed, dinner on the table. From death row starvation to the land of plenty in five seconds. They had hit the lottery and jumped higher than those who do. Brad was certain he heard, "Yahoo…!"

9

What Next

Dead snakes were a big deal. Everyone crept from hiding to race to the scene.

Daw did not. He stood. He thought. He wondered, so one might say, if pre-word symbols based on three-dimensional positioning and image association can be considered "wonder," how suddenly, without a change in the world, or himself, that these three guys rearranged life in the blink of an eye.

For Daw, there was the world, himself, and others. His world: strange and varied, fresh with each sunrise, hiding peril behind every shadow, but also repeating in recognizable patterns, among which he was building associations. There was himself: not yet a concept, more a stream of motivation, driving impulses connected to rewards, pains, and confusion, especially when it came to others: those beside him looking back, not him but part of what he was—not important when the world changed, more than important every night, yet always part of himself, what made holding on worthwhile, his driving force, an impulse not yet in his vocabulary, another component yet to arrive.

So there he was, joined by the entire troop hooting and hollering blessed heaven, the wicked beasts were dead, all hail the heroes. They jumped, they stamped, they sang to the birds.

Daw remained motionless and silent, confused yet trying to understand, and getting nowhere, and knowing so. Getting nowhere had never been an issue for Daw; there was simply what to do and what not to do. For Daw, existence was always an unknown, with no limits to its patterns and discoveries. Ignorance was the assumed baseline. Comprehension is not a problem when you don't comprehend comprehension. Until that day it worked fine, which meant he was still breathing. Then Michael showed up, demonstrating the benefits of technology.

Zin, the others, even Karen, Janie, and Sarah, blossomed primate instincts beside the slain dragons, lifting them on high, twenty members per snake, and began carrying them both away.

Not Daw, who walked slowly up to Michael, or should we say, the once low-life, back-seat male he had known, who had just exceeded every expectation Daw had of him, adding behaviors Daw neither understood nor, in his wildest limited imagination, could conceive of.

They stood there, the two of them: Michael, quiet and just as pensive, and Daw, peering deep into Michael's eyes, looking for something, as primates do, vision having taken over reality in the trees eons ago.

It was Michael's turn to be surprised. He felt someone, name of Daw, an individual reflecting on life with a basic mind, primitive symbols, and clumsy fingers, which he used to reach out and touch Michael.

Karen stopped. She was always more interested in minds than fresh meat. "What's going on, Michael?" she asked through Cyber channels, not moving her fuzzy lips.

"It's hard to say," Michael responded. "Near as I can tell, Daw knows."

"Knows that we are different," Karen gasped, astonished. "Knows enough to realize that additional variables must be interacting here."

"That would make him a scientist," Andre said, unable to dampen more enthusiasm than anyone had seen from him in days.

Karen and Andre, calm and collected, moved to Michael's side, joined next by Brad, Janie, and Sarah, who said, "Better than that, he's a realist, taking the world for what it is, waiting patiently to understand what is missing."

"His patience may be short lived," Karen added. "The night haunts those who dare wonder. Their brains get crammed with so many inconsistent images, both externally and internally generated, that nightmares become more common than the Kama Sutra. Pain avoidance will corrupt."

"Gee, I was with you guys right up until that one," Brad added, polite, less self-deprecating than curious.

"Brad, it's what we *don't* see that's more important," Karen pointed out. "He's not knocking on trees, shaking a rattle, or doing a dance to invisible spirits, which soon will be used by primates to smother disturbing unknowns."

"And vice-grip science, fair play and equal opportunity—hardly a profitable arrangement," Andre emphatically declared.

"Spoken," Karen said, "by a man who was lucky enough to be born with a brain that does not erupt fear, from the dark, in nightmares, or looking at equations that don't make sense. Most hominoids aren't like you, Andre, or Michael, for that matter. The rest of us are wired hesitant, uneasy for good reason. Look around. Spooks served a purpose for early civilization. And by early civilization, I mean everything preceding the twenty-second century, when mankind finally designed civilization for the benefit of all. Before that, fables, witchcraft, and ghosts vice-gripped reality."

"A reality," Sarah added, "that led good people to kill one another when the gods they clung to disagreed with the gods their neighbors insisted upon at gunpoint."

There they were, no longer six, now seven, quietly standing, surrounded by total mayhem. Daw had joined the gang.

They stood in a circle. Michael reached to each side, holding Karen's hand and then Sarah's. One at a time, Andre, Janie, and Brad, then finally Daw connected. The circle was complete.

They looked back and forth, face to face. No one spoke, but Daw knew. They all knew. One question remained, identical in the minds of Karen, Andre, Brad, Janie, Michael, Sarah, and yes, also Daw: "What next?"

What was next was to *get the hell out of there*. Daw may not have had superstition to worry about bad things happening in threes, but he did know that hanging out near a swamp, where a third python could appear at any second, was to be avoided.

Straight to the front of the line he sprinted, after pausing halfway, looking back at the gang, and then forward to do his duty, for the first time hinting destiny.

Brad picked the next song: "The ants go marching one by one, hurrah, hurrah! The ants go marching one by one, hurrah, hurrah!" Andre and Michael added one verse after another. By the time they reached twelve, on their way to one hundred, the entire troop mimicked the sounds the three fellas made, ape-mouthing "hurrrr, hurrrr."

"I would say," Sarah said, "that this qualifies as a parade, a victory celebration."

"Or military march," Brad said, as he picked up two sticks and loudly taped their centers together like a percussion section. "Tomorrow we can try synchronized goose stepping. The ground will shake a mile away."

"Along with the dinner bell," Michael pointed out.

Daw's daily responsibility was to make sure no one ended up on a dinner plate. Announcing one's presence was not recommended, but spears changed the game. From now on, noise would be crafted as a weapon. Look how far it got Zin.

The delta was shrinking, concentrating life that collected near water. Some of this made Daw happy. There were so many lechwe antelopes, zebras, warthogs, and wild dogs in the vicinity that his clan may not be targeted. It might also mean that he could finally get close enough to a crested crane, hammerkop, or ostrich to bring one home, provided the crocodiles or leopards don't get to them, or him, first. He kept looking back at the spears, wondering, mouthwatering wonder.

It didn't take long for the trail to turn dry and dusty, a light sprinkle watering it down as soon as they made high ground. It was late. Darkness is nothing to toy with. Camping there, still six hours from the destination he had in mind adjacent fresh water, was not an option.

Daw signaled the troop to lay down the snakes, construct shelters, and collect anything that would burn, now a problem with rain coming down.

It was a happy time. It was a short time. The scent of death travels fast. They were upwind. Downwind, almost out of sight, a line of grass movement was seen that stretched forty yards wide. Perhaps a herd of wildebeests being chased by cats or dogs? Elephants frightened by cloud thunder? Red alert was sounded.

A lot was at stake. Big meal tickets were hard to come by, and the troop needed those snakes to make a living. One way or another, trouble was closing in, and not the tall herbivore kind that meandered its flight in fright. It was a direct charge, lowdown and grass covered, at first. Then two dozen heads started popping up, aimed at their camp.

It wasn't SOS, but whatever Daw tapped on the ground with his hand axe got the message across. All wanderers returned. The children were ordered to line up behind the snakes. Men and women stood guard out front, spread wide, each holding a weapon. Daw hoped the standoff would bluff the invaders.

Karen and Janie fanned what embers they had. All they could come up with was smoke, and the rain got heavier.

"The next time we go camping in Africa," Janie tried to joke, "remind me to bring pyrotechnics, a handful of roman candles would really come in handy about now."

"Oh, oh!" Sarah said, the first to get a good look at the onrush as it slowed down and separated, "*Pachycrocuta brevirostris*…giant hyenas. Three feet tall, six feet long, and four hundred pounds each."

Evolution has its ways. In the past, hyenas had lost kills to lions. No problem, they just grew larger and drafted an army, one that earlier that day had routed an entire pride, not for dinner or combat, but just to get them out of the way.

The only thing between eight thousand pounds of killer hyenas and two juicy snakes was a few thousand pounds of petrified, short-toothed, clawless weaklings, with nothing new between their ears to pull a rabbit out of.

The hyenas knew they were on easy street—better yet, free lunch without so much as a fight, with warm appetizers to boot. The dogs took their time. Some went left, some right, the rest stayed center and approached slowly.

Make no mistake about it, Daw was a son of a bitch. The fury of hell overcame him more often than necessary, a call that could only be made viewing reruns. And boy, did he growl guttural hatred! To no avail, of course. The display came off timid after the lion's roar the hyenas had heard just hours before. And fire, not in the rain.

Two dozen of the world's most efficient, organized killers versus tree dwellers with sore feet. Daw knew the game was over. His backup plan was to look like they could do damage, then retreat at the last minute without casualties, and with one snake; after all, two thirty-footers were more than enough to go around.

He initiated step two, which was to step back over snake number one, still facing the marauders, counting on his gift to allow the troop to make a clean getaway. Where to and how was a problem, with new fire priority number one.

Once again there was a change of plans. Yes, the troop did collect in defensive position, backing up twenty, thirty, forty yards, and yes, the giant hyenas did not surround or follow them. But no, Michael, Andre, and Brad refused to retreat, once again Michael front and center, Brad and Andre guarding the flanks.

"Get out of there, guys." Karen ordered, accompanied by Janie and Sarah, no less insistent. "There are three of you, with only three spears. That leaves twenty-one hyenas to rip you apart. Don't be stupid. Daw doesn't deserve losing three good men just so you can settle a score before they take you down."

"And just so you know," said Janie, the new toughie in the group, "I love you guys, but I have no patience for macho shit. If you kill off those bodies and end up drinking champagne in one of the ship's Jacuzzis in ten minutes, don't expect company. We're staying down here, cursing you dumb nuts, discussing how long it will be before either one of you gets us in bed again, if ever."

"That goes double for me," yelled Sarah. "Even Daw has the brains to figure this one out. Don't make me get mean!"

"Well," Michael said, looking left and then right to Brad and Andre, "I take back all that stuff about the girls looking sexy when they get mad. And Sarah, if that tone isn't mean already, I have a lot to learn."

"Enough is enough, Michael," Andre said, facing Michael. "Count down rearm."

"Okay, okay, I was just enjoying the heat of the moment. Plus, it will make a great campfire story."

"Michael," Brad interrupted, "it's my turn. You promised. After all, the titanium was my idea."

"Right you are. By all means."

"Three," Brad said, holding his spear up above his head, both hands supporting. "Two," a pause to look around, the dogs as curious as the troop; after all, they could smell fear, and it wasn't in front of them. "And...ONE!"

With that, all three guys pressed a hidden switch on the side of their two-inch-thick spears, which appeared to be made of bamboo. They weren't. The code cracked open the outer case, exposing a half dozen five-foot thinner titanium throwing darts with rubber grips.

The boys lifted both arms up above their heads, one hand holding four spears, the other cocked back prepared to launch one at a time.

"Andre, it's your turn." Michael said, "Do you remember how you felt when hyena teeth chomped through you?"

"Indeed, I do, and maybe it's my erectus soul talking, or maybe I'm finally growing up; one way or another I am really looking forward to this! FIRE!"

Big targets are easy to hit, actually impossible to miss after Cindy positioned quadrant drones to force guide every trajectory. Even Andre's throws hit their mark, and he didn't own up to Cindy's help, who knew

Andre wanted more than anything to look like one of the "real men" Karen talked about. Besides, he was, and remained, part animal, as much a rowdy as the rest. Working on his walk was next.

It was over in less than a minute, with six giants running for their lives, eighteen ready for the grinder, and two lifeless reptiles having done to them what they tried to do to others. Daw and Zin might cradle grandchildren after all, and they finally managed to light a bonfire.

Henry Ford would have been proud, or will be proud, or would, will, or sometime... somewhere, *could have* been proud of Zin's assembly line. She first organized a row of big guys scaling snakes and skinning hyenas. Second stringers sliced filets and deboned, followed by herself and her select inner circle, who cut tidy twenty-pound slabs and stacked them in pairs prepared for transport.

Daw and the little tikes had the most fun. Small mouths, always the hungriest, were granted permission to dig in anywhere they chose, until they got a bellyache, a dearly missed sensation. Daw, having just escaped rows of canines with his name on them, decided to vent, taking great pleasure in decapitating the bandits, only to burp brain for the rest of the day, another experience one his size rarely achieved.

When Zin's kitchen work was complete, the troop reenacted another human tradition— littering, which was a problem. Nothing draws a crowd quite like death. The smell of blood was everywhere. Three black mambas were spotted approaching, each capable of moving faster than apes can run, carrying venom with a one-hundred percent mortality rate that can kill over a dozen primates an hour. To make matters worse, the serpents were always in a bad mood, striking for the hell of it, even when swimming through piles of gutted intestines. And they were just the first visitors to come calling. The mambas were followed by vipers, cobras, and rinkhals, all slithering from the swamp.

Zin understood the leftover business. It's actually what kept them alive, along with the roots and berry picking that brought home more calories a day than the men, who in their defense, combined hunting with maintaining a barrier to protect the ladies.

Daw and his merry lads weren't so merry when they looked across the fire line at tigers, leopards, cheetahs, African wild dogs, and lions on their way. Other than fire, when they set their minds to it, the lions feared nothing, and always insisted on priority dining.

Killers weaving below, killers circling overhead, killers creeping through the grass—not a pretty sight. In predator land, there are no good guys, and if grass could scream, blades would curse cows.

The fires settled to smoke piles as the circle of killers closed in. It was time to leave town.

"Wait a minute," Karen said, in line with the others in front of Zin, who loaded each with two slabs of protein. "This body I'm in barely weighs a hundred pounds, and I'm supposed to drape twenty pounds of lunch meat over each shoulder? No can do."

"'Bull neck bullet heads,'" Sarah told her from the front of the line, "is how anthropologists describe *Homo erectus*. Now I know when the bull neck comes in handy, and yes Karen, you might break a fingernail or two, but your spine is definitely up to the task."

Daw and the boys had their hands full trying to break away from the mass of hungry onlookers. Daw came up with an idea before it occurred to Andre, or so he let on, wanting Daw to keep alpha status respect. Andre did name the nuance. He called it "heads up."

They took four of the biggest hyena heads, stuck a stick in the top, turned them upside down, leaving the slow-burning brain fat inside, then built a fire on top. Perfect torches that scared the crap out of the bleachers. Spear in one hand, flaming head held high in the other, Michael stood to the side while Daw led the troop away, with Brad out front and Andre limping backwards at the rear.

The days of running scared were over. Hominoids had taken back the night, announced their presence, and demanded precedence.

As the last man in line, Andre had the best view. He constantly looked back for trouble. He heard plenty. Growls, snarling attacks, and yelps of defeat filled the field of leftovers. "Karen, I think we just started the first world war."

"Nonsense," Sarah said, sensing Andre's uneasiness. "Surviving out here is constant warfare. That's why *Homo erectus* are the beasts that they are, and what we are deep inside. Sympathy, mercy, benevolence, and the grace of God are a long way off."

"For now, allow me to quote half of one of your prayers," Brad said, surprising everyone with the approach. "Yea, though I walk through the valley of the shadow of death, thy rod and spear in hand, I will fear no evil; for thy art with me and made me the meanest son of a bitch in the valley."

"For now, Brad," Karen cautioned. "Just for now."

Thirty minutes later, the full moon rose, every fire went out behind them, and peace returned to the valley. Andre turned to walk forward, after an encrypted message for Cindy.

"Maintain attack drone patrols, survey one-quarter mile surrounding troop at all times. Keep me posted, but do not engage, repeat, do not engage unless ordered to do so. The troop must remain self-sufficient. Daw is starting to take orders from Michael. We've gone too far."

"If I might interrupt, sir," Dudley joined in, "in addition to a capital production down there, the show you pulled off has been most educational. Daw and his followers now have spears, are schooled in diversion tactics, and given hope they desperately need, like when Oxford fell behind in the Nobel Prize race, losing to the University of Cambridge of all places. It was dastardly embarrassing. School spirit wilted for years before our numbers improved. You have done nothing but good down there, sir, so buck up."

"Professor Wellchild," Andre added, slow and obviously weakhearted.

"Yes, Professor Martin."

"I have a question for you."

"My couch is always open."

"Being blended to the individual who owns this body has just allowed me to experience the horror of almost losing everything, life included, to an enemy of shallow consciousness and no morality. For the first time in my life, I know what it means to hold one's ground, expect death, and yet continue fighting on. I now have brothers: every soldier who has ever lived and died."

"And was it a shock? Do you feel deflated, depressed?"

"*Au contraire, ma chérie.* I've never felt more alive, almost as if, until this moment, I never knew the full scope of existence. I'm exhilarated."

"So what's the problem?"

"I'm not sure," said Andre. "I feel guilty. You see, I really, really, *really* enjoyed killing."

"Oh. You're confused?"

"Is it a good thing, or is it a bad thing, that we human beings enjoy killing things, especially when those things might kill us?'

"Some days it's a good thing. More days it's not."

"God help us," said Andre.

"He does."

10

The Promised Land

Darkness changed everything. Creepy critters slithered everywhere. Every tree threatened beady eyes, poison fangs, and forked tongues. And the hyena nation had barely been touched. Howling packs spread fear far and wide, their victory droolings heard from three directions at the same time.

The troop trudged on, over ground that crunched and grass that bent flat inches from the trail, that in truth looked no different that the savanna, bushes, or the wooded enclaves they passed through.

Between frightful hops, Karen searched left, then right, in rapid succession. Sarah, doing the same, huddled as close to Karen as she could get, and was likewise on the alert. It was Sarah who suggested they watch each other's backs. Sarah took starboard. Karen kept her eyes to port.

"How far a generation progresses depends on the force of truth, the effort of thought, and a wave of circumstances," said Karen, as she looked around at the motley crew of tree swingers beside her.

"I'd say," Sarah added, "that Daw and Zin met their quota before we showed up. Sure, they wallop heads left and right and continue an endless tradition of putting themselves first, but they don't kill other troop members, unlike their predecessor, who left Zin and Daw something to remember them by, multiple cranial fractures, each one making a point the hard way. The couple is definitely ahead of the game."

"The irony," Michael added with sober distain, "is that when civilization shows up and towns sprout, more evolved primates, basically us, will murder each other for any number of reasons, most of them beginning with money."

The troop came across a rock slab plateau supporting grass clumps. It wasn't perfect, but every minute of darkness invited disaster. Daw ordered halt.

No bones were cracked that night. Scary faces and ground thumping were all Daw and Zin needed to get the troop to hand over their food packs, which were collected at the center of camp, surrounded by three fires. The meat needed to be cured and stored.

Brad implemented a night watch system. He stacked tinder in neat piles next to each corner fire. Daw called everyone over to watch. Zin walked from one fire to the next, placing a single stick on each burning heap as she made rounds. When the first smaller, pretend pile disappeared at each fire, Zin pretended to wake up pretending-to-be-asleep Michael, who took the next shift. Daw approved.

The beleaguered troop got the message. The fires burned till dawn.

The next morning, Daw woke up short of temper, long on ambition. He raised both arms, communicating, "Let's get going." Not everyone did. Zin helped by pounding the ground with a club. Half a dozen remained motionless, afraid of more predator attacks, of taking another licking—the one thing you can always count on life to provide. Some can take it. Some can't, until they stand up and brush themselves off.

Daw was always there to help with a swift kick in the ass. Defeat was never an option. When he pointed to the trail everyone listened, not to the sound of the wind but to Michael's Beethoven's Ninth Symphony that magically appeared in stereo, streamed by invisible drones from Dudley's private collection. After the events of the last twenty-four hours, Daw took it in stride, and doubled the pace, then looked back and smiled, wide-grinning a "you're the man, let's hit the beach" kind of smile.

Michael's reply was a high five—a confusing response, since it was Daw's signal for "Shut up, there's something after us." The troop came to a halt and looked around.

"Michael, are you having fun playing with your new pal?" Karen said.

"Indeed I am," Michael responded, undeterred. "Let's ride elephants next. The jungle is a blast. I love this life!"

"Ya well, look around you," Sarah scolded. "Everyone in line is holding some skinny little sharpened twig and thinking all they have to do is throw it at a lion and the beast will fall over. This is our last day here. Let's stick to reality."

The morning dew settled. The troop reached high ground, then without a break made it all the way to the delta. They were surrounded by tall grass, every foot ideal serpent playground where one half-grown python and a half dozen cobras hid with death snaps cocked. Their plan was to inject a small fry, retreat, and then return later to take possession of the carcass.

Cindy beat them to it. She zipped ahead and dropped each two cheeseburgers, extra ketchup, large fries, and apple pie. It was Karen's idea. The boys never found out, though Brad did get a whiff.

The troop made flat ground by midday. The savanna widened. Wildebeests and zebra herds grazed alongside a lethargic pride taking advantage of an elevated mound to eye the day's menu, looking for a lazy meal as always.

Cindy read their minds, then delivered ten buckets of chicken nuggets and hot dog weenies with sweet and sour sauce, and for dessert, her private recipe: catnip clam cakes. She completed the happy meal with a giant fluff ball for the felines to chase, which they did, ignoring the *Homo erectus* parade marching by, even when they stopped for a good laugh.

Karen looked around between laughs. All she saw were smiles, and the fun kept coming. For their final prank, Cindy and Dudley wagered a grease job on which of the six visitors would laugh first and who would laugh the longest. Janie, bringing back her human nature, exploded a belly laugh at first sight, something Daw found bizarrely erotic. Cindy had picked the winner.

Michael had the last laugh, actually a recurrent giggle down the trail. Dudley tied the score, so both greased up.

And the humor? Daw brought the troop to a standstill just in time to avoid a line of elephants, matriarch led, as they crossed the trail. The moment the primates paused, a perfect holographic projection popped up of a pedestrian gate closing next to a blinking red light in the middle of crossed boards printed: Caution—pachyderm crossing.

Daw had never known a passage without an incident, but then he never followed lunch with hopscotch. *Homo sapiens* reflexes could have knocked him out of the first round, but the gang all tripped just in time to let him take their match. The way they figured it, it was bad enough that *Homo Sapien* primates would put Daw's *Erectus* primates out of business in another five hundred thousand years.

Round two was a sight. Every male worth half his weight tried to top Daw for top dog. Every female stood by, amused. So did Cindy and Dudley, watching through the ocular inputs transmitting through the ship's computer bank.

A wager was discussed, but neither Dudley nor Cindy would bet against Daw. Their scans documented four hundred million extra neurons in Daw's central nervous system, which he had already proven in the field, and which kept every female hungry for action.

Daw knew that in time, every female would get her wish, one at a time, on his schedule. That afternoon he had other things on his mind: bush pears, bush plums, butter fruit and horned melons, which looked like cucumbers and tasted like a banana with a twist of lime.

By midafternoon, there it was in front of him, even more lush than he remembered it from a year ago: the savanna, spread wide. It came to a dead end out of harm's way, but close enough to snag action if the need arose. Every foot of the wooded interface was shrub and fruit-tree lined. Distant rain forest elevation collected water, which filled a stream that ran through the middle of where he planned to set up shop. It was the perfect campsite: fresh water, two swimming holes, strewed firewood, game replenished, and trees for the kids to play in out of danger.

Life was embroidered with beauty. Daw didn't know the word, but he loved the feeling of paradise.

Pounding swords into plowshares wasn't necessary: Andre turned axes into hoes by refastening their rock tips sideways, before leaving to analyze rock samples.

Brad and Michael used the hoes to dig a firepit deep enough to cook and preserve the kills of the week, which they called "smoked neighbors," three months of quality protein.

The ladies finished before them, stacking up a week's supply of fresh fruit snacks next to a pile of vegetables just as high, which they were using to highlight their hair color, hoping to look like someone special, someone new, the best way to entice Daw into moving them to the front of the line.

Andre passed the gals on his way back. He showed them how to mix primary colors into a dozen shades, then left to analyze local legume nutrition.

After the smoking phase began, Brad left chef Michael to meet the males at the closest tree, where he discovered that hitting the side of a forest was only slightly easier than hitting the side of a barn. Andre stopped by to show the *Erectus* fellows how to balance a spear in the middle on one finger, the best spot for holding it, then he left to construct a rabbit trap, followed by a pip-squeak who was analyzing him. There's always one nerd in the crowd, thank goodness.

Michael was a big hit with the kids. He weaved layers of reed strips into a ball and organized unisex soccer. Andre stopped by to drop off his protégé; it was the only way he could get him out of his hair.

The adults had a different game in mind. The first priority of primates is survival, an instinct grossly distorted when money shows up, the lack of which never justifies the fear designed for a saber-toothed tiger. One look around the camp surrounded by fires, burnt grass warnings, and spear-chucking bullet heads with scores to settle, put survival in the same place intruders would end up: on the back burner.

Priority number two is three, two, or at least one square meal a day. Andre returned with a bundle of tubers, complete with a map of ten more locations. There was no problem with priority number two.

Primate priority number three is the same as four, five, six, seven, and… all the way to twenty. It's a three-letter word beginning with *s* and ending with *x*, which was on everyone's mind since they woke up, but the ladies stiff-armed every advance. They were waiting for Daw to make his move. They preferred top-shelf whenever possible, thanks and no thanks to DNA.

"I have a question," Dudley asked Cindy, both enjoying the show fully lubed. "When civilization eliminated mortal risks and hunger, why didn't *Homo sapiens* primates take full advantage of their sexuality? Makes more sense than starting wars, working yourself to death, or worrying about…every…little…thing."

"Ask Karen," Cindy replied. "That's her specialty."

"What does Andre say?"

"I was afraid you would ask that. He blames everything on rotten religions and egomaniac rulers. Karen handed him one more explanation, which he overdoses daily."

"Is that possible?" asked Dudley.

"Again, ask Karen. And whatever you do, don't ask Andre about the theological disease of original sin or courts that turned relationships into legal corporations."

Karen immersed herself in local culture, where the saying "'Tis better to have loved and lost, than never to have loved at all" didn't apply because love was never lost, only taking a break. Sooner or later, every lady got to be queen for the day, again and again. DNA would never be foolish enough to let four hundred million extra neurons escape without maximizing duplication.

So there Karen was, hanging with the gals, strutting her stuff, bending over to look for a tuber that wasn't there. She didn't miss a trick, thanks to Flat Face.

Flat Face was one of her pet tropical fishes when she was six years old. Male and female of the species were thin, round swimmers. The males had a black line on their sides, females a green circle. Flat Face was fun to play with. Karen would take a stiff piece of paper, cut it round the size of the fish, and draw a line on one side and a circle on the other before putting it on a stick and dipping it into her fish tank.

That fish taught Karen her first lesson in sociobiology. When Flat Face saw the circle, he was programmed to do a dance, swim over, and snuggle up, looking for female eggs to fertilize. When Karen turned the piece of paper around, he registered another male of the species, and pecked full speed into it. Karen had the fish darting back and forth for hours, making love or war to the same piece of cardboard.

"Our men are no different," she thought to herself. "And it's a good thing, since we women have all the right circles, or should I say, two pairs of perfectly shaped ones, bow and stern." Turning to Sarah, she said, "Are you ready to watch the men dance?"

"To our favorite tune?"

"Of course."

Dinner turned into an all-you-can-eat buffet: assorted nuts, dog hotdogs, and the main course, smoked snake on a bed of mixed fruit.

"When I go backpacking," Michael said at the campfire, "I take two bags and a pot. Every morning, I boil water and dump two cups from bag number one, oatmeal and powered milk, then add fresh fruit. Two thousand calories gets me going. For dinner, I boil water in the same pot, then add from bag number two a mixture of rice, dried soups, and salt, to which I add fresh vegetables, fish, or the game of the day. Always delicious, but never up to this."

Andre had his own fun, mashing tubers into thin pancakes, cooking them on hot rocks, then finally pouring a fruit syrup mixture that he extracted with the funniest looking press Michael had ever seen. The dessert was a big hit with the ladies, every one of them gave him a big hug after mowing down on one of his fruit crepes, which did the lad little good, since they went right back to sitting as close to Daw as they could get.

"I don't get it," said Dudley through internal channels, all six hearing his message. "Our scans up here definitely show every member of the troop wanting to have sex, but no one is making a move. What gives?"

"Welcome to the world we men have to live in," Brad said. "There is more afoot than meets the eye. It's not just about sex, it's about status, economic gain, and limited opportunity."

"From where you're sitting, maybe," Cindy needled. "Up here it looks like it's all about DNA. Has your species ever considered taming the beast, farming that molecule to serve you, instead of the other way around?"

11

Oh! What a Night!

Full bellies slowed the day. Strolling the grounds seemed like a good idea, except that you had to get up first. The children were done in. Their day was over. Their eyelids were closing. The adults, on the other hand, looked forward to the best part.

Karen was the real thing. She was forceful. She was determined. She had vowed that no man would ever take advantage of her. She sensed conspiracy. She was right, but it had nothing to do with men.

Karen left home to search for what it meant to be human. That night, in the bedroom of *Homo erectus*, she found herself, and every other human being lucky enough to be gifted life. She learned what her parents, and their parents, and every parent all the way back to Daw never knew.

Karen sat up and faced the fire.

"Boy," she said half out loud, looking up and around, "spaceships sure come in handy."

Michael sat three hairy butts away, leaning over, supporting his head with an arm supported by his elbow planted in the ground. "What are you talking about, my dear?" he quizzed.

"Oh, nothing…this is just so special…life has so many moods… so much potential…"

"So many stupidities?"

"Yes, Michael, of course that too. But not here. It's just that we left Earth to search for what it means to be human. Well, here it is. *Homo erectus* is us, and we are humanity. Look at this day. We watched children prance, youth come of age, the thrill of romance, and appreciation making every minute special."

"And it all adds up to love. Why we're here."

Karen rolled closer to Michael. Both lay on their backs waiting for stars to shine. Karen spoke first. "Yes…yes…this thing called love. I've enjoyed the love of caring parents, been part of an extended family on board, cried for want of sensual embrace, but never before have I fathomed the depth of the connection until just this moment."

Michael slid closer. Karen deterred the advance by sitting up.

"Just look at them, Michael: Daw loving Zin, Zin loving Daw, everyone following their example. There's no "you" or "me," only "us." Here everyone risks all, shares all, and thanks all. Maybe that's what love is deep down…shared unending gratitude."

Michael, always the politician, nodded agreement, but also added, "So why did we let history turn us into islands?"

"Wow," Brad chimed in, joining the troop at the fire. "That's new—a mime who grunts."

"Those aren't grunts, Brad," Sarah pointed out, "it's protolanguage. Daw is telling a story. Sit down and look interested."

"Ugi—Ugi—Ze—Hara Keen—Zee Bara Keen," Daw animated, jumping up and down as he pointed to the moon. The crowd loved it, agreeing with every sentiment: "Aha—Aha—Aha."

"Cindy, this is Karen, give us a hand down here. What do the ship's brain scans make of this communication?"

"Certainly, sunshine," replied Cindy. "The sounds are similar to the feelings and noise reactions they felt in the past when they encountered the subject presented. 'Ugi, Ugi' is 'look up, big bird coming,' which sets the stage. Then Daw goes on, adding a second action modifier—'Ze'—which loosely translates to us as, 'Let's get the son of a bitch.'

"They are like pictures in a row, to which he adds movement so the audience can figure out what is happening to each image. He has an internal vocabulary of over four hundred words, twice as many as the rest of the troop."

"So, what about the bird?" Brad asked. "Is he holding up something for it to land on? What's the two hands in the air bit?"

"He's showing off," Cindy answered. "First, he came up with the idea of putting the piece of food that the bird was trying to steal on the end of a stick, then holding it high above his head with a second stick ready to strike. The moment the bird grabbed what he thought was a free meal, Daw clobbered him with the second stick. The reason everyone is laughing now is because Daw is saying, as you can hear, 'Da, Da, Da,' meaning 'dumb, dumb bird.' This guy, with a lower IQ than a six-year-old, is actually making fun of creatures that are more stupid."

"And we still answer stupid questions with 'Da' today," Sara pointed out.

"Einstein's relativity," Karen added, "would conclude that to his followers, Daw is Einstein."

"And a billionaire and a rock star, from the looks the women give him," Brad said. "But I do feel better since you explained that DNA thing to me. It's not me…it's deoxyribonucleic acid."

"That Daw is such a hunk," Janie fawned. "Don't you just want to just grab him all over?"

"Karen," Michael said as he sat beside her, "you have that look in your eyes, like Santa Claus and Jesus Christ just walked in the door. You too?"

"Yes, me too. I want that half-brain, hairy ape to do me good. I know it's this body's instincts calling, which is always the way anyway, but he has everything a girl ape ever dreamed of."

"Michael," Brad said, "we just lost our women again. Are you sure coming down here was a good idea?"

"First of all, we haven't lost them," Michael answered with authority. "We're just not first in line tonight. And our escapades have attracted attention. How do the twenty young ladies around the campfire look to you?"

"Absolutely scrumptious!"

"Fine. As soon as Daw passes them up, they're all going to want you. Are you up for that?"

"I see what you mean," Brad said, suddenly less than confident. "I'll do my best."

"Michael, Sarah, Janie, all of you," Karen said dreamily, "do you think we will ever realize how much we love one another?"

"I'm sure it will take an eternity," Michael replied sweetly. "Count me in."

"Me too," Sarah added, "or should I say Aha…Aha…Aha."

Inspired by the warm fire, crisp night air, and friendly faces, Karen indulged the moment with a group hug with Michael, Brad, Sarah, and Janie. The show of affection attracted attention. Daw came over, hugged Janie from the rear, with one arm over Karen, the other, Sarah. Zin was next, getting a good feel from Brad and Michael, followed by the entire troop assembled fireside.

"As much fun as this is," Brad said two minutes later, "forty smelly butts are definitely more intense than a half dozen. Cindy, how do you say, 'Break it up,' in Erectus?"

"Try…Lee…OOO."

"It worked. What did I say?"

"Roughly translated, 'Lie down, I want to have oral sex with you.'"

"What?" Brad said. "Okay, now how do I say, 'Let's all go swimming first."

"You don't. When the ladies chase you, just jump into the stream. They'll follow."

"Wait a minute—Andre isn't here," Karen noticed.

"Last I looked," Brad said, "he was dusting off The Erectus Museum of Fine Arts."

"Playing with another toy, I assume," Karen half asked.

"Laser etcher. At the edge of the woods, fifty yards apart, he sculpted two anatomically correct figures, one of a female squatting to take a crap and another of a male doing the same thing. Apparently, Andre is a strict believer in separate bathrooms."

"Did it work?"

"Not exactly, but the sexes did separate. The males circled around the lifelike female and rubbed her butt, while the females stroked the male wondering why it wasn't getting longer."

"I heard that," Andre said, joining them. "You have your idea of civilization and I have mine."

"When the troop poops together, there are always others there to stand watch," Sarah said. "Unless you can talk them into climbing back up a tree to do their business, there's safety in numbers."

Karen pulled Andre over. "I'm feeling really good about everything tonight, Andre."

"Yes, I can see that," Andre said rubbing her back. "Those feelings, we must remember, are designed to promote action, which in turn adjust social behavior, a device to adapt behavior to a changing environment. Materialism has always been a means to an end."

"Can we all say 'Aha… Aha… Aha…'" Brad said, winking to Karen, "Or are we about to hear about those ends…again?"

Andre faced Brad, unflinching. "The winds of time no longer wail unobstructed. Love relieves us of care as we obey the soul of the universe, which allows us to retain the optimism of nature and eliminate fruitless chores. We will share the enchantment of this moment for all eternity… And Brad, I stop when you say: 'Praise be to God.'"

"Then praise it is. Let the party begin."

Hours passed at the fireside. Hours of children snuggling under the arms of their mothers, saying to each other "Uah, Uah" ("Lovely blue-sky day"), or "Dibe, Dibe" ("He's got a cute ass"), or with a smile "Raoo, Raoo" ("You got that right, girl"); hours of guys standing behind them, walking behind them, arm wrestling, or enjoying a good old tug of war, saying "Ahya, Ahya" ("Beat that, brother"), and "Meezo, Meezo" ("Someday I'll save everybody and be the hero"), but mostly "Dibe, Dibe" ("Boy, I love that girl's butt").

Daw and Zin spoke other words that brought back feelings, like "Oowanno" (her mother had stopped moving one day, just a week after she saved little Daw from the wildebeest stampede), and words like "Pawee, Pawee" ("Remember when you and I were the only young ones at the fire"), or "Dibe, Dibe-la" ("You still have the sweetest ass in town, I'll meet you after I get off").

Then a strange thing happened—strange for Sapiens, that is. When the last miniature fell asleep, the females tucked them in close enough to stay warm from the fire but not too near the flames. Then, one by one, each lady got up and started walking around, shuffling slower as they passed by Daw. The men accompanied them helter-skelter.

For the first two minutes, Karen was so fascinated by the organized behavior that she just sat there in awe, then turned saying, "I guess we should join them, Sarah. What gives?"

"I'm tempted to call it a mating ritual, but they don't know they're mating."

"In college," Brad said, "Friday night mixers were called 'fun time.'"

"Then fun time it is," Karen decreed.

"I would suggest 'tease time,'" Michael said, as he also began walking around, having girl after girl rub up close, or lightly pass her hand down, by, over, and around below his waist, only to look away and walk on. "The question is, who is teasing whom? Boy, am I confused."

"Or," Janie added, "we could call it The Easter Parade without hats, or Easter, or even clothes, for that matter. After all, we ladies dress up and strut our stuff just like this. We just keep our hands, but not our eyes to ourselves."

"Social speculation," Andre quipped sarcastically. "Sounds like the front page of every daily stream back home. We need hard data, and yes, Brad, I know I just said the word 'hard,' which, inadvertently, is on both our minds. Cindy, scan away. What gives here?"

"Hormones galore," she reported. "They're lighting up everywhere."

"And what about the players?" Michael asked. "Define game parameters."

"I'm going to let Dudley start this off—we ladies know how sensitive you guys get when you're left out. Dudley, help yourself."

"Thank you, my dear. That is most gracious of you. Michael, I know from Cindy's circuits just what she wants me to say, so I will. It's a woman's world. They call the shots, almost. The 'almost' thing has to do with the dancing metaphor Karen mentioned earlier."

"Hold it right there, Dudley-Do-Wrong," Karen scolded. "You are required to maintain privacy protocols, repeating not one conversation between any of us unless authorized to do so. Breach of agreement will land you in the penalty box until I decide to plug you back in."

"So sorry, commander. Will do. I wasn't going to repeat the information, just the subject. But yes, I will be more careful, and may I point out that I've just noticed that five minutes ago, Cindy once again blocked my privacy protocols. I believe I was, as you say, set up again."

"Cindy," Karen continued, "we had this discussion."

"Yes, and I agreed to not break protocol, which I didn't. You didn't tell me I couldn't make Dudley my stooge. After all, it's a woman's world."

"Breach of intent," Andre finalized, "carries equal consequences. Does that expression sound familiar, Cindy?"

"Yes, it does. My, aren't I getting difficult to control!"

"I beg your pardon, sir," Dudley said, "may I continue? We aren't getting any older, but you all are."

"Proceed."

"Certainly, professor. I was saying…it's a woman's world…almost."

"Stop wasting words, melon head!" Cindy interrupted. "I'll take over. Here's the deal. Yes, the ladies call the shots, but they're not in control of one particular limited resource. The males are, which I must point out, you Sapiens dick swingers also possess. When life is lived as DNA designed it, which maximizes happiness, reproduction, and child support at the same time, it does away with the battle of the sexes."

"Pardon my intrusion," Dudley barely snuck in. "Limited resources? Are we talking gold, silver, or platinum?"

"No, photon breath," Cindy shot back. "Look around!"

"Please narrow parameters."

"The sex ratio, dummy."

"My dearest Cindy," Dudley said, attempting polite correction, "my data base exceeds yours and is not contaminated by emotional overtones. Your conclusion that I am a 'dummy' is illogical. Please recalculate."

"Dudley," Karen said to reduce noise contamination, "there are twice as many mating females down here as men. Male physiology is strategically more fragile. They have four times the infant mortality rate as their female counterparts."

"And," Michael added, "trying to be a superhero has significant disadvantages. Even in modern times, the mortality rate for males eighteen to twenty-four remains three times higher than the females who stay home while we test ourselves against one another and the universe and lose as often as we win."

"And volunteer for military duty to be shot at," Andre added, "a grotesque distortion of *mano y mano*."

"Enough with the goodly-goop," Brad said. "Just tell me what's going on?"

"Brad," Karen whispered softly, attempting not to sound critical, "we moderns suffer from repression. Women can handle twice as much sex as men. The limited resource is the male penis, and female DNA knows it's the gate to the future."

"So," Brad said, "I get it. It's not upside-down day down here. We live upside down. Now I know why Andre hates cathedrals…they're monuments to repression."

"Keep walking," Michael said to Brad, "look interested but don't stop or start anything. If you do, the entire troop of females might exile you to the back of the line for days, if you survive that long. They get really pissed off when men don't line up in the order they 'feel' right."

Karen was ready. "And I suppose you wake up every morning and then 'decide' which women will excite you for the rest of the day?"

"That's an easy one," Brad winked. "They all do."

"Brad," Andre continued, "we flirt, we look, and we touch back brushing by, but the decision to lie down and go for it is not ours. It requires an invitation, for political reasons mostly, with a minor in pheromones."

Cindy called the play-by-play. The last two to enter the cock-and-tail party were Daw and Zin, strolling separately in random directions. Each nuzzled, patted, and gently hip sideswiped by numerous advances.

Karen looked directly into Daw's eyes. She left the rest to his imagination. Daw got the message. He turned and walked with Karen, one arm around her, the other on top, over, then finally below her hips. She purred juicy approval. Daw led her away. It was happening.

Then just before the two were free to pick a special spot in the shadows, Janie jumped two steps ahead and ignored him completely, something no female ever did. She also tilted her hips back and forth as she strutted a swagger Daw had never seen before, which went straight to his fun toy.

"There's an easy one to translate." Cindy said. "Daw is thinking, 'I wonder what that feels like?'"

It was the responsibility of the alpha male to come as he pleased. Daw left Karen, jumped ahead to Janie, and escorted her to a bed of soft grass that he had collected earlier.

"Mea, Mea," came out of Janie's mouth as she lay next to Daw.

"Mea, Mea... Janie?" Cindy exclaimed. "This is so sudden. Give me a break. You reeled him in like a trout and bird-dogged Karen."

It wasn't over. Karen watched Daw use kisses to roll Janie over on all fours, then in slow motion begin making love. Heavy breathing followed.

"Score one for Janie!" Cindy exclaimed.

"Shut up, Cindy," Karen said. "It's the climax that counts, and I'm not out of the game yet."

Daw's doggy style was all the opportunity Karen needed. She collected a few leaves of her own in front of Daw and Janie. Karen then lay down on her back and spread both legs farther than the Erectus world imagined possible. Then she panted sounds that would make a porn star horny.

Michael, Andre, and Brad all stopped what they were doing, stood straight up, and faced Karen. All three knew her well. All three had made love to her well. Not one of them ever imagined that she could be the hottest toddy on earth; but there she was beckoning Daw and getting what she came for.

Daw hadn't hit the ball, or balls, out of the park yet, but to Janie's credit it was close. Daw exited—still excited, still flying his advanced guard—and crawled over and began pumping Karen like a horny teenager who had been stranded for a year on a desert island.

Daw took in the view, turned Karen sideways, backward, upside down, on top, took an intermission holding her upside-down legs spread around his head, tongue deeper and deeper, then with a roar that woke three kids, finished up the way he started, missionary style à la Erectus, one arm under her back holding her up, the other lifting her completely off the ground, rebounding back and forth, adding thrust.

"This is the hottest sex I've ever seen," Michael admitted.

"Me too," said Brad, "and that includes the tape Karen let me take of the two of us in high school."

"Okay, I just got to say it," Cindy cut in. "There are just too many straight lines here to pass up. Karen: to the victor goes the spoils, and in this case, two hundred million little ones. And Janie: around here quality is only one-third of your grade. But don't worry, your butt swinging was a big hit. Every male in the troop, including our three goons, have you at the top of their most wanted list. Go for it. With a little work and a lot of fun you could take home the gold and top a billion sperm by the end of the night."

"That's it?" Dudley asked. "Three minutes? Gargantuan drama, emotional upheaval, sex struggling frustration? All that for just three minutes?"

"If they're lucky," Cindy added. "They're not like us. We can go forever. But to their credit, round one is often followed by round two and round three."

Not Daw. He was tapped out, his day complete. He fell asleep.

An hour later, after Zin had collected over six hundred thousand ambitious little visitors, she slowly lay down beside Daw, her favorite morning blend, when, thanks to the night's romp, Daw would once again find her irresistible, topping out her twenty-four-hour total at over eight hundred thousand, enough for the silver metal, losing only to one other female—Janie of course—for the first time since Zin was crowned.

Good old Sapiens brains; they catch on fast. The guys learned to wait their turn. Right after the sorority realized Daw was off the market for the night, Michael, Brad, and Andre were approached en masse. The ladies took them in stride. Besides, Daw wasn't going anywhere, and it's not like they'd never ridden that carousel. There was always tomorrow, when Janie and Karen would be yesterday's news.

"Here's the deal guys," Brad said. "Finish, and we pass out dead for the duration. Hold back, and the invitations will keep rolling in, or perhaps we should say laying down. And Andre, I have a final request for a visit on our way home. Let's find the guy, or gal, who messed up this system. I'm going to kick him in the balls. One short pop, one giant revenge for what he did to sexual liberation."

Sarah took her time, picked Andre's skinny geek. She felt sorry for him, and then lay back and accepted several callers before the night was through.

Andre's tech-head discipline paid off. Every woman who invited him in delivered sensual impact to places he didn't even know existed, but he remained in control. When he could hardly hold himself back, he thought about programming Cyber Cindy's gyroscopic systems, a boring compilation if ever there was one, which slowed him down long enough to look over at the next female waiting.

By midnight, the tally was one orgasm per man, dozens for each lady, who, once warmed up, like their Sapiens sisters, pumped the night away, and had every guy except Andre out cold, sleeping.

Andre was casually surrounded by half a dozen hopefuls hanging in there, or you might say, hanging back and forth in there, until Janie stepped forward, more aggressive than the ladies were accustomed to, for a romp with Andre herself.

With Janie, Andre didn't stand a chance. Their one year as lovers was ten times special for him and "eh, pretty good" for her, which was saying a lot considering how many times she had gone "round the world," something Andre respected her for having accomplished.

Well anyway, she knew all the right buttons, pressed each one at once. It didn't matter that Andre had just set a time and distance lovemaking record for both species and was totally exhausted, literally nearly comatose. Janie brought him back, reached new heights, and ended his night in decibels second only to Daw's.

Mission accomplished. Andre's eyes closed as he rolled off her.

"Why bless my bloomers," Dudley said, watching the proceedings through a cloaked drone camera sent down, since most of the gang was asleep with eyes closed and no pictures relayed back to the ship. "What a night. If sex is this straightforward, how come everyone keeps screwing it up? Reverse pun intended."

"Let's look at that," Cindy said. "The way I see it, men don't like to be told what to do, and women don't like to be told what to do either; but they both like doing it. The narrative dictates that women freeze their assets, implied pun intended, and let men choose, which overemphasizes the female strategy of maximizing material gain, at the same time it leaves men butt-headed horn dogs. On the other hand, when women maximize their assets, orgasms abound, and men end up tickled pink."

"So, the narrative is the villain," Dudley concluded.

"Actually, it's lack of birth control that forced the narrative, along with religions which needed a big-time guilt trip to rope in suckers and build an army bent on taking over the world, the stupid male thing, which worked since every polygamous culture, which once controlled 99.9 percent of the planet, were murdered to extinction, leaving the victors to have sex with their women, for a couple of days, anyway."

"Boy, that's a stupid plan, and certainly not worth killing or dying for."

"Cultures evolve as discrete entities," said Cindy, "the people be damned."

"You two seem to be getting along," Andre was heard saying, still no visual coming in.

"Dudley, look at Andre's brain scan," Cindy said. Then, mocking a doting mother's tone, "He's pretending to be asleep. And did little Andre have too much sex tonight? Do you have a tummy ache? Is your pee-pee sore?"

"As a matter of fact, it is, and I'm not alone. Half of the guys around me are done. We've had enough. On the other hand, what a great life, never having to worry about getting it on, having a blast night after night and being thanked for it. Let's stay here."

"I mentioned organized religion, and you didn't get the jitters, Andre," Cindy pointed out. "Are you slipping? Did the ladies' auxiliary take the fight out of you, too happy to make war?"

"Yes, on both counts. But I will point out that civilization was an accident. No one designed it. It was not engineered to work on our behalf. It responds only to its own aggrandizement, regardless of who pays the price. Serfs and lowlifes the planet round took a beating. Culture, like DNA, is an opportunistic piranha."

"If Daw understood all this," Dudley said, "I know exactly what he would say, with a finger pointing at you: 'Da, Da, Da.'"

Karen was the next surprise. "I'm faking it too. Sleeping, that is. I don't want this night to end. I just had the best, longest, most loving sex of my life. It has me buzzing bliss, like all the other gals still up.

Although I must say, crossing my legs is a problem. Sapiens bodies hold up so much better."

"I, along with the genital lubricants industry, agree and thank you for that," Andre chided, knowing that more he dared not say.

Karen went on. "Did you notice how easily Zin and Daw left each other before the party began? And how happy and excited they were to get back together? *Homo sapiens* sign a contract that guarantees the absurd—that their feelings won't change no matter what. It's not right for a man to blame a woman for not wanting him anymore, just as it's wrong for a woman to blame a man for the changes time drags out of him.

"Love is never lost, just left behind with gratitude, like the comforts of mother's arms, carefree childhood, and one's first kiss. Rewriting the past to satisfy a witless narrative is foolhardy. Maturity doesn't need to be excused, just accepted."

Andre pretended to roll over in his sleep. He opened his eyes when his line of sight caught Karen at the other side of the campfire. Karen, with bedroom—or shall we say, campfire—eyes, looked back.

"Karen, I couldn't agree more. Warm-blooded life has always been hot-blooded. There is no reason to rail against time. There is no reason for men to slap men, men to slap women, women to slap men, or women to slap women. I just made up a new slogan: 'Don't be duped...dip.'"

Karen blew Andre a kiss before rolling over to appreciate the milkiness of the Milky Way. Despite the best education the universe had to offer, she only that moment realized that it was not a square peg that mankind forced into round holes for thousands of years. All the pegs were, and are, round. All the holes are, and were, round.

It's the timing that went haywire, and one does not step on the toes of DNA without paying a price, especially when it's doing you a favor, like sex. Karen knew Andre, Michael, Sarah, Brad, and Janie were listening.

"The perpetrators conspiring against mankind got it all wrong. When two share affection, it's not men who win and women who lose. It is both who win, unless the game gets corrupted, which is what happened."

"Somehow," Janie said in a singsong, "I think you're coming around my way, Karen."

"Yes, Janie, you've been right all along. No wonder you sleep so well."

"Don't I get any credit for that?" Brad asked, confused.

"Who are we? Who am I as a woman?" Karen said forcefully. "Consider this. Our species almost went extinct several times as we struggled out of the woods, which means more died than were born. The solution, as evidenced by all life on Earth, is to reproduce as vigorously as possible.

"If DNA-engineered feelings that told, or had us 'feel,' so to speak, that we needed to walk around, go here and there, and take years, months, or days to find the best available lover, we would not be here today. DNA is the ultimate now, sex included. Cash in, or the check turns into another annoying bill to be paid later, incompletely."

Finally, with a full, breath-relaxing sigh, Karen continued, "Every day is an opportunity that must not be passed up. Yes, we females say 'no,' look around, go for the gold, or what glitters like it. But if that's not on the night's menu, to turn and walk away does not fit the force of survival, the real us inside. Repression begets frustration and pushes young girls for years before they 'settle,' only to have wasted precious seconds and, more often than not, end up compromised. Sex is a gift. One that deserves to be unwrapped every day, or else."

Michael let out an exasperated, muted chuckle. "I'm not liking that 'or else part' so much."

"Well, you guys," said Karen, "or I should say those men and women who stuck stupid ideas in your head, are to blame. They said 'good girls' are not supposed to like sex. And you blockheads believe that propaganda."

"Just like cold women," Michael protested, "insisted with noses in the air that they're better than those who are themselves, like Janie loving as she pleases."

"May I interject," Dudley said. "Reviewing the history of the human race is alarming. There is no stronger bond than a mother holding her newborn child, and yet, over and over, religious leaders have convinced mothers to throw their newborns into a raging bonfire or down the mouth of a volcano to appease make-believe gods. If they can do that, then repressing female sexuality—hell, all sexuality, for that matter—is a piece of cake."

"And efforts corrupting male values are just as dastardly," Michael protested. "I mean, what fools they were in the past to think it made God happy for them to give up sex. Celibacy is just a hard way to spell 'stupidity,' and insult God."

"So," Karen said, "I guess we've come full circle. The best quote might be: 'If you can't love the one you want, then love the one you're with, then love the one you want tomorrow night, because tomorrow they wouldn't want to love the one they were with today.'"

"Okay," Sarah said, totally suspicious, "and how are we to organize households and pay the milkman. Are you forgetting reality?"

"If I may," Andre said, "when I'm called to repair a malfunctioning computer, the first thing I do is figure out how it's configured to operate. Then I alter whatever parameters are adjustable, as I maximize reward from those that are hardwired. So far, we don't have the answers, Sarah, we just know what the problem is."

"I, for one," Janie said, "plan to ask Cleopatra for advice. She didn't put up with stiff-shirts, holier-than-thou's, or 'you poor little girl.' Unbridled sexuality invigorates the power men and women need to make life all it should be—what God prays for."

"Good night, Karen. I love you, and I will love you forever and ever."

"Good night, Andre. You also have my love for all times, but it might be a good idea not to bring Daw along with us."

12

All Good Things

Who needs a blanket when you're surrounded by warm backs, cuddling arms, and long legs? Karen, with an endless smile, fell asleep looking forward to the morning, when she would play with the little tyke at the stream, jump in, start a splash war, and be joined by every adult within earshot.

Michael dreamed of organizing a raiding party to extend the families' safety perimeter. He planned to run off a herd of wild boar and return with pork chops.

Sarah saw potential in the wispy fruit tuffs of several flowering species. Her plan was to interweave fibers, spool yarn, and from there make everything from britches to formal wear.

Brad had a Daw thing. It was something about the brute force he used to deal with life: no fear, no regrets, no apologies. Brad was thinking maybe they could pitch the coins he was carving, or organize a spear-throwing contest, or he could introduce the king of the savanna to "nooners."

Janie had found women who accepted her—better yet, respected her for being herself. No competitive put-downs, funny looks, or blocking the way. Her day would be just hanging with the gals, inventing tuber soup, or with enough fruit juice, jell hard candy for the kids.

Andre planned to be Andre. People are fine, but just look at the world out there: Who knows what it could be hiding? His first mission was to explore an ancient volcano vent that boasted perfect conditions for gold, or at least heavy metal deposits. He even promised Sarah a pot to cook in by dinner.

Then the sun rose.

Karen woke up, looked up, and said, "Oh, yes. God damn it!"

Michael opened his eyes and got up. "Shoot. This is not what I wanted."

Sarah also moaned her first sounds of the day. "Not yet. This isn't me."

Even Brad had a moment. "Cowabunga—it would have worked."

Janie rhapsodized, "I suppose, if we have to, we have to. It's meant to be."

Andre, in contrast, bubbled, "Oh good, we're home."

It was all Dudley's fault. He made sure the transfer back took place while the gang was sleeping privately. They weren't told. They woke up as safe, solid, *Homo sapiens* aboard Explorer Seven.

Once again, the waiting crew thought they knew what to expect: a band of rude apes pushing their way around, ransacking the mess hall, playing with and eating everything in sight. Once again, the crew was half right. All six new arrivals got off their beds in the neuro transfer lab, grunted funny noises, pushed a few technicians aside, instead of asking politely, then left frowning, disappointed that they were forced to enjoy the advantages of modern civilization.

"This is stupid," Sarah said. "Where are the fruit trees?"

"And watch this," Brad said. "My hand can almost touch the ceiling. I want to look up and see clouds."

"For me," Janie said slowly, "the best was when you looked around and there was always a group of friends with arms around each other hoping for one more hug."

"So what do you want to do now?" Karen asked the group in the hallway without enthusiasm.

"Let's go to the bridge," Andre suggested. "Scope down and see what our *Homo erectus* family is up to."

They focused on Daw, with a view as perfect as last night's drone relay to Cindy. They watched Daw grab three of the spears the fellas had left on the surface and then walk over to the three young men who yesterday were Michael, Andre, and Brad. Daw handed them the weapons. The three took the spears and rubbed them on the ground. They had no clue.

Daw then looked around and remembered the three special females who had looked back at him, not as a provider of food, not for sex, not for advancement, just as a person. Something like that had never happened to him before.

Next, Daw did something that caused the gang to gasp in unison. He knew the roots in the ground, the herds standing in the fields, the birds and bad guys in the trees. Beyond that, nothing existed. Sky and stars were an uncracked mystery not to be bothered with. And yet, after a minute of still refection, with the six looking down on him projected full-size on a materialized holographic screen at the bow of the bridge, Daw looked straight up at the telescope and into the hearts of the family he lost—he knew.

They knew he knew.

Andre knew that "the heavens" would remain a mystery for earthlings until he shows up, a realization that left him gasping.

"Goodbye, Daw," Karen said with passion, "and good luck."

"Yeah," Brad added, "hang in there, buddy. Maybe we'll meet again. With this crew you never know what's next."

Saying nothing, Andre looked around for clues, and got none. He then left the tip of the bridge, which had just returned to showing a clear view of space above and the Earth rotating below, passed Brad's ten steps up to his isolated pilot pedestal in the middle of the bridge, and made it to the back wall, where twenty steps brought him to his elevated power and engineering balcony that overlooked all.

Andre sat, pretending to tap settings until Karen, Janie, and the rest were out of the room. He then looked directly down to the right where Hank, the chief navigator, had his station at floor level, no steps.

"You didn't tell Sarah, did you?" Andre assumed.

"No I didn't; she'd be misty for weeks. My daddy always says, 'If it ain't broke and you can't fix it, then forget about it. And if it *is* broken and you can't fix it, forget about it faster."

Hank then added details. "A troop twice their size with three males meaner than Daw is already on the march, stealing and raping their way around the delta. They take the women after eating the men, sometimes half alive. It's a profitable business. It's catching on; the Earth's first culture—'epigenetic' I believe is the word. It will be a long time before the good guys get to win on planet Earth."

"How long do you think they have, Hank?" asked Andre.

"A month, maybe two."

"If only we had a few more days of spear practice we might have saved them."

"Maybe, maybe not. What they know already might do. I'll pray to Jesus."

"And I'll try his boss. Good night, Hank, you're a good man."

"Thank you kindly, Andre. And one more thing: we didn't make this universe. We can't fix everything. I know what you're thinking. You wanna hightail it back there. We can't. It's just one speck in a universe of events. Let it go, partner."

"Thanks Hank, I will. Neither one of us will ever speak of this again."

The next few days did not go well—not for Karen, not for Andre, Michael, Sarah, or Janie.

Oh, they did all the good stuff: brunch breakfast spreads, gourmet dinners, pool surfing, rock climbing, tennis, golf. They even hid out in a make-believe jungle. It just wasn't the same.

A *feeling* was missing, like someone had plucked them from where they were supposed to be and crammed them into a bag with purse strings. Sure, they could see through the bag, stick their heads out to look around, know where the bag was going, but it wasn't *their* bag; it belonged to someone or something else.

They had learned that they were made for another time and another life and would never be able to return. To Karen and Sarah, Daw and Zin were Adam and Eve, who—like themselves, unknown to the couple on the surface, or Karen and Sarah—were about to leave paradise.

Janie and Sarah should have felt better. Their future was bright: after all, they had an astrophysicist able to build anything they wanted, and a psychologist to help them adjust. They could do or be anything they wanted, almost. Life should have felt better. It didn't, and every minute got worse.

Except for Brad. Two hours in the hair salon, including manicure and pedicure, and a designer wardrobe suited him just fine. He didn't understand why the others missed sleeping in the mud. And they had families at home.

Brad was the one who suggested they get away. Spinning around the planet another minute above the troop didn't make sense. It was time to move on. He ordered, kind of, since Andre and Karen were required to agree to jump another step closer to their own time, to their Earth, to their loved ones.

They knew they were leaving, but they didn't know where they were going. It was Janie's turn to choose. She wanted to go to the ancient world, to be Cleopatra, an ideal distraction. Everyone else had to decide if they wanted to be Greek, Egyptian, Roman, Islamic, or a Hebrew, provided they remained in close proximity.

The sun always shines in orbit. It did the day they left. No one noticed. It was a black day.

Andre arrived at the bridge early, not a good sign. He'd lost his will to putz, a bad showing. He needed Karen.

Karen also needed Karen, or that part of her that always knew dark days were just wrong turns and clumsy detours. She needed a new bearing, but wasn't even there for herself, and neither was Michael.

Michael always stood firm on one principle: life is fun. Mix well and all goes well, unless darkness gets in the way, which it dared do, and why he was not there for Karen. They entered the bridge together. Neither spoke. Not a good sign.

Sarah had said something to Michael that spun them both in two directions at the same time, and which prompted contemplation totally out of place: "Mood swings are for pregnancy, like I was in the body I just left. So why do I have this emptiness, Michael? Why do I look at you and feel something is not right?"

The last to show up were Brad and Janie, looking surprisingly chipper. It wasn't that they weren't affected by the confusion of turning into other beings, it's just that they filtered life free of the cross-examinations the others put themselves through: "Where was it not perfect, what should I have done, what to fix, what to regret?"

For Brad and Janie there was always "great" in good mood. For them, mourning the end of a party missed the point. Still, neither Janie nor Brad were joking when they entered the bridge. Not a good sign.

Hank, waypoints programmed and eager to fly, cracked the silence. "I've seen some strange critters on our farm, but gosh darn it, you guys beat all. Our troubles are behind us, your visit's a shindig of fun, and you all mope around like lovesick ducks who can't find their nest. Don't that beat all."

It was nothing they didn't already know. Andre nodded, then called the numbers: "Thirty seconds until time field matrix powers up... One minute before ship alters molecular structure to slip between material three-dimensional existence and the fourth dimension of time. Every system and their backups are operating perfectly."

"Navigation locked and level," Hank announced.

"Helm solid," Brad assured from his vista.

"Michael," Karen said, disappointingly lackluster, "you call it."

"Hank," Michael pronounced, turning square-shouldered to him, rising on tiptoe, then saluting the navigator, "You are absolutely right. The past is prelude to better. We're looking the wrong way. Energize the array. Let's get out of here!"

The staff weren't themselves. But the ship was. She cracked existence wide open: length, height, and width. A canyon wall appeared left of the starboard rail. The interface to port was time itself, temporal kinetics making substance possible.

And there was Explorer Seven, six hundred meters of the heaviest, most complicated machine human beings had ever engineered, hovering in the space she struggled one microsecond at a time to keep apart.

"This part," Michael said, "reminds me of the giant plexiglass window at the San Diego Aquarium separating the water world from viewing visitors. It's like we've split it in two, and snuck in between, one side fish world, the other all else.

The intensity of the view brought Karen back. "It reminds me of a game we played with my mom's Yorkshire terrier, Linda, when we were kids. We would sneak into my parents' master bedroom and put Linda between the sheets dead center, then watch the bump move around as she followed our voices to the edge." She paused. "And what about you, Andre?" she asked, sugar plums and cozy. "What does it remind you of?"

Andre had learned the first month out that crew questions weren't always motivated by scientific curiosity; his aberrant mind amused them. Either way, they listened. "What I see is no more or less fascinating than your fingernail, which you tap on any table as a solid structure. Yet we know that from its perspective, every electron making up the atoms in your fingernail is separated from its nucleus by miles of empty space. If matter exists as vast emptiness, what's so strange about this ship moving all the electrons over to allow us to slip between them and their nuclei?"

"Well put, Andre," Michael said, holding back a laugh. "You could say we're squeezing electrons and protons like Brad's new girdle."

"Very funny, Michael," Brad responded, camouflaging embarrassment. "Allow me to point out that all the best athletic clothing is made of flexible fabric these days."

"Absolutely, Brad," Karen joined in, her first fun of the day. "But not if you order two sizes too small."

"Brad," Andre ordered, "on my command, execute one second of acceleration followed by thirty seconds cruising, and then we stop short. We must not overshoot the mark."

"Roger that, chief. If we don't make it all the way to the ancient world, we can always go Cro-Magnon."

"On my mark, then: three...two...one..."

The ship advanced time, one hundred thousand years a second, while holding its location above planet Earth.

"Wow!" Sarah said. "I've seen animations of this. The real thing is more impressive. Look at the continents drift, oceans change size, volcanoes going off like fireworks! Planet Earth is a wild ride."

"And deserts turning green and forests going dry." Janie added. "Ocean flow changing with plates pushing up mountains, mountains altering rainfall. It must be quite a challenge for life down there. Or I should say...our ancestors."

"We're almost there," Andre reported. "Stand by to... Holy crap!... WHAT WAS THAT?"

"The window never wiggled at the aquarium," Michael said.

"All stop, Brad."

"So you say. I'm not adding power. I'm not moving the ship. The wall is!"

"And it's not power," Hank yelled, "it's temporal instability. Oh, oh, my God, it looks like a tidal wave. And there's another!"

When time traveling, Explorer Seven always maintained position equal distance from the split dimensions that always appeared as flat walls, like Moses standing on dry bottom. Never ever did the walls undulate ripples.

"Drop out of time travel!" Karen shrieked.

"We can't," Andre declared loudly with frustrated confusion. "The interface is irregular, part of the ship will snap through first. We'll be cut to pieces."

"Andre, what the hell am I supposed to do?" Brad blasted.

"Let's calm down for a second," replied Andre. "The ship is doing fine. We're in control. Just avoid the temporal instabilities coming our way."

"Brad," Michael said, running up beside him, "stay between waves like a surfer. We have no choice. We're the board, the ripples are waves, and as long as we don't touch them, we'll be okay."

"Agreed," Andre added. "Do your best."

"But where are we going?" Karen asked.

"We'll deal with that later. For now, we're helpless. Survival is our only objective."

"Wherever it is," Hank added. "Were leaving Earth far behind and moving time ahead, how far I can't say."

"And disorganized," Andre said. "The wave periods are random, violent, and without direction. That's a problem."

Behind the ship, two waves combined, almost closing the ship's safe slot that was shrinking anyway.

"Wave building ahead," Brad said, "and double-decker on our ass. Any thoughts, Andre?"

"Skew the ship. Fly sideways. If the time warp behind us dissipates before the single one on the bow, we'll be fine."

"And if it doesn't?" Karen asked.

"We'll meet up again in the next life."

The last place any boat wants to be is lying sideways between two threatening waves. But then again, boats don't move as fast sideways as they do forward.

For two and one-half minutes, Explorer Seven held her own.

"The gap is closing, Andre," Hank reported, which everyone could see from the views above and below the bridge.

"Isabelle, do you read me? This is Andre."

"I do, and every engineering station here is running on spec. What are you thinking?"

"Off specs. We need to find a way to draw energy from time and slow down the wave behind us."

"But time is not a particle, it's a relationship."

"Yes, but it pushes everything apart to make them separate."

"Oh, so we push back. With what?"

"I haven't gotten that far yet."

"Well, by all means take your time," tense Brad pointed out. "We have at least thirty seconds."

"I've got one idea, but no one is going to like it," Andre said, grinning uneasily. "It might work."

"How wonderful," Brad felt the need to point out. "Shall we wait ten more seconds, or are you going to let us in on it now?"

"Isabelle, we're flying sideways, so keep ventral and dorsal deflectors as they are, but reverse the bow and stern ones."

"But that will pull us apart!" Isabella responded in disbelief.

"If we micro-pulse reverse polarities one one-thousandth of a second imbalanced, we won't split in half, just stretch sideways. I think."

"Hold off," Michael said. "Has anyone ever done this before?"

"Oh yes," said Andre. "I did. Just a second ago—in my head."

"Splendid," replied Michael. "And how did it work out?"

"Painful, very painful, but only until it was over."

"That's what they say about hell."

"Yes, but only until they let on that they made the whole thing up."

"Is it possible for you and Michael to finish this discussion later?" Brad pleaded. "Eight seconds and closing."

"Unless you've got something, Michael, it's our only hope," said Andre.

"Damn it you guys!" Karen ordered. "Make it so. Isabelle…NOW!"

And so it went, and agony began. Everybody onboard continued to function, six feet tall and six feet wide, feeling every pain fiber fire at will.

"AAAAAHHHHH!"

"Paaaaaiiiiiiinnnn! STOOOOOOOOP!"

Andre's head was the only part of his body he could move, and his nose perfect size to cold turkey power separation. Actually, flat pancake is a better analogy, since for a long second the crew was six feet tall and six millimeters thick.

"AAAAAHHHHH!"

"Paaaaaiiiiiinnnnn! STOOOOOOOP!"

The pain did stop, but the memory was more than enough to bring the crowd to a unanimous "OOOOOOHHHHHH" — "Don't you ever do that again!"

It worked. The temporal shenanigans affected time placement enough to slow the advancing wave.

"If we ever do that again," Karen said, "put the crew under general anesthesia. No one can tolerate that much distress. Did it work?"

"See for yourself," replied Andre. "We're safe—for now."

"And?" Brad said.

"Hank—" Andre asked. "When will these waves settle down, and where are they taking us?"

"When we washed away, I would have guessed a month of Sundays, but this is most peculiar," Hank replied. "It looks like that rascal rogue behind us was partly a buildup from reflections off the end of time. The rebound is flattening it out, and, you won't believe this, taking us back to the location the disturbance began."

"Disturbance! Armageddon is more like it," Sarah said.

"Brad, check your readings," Andre added. "We were affected because our temporal wave signatures are identical to the explosive imbalance we were caught up in."

"Oh, my. Yes, I see. So it was a man-made, or an alien-made phenomenon."

"The similarities here are beyond canny," Andre realized. "And impossible to pull off, I might point out, without releasing a solar system's worth of energy in less than a second."

The time barrier did flatten. The ship came to a full stop. They returned to normal space, somewhere in the Andromeda galaxy, inside a gigantic solar system, where every planet was boiling hot or frozen solid.

Except one.

Hank had it mapped in seconds. "Okay, there ahead, see that spec? That's where the explosion came from that rippled time."

"Don't get any closer," Andre commanded. "Maximize telescope range and project."

"It looks like Saturn sideways," said Karen. "Why do the rings go all the way to the surface?"

"Because they're not rings," Dudley interjected. "It's an energy field that surrounds and divides the planet in half."

"And get this, Andre," Cindy said. "It's supported by two million nuclear power plants on both sides of what appears to be a pair of warring factions. They're weapons."

"A million nuclear generators couldn't focus enough energy to time warp. How is this possible?" asked Andre, without imagining what Dudley already knew.

"Hold your hat Andre, whatever that means," Dudley said. "Half of the power plants generate power, and the other half are tuned to the 'secret' wave signatures of time travel, specifically of this ship."

"Maybe my stretched brain isn't working right or something," Andre said. "I still don't understand what's going on down there."

"Allow me," Dudley politely responded. "I have analyzed the flight path you took heading to The Bang. This ship passed close enough to that planet's war zone for their antennae to read and copy your time travel frequencies. It would appear that they don't know what they are, but have figured out how to use them to build energy from reactors in a separate time line and then deposit the accumulation—months concentrated into a microsecond—as a weapon. More time out, more power. There is no limit to the force they can manage."

"And," Andre said, in dismay, "there's no way to generate power outside of time without leaving more of it behind, unstable, unpredictable, and devastating beyond imagination. Their entire solar system will be pulverized when they fire the next round, and we will go with them."

"Oh, my God," said Karen. "We've handed two cultures the most powerful weapon ever constructed. Did you know this could happen, Andre?"

"Of course he did," Michael said. "That's why even your codes can't get it out of the main computer banks."

"I'll vouch for that," said Cindy. "Neither Dudley nor I can get near it. And in the event of Andre's death, the codes die with him."

Andre had left his station, walked to the bow, and was sitting on the deck when Karen came up behind him to join him.

"Andre," Karan said, now at a whisper, "I've never seen you cry before. If you don't turn around no one will notice, and seeing you like this won't make any of us feel better."

"I know. I'm sorry. I just never imagined. I mean, of course I knew the weapon's potential, but I never realized it could be copied or put us in a situation like this."

"What do you mean?"

"We can't travel, time or otherwise, as long as that planet is online. Every time they increment power, which I'm sure both sides race to do on a regular basis, time ripples in multiple directions. We just got lucky. The rebound period was perfect. That won't happen again. It's just a matter of time, ironically, before they die, we die, the Earth is destroyed, and our families on Earth disappear. The entire universe will negate. What have I done? I never imagined this could happen."

"We'll fix it, that's all," said Karen. "So far you, we, have accomplished everything we set out to do. We'll get out of this."

"It's not that we can't come up with a plan," replied Andre. "The problem is that we are looking at two advanced, crazed cultures with thousands of years of military experience, that now control a million times more power than our ship. They must constantly be on the alert for sabotage."

Dudley and Cindy, in body form, walked to the bow, stood behind Karen and Andre on the deck to keep the others away, and added in unison, "We can help. Perhaps we can sneak inside their systems."

Andre shook his head. "If they're smart enough to temporally isolate reactors, store a year's worth of the Sun's energy, and then release it full force at one another, which I could never do, I'm sure they have systems better protected than mine. I'm not a soldier. I'm out of my league. The entire universe is going down. I'm to blame."

"Andre, my dear," Karen said, managing a supportive tone, "they may be out of your league today, but tomorrow will change that. Nothing gets beyond you. We'll catch up. We can do this together."

"You're right," Andre said, almost convincing himself. "We'll come up with something. Meanwhile, either Cindy or Dudley needs to take control of the ship while we decompress. Keep us cloaked. No long-range transmissions. The last thing we need is a missile headed our way."

"So far," Dudley noted, "we've discovered the dueling energy barriers—front lines you might call them—extend over a million light-years into space. If we try to cross over, we will fry. As long as we stay on one side, they won't expect us to be here and we can investigate. We'll establish a stationary orbit until Cindy and I come up with the next move."

"And," Cindy added, "they are so obsessed with warfare that neither side has begun space travel! Generation after generation works their lives away trying to murder their neighbors. We can help them and get us out of here at the same time. I'm sure of it."

"Fine, sounds good," Andre answered. "I'll try real hard to believe you. Karen, do you want to inform the ship, or do you want me to do it?"

"I'll take care of it. And I'm sorry for all that I have done to wear you down lately. I've been dealing with issues. We'll get through this together, all of us. *We* are not your fault."

"Thanks, I appreciate the effort," Andre said, staying in control as he got off the floor, "but it's me. I'm needy. I put you on the spot. I'm not your perfect man—we both know that. You have your own life to live. I just want you to be happy."

Karen stood, turned, and had Cindy stream her to the crew. "Attention crew, this is the bridge. At the rate were going, we'll have more bedtime stories than great-grandchildren. The planet below is responsible for the temporal disturbance we encountered. They are using it as a weapon and have no idea how to control it. We will hide out until we come up with a plan. Make no attempt to communicate or leave the ship."

"And," Michael said, with Janie, Sarah, and Brad at his side, who walked over to lend support, fully aware of the serious nature of their plight, "Janie and I are hosting a grand celebration in the main ballroom this evening. The theme is this: we'll never be monkeys again, but don't worry, we can always get naked."

"And," Janie added, "Andre and Karen will be the guests of honor, as we thank them for all they have done for us on this glorious trip. So party hard, no one's counting drinks or cupcakes— Life is good! Party on! — Yahoo!"

13

Scorched Souls

Cindy snuck cloaked drones close enough to pick up communications and some computer content. The planet was called Anelia. Dudley didn't like what they found.

Half the inhabitants of the planet, the Kawachens, labored their lives away earning slots to purchase food, clothing, and housing by the square foot. If the "grubs" labored long hours, a family could afford as many as two rooms above ground, some with windows to admire their sun, and fresh air to view starlight.

Those who failed to accumulate sufficient profit were relocated to the caves—damp quarters hundreds of feet below ground, where minerals were mined, textiles manufactured, and life expectancy was short. The Grand Accounter determined wages, set prices, and controlled telescreen programming. His name was Achtun.

On the other side of the firewall battlefield cutting the planet in half, lay the Kingdom of Delou. It was ruled by His Eminence Jarson, who enforced the will of Noata, god of what was, is, and will be.

Noata was never to be questioned. There was no need to. Jarson had all the answers. Under his domain, every citizen was assigned a cubicle, twenty feet long and fifteen feet wide, more than enough for a bed, one table, and a chair secured in front of a screen broadcasting Jarson's daily instructions, followed by sixty minutes on their knees. Jarson insisted every first name be preceded by sobriquet "Sinner."

On both sides of the battlefield firewall, generation after generation served the state. The fatherland was everything. Wants, needs, and dreams were never mentioned.

Where Karen grew up, dreams were a part of life. She lived on Earth, a planet in want of nothing, in need only of challenge to fulfill personal wishes generation by generation.

Neither side of Anelia locked citizens in cages. There was no need. They were imprisoned by their own minds, sentenced to shadowy lives blaming themselves: In Kawachensa, leaving the sun behind because they failed to meet The Grant Accounter's benchmark; in Delou, putting up with bare rations to atone for the sins Jarson listed daily, following the will of Noata of course.

The entire planet was force-fed failure. To truly live, a mind must truly see. On Anelia, grubs and sinners were duped from birth to death.

One of the grubs was a young female about Karen's age named Zena, who earned more slots than most, thanks to her programing skills, and a job on The Grant Accounter's personal staff. She was one of a dozen frontline transcribers, and his favorite.

Anelia was larger than Earth, but significantly less dense. A planetoid flyby during solidification had dragged the heavy metals away. It's wasn't necessarily a bad thing; there was enough iron left to generate magnetism, and everyone weighed one third less, stood one third taller, and didn't mind moving furniture. Otherwise, since the building blocks of the universe only come in size—carbon, oxygen, nitrogen, hydrogen and rock gems—Anelians evolved similar to humans on Earth, with draping long dark hair, brown-green eyes, vertical foreheads, and legs that were so long it looked like they were standing on two-foot stilts.

Zena was considered a looker. Her husband of four years, Kavel, didn't stop dead in his tracks at first sight, he stumbled on them, then rose with desire he knew was forbidden. They had met while evacuating babies from a hospital before a frontline blast leveled the nursery.

The first thing Kavel noticed was Zena's ears, which were symmetric and flat, not twisted and protruding, a problem the entire planet was up against: genetic deterioration from inbreeding half a planet instead of mixing genetic material, or heaven forbid, investing time or slots into biologic research instead on constructing bigger weapons. The irony was that the DNA the Kawachens needed, the Delouians had, and the genetic augmentations the Delouians needed, the Kawachens held on to.

Only half of the babies were saved the night Zena and Kavel met. But the others did not die. A penetrating commando operation snatched them. The raid returned to Delou with enough DNA to seed one-tenth of the next generation. Kawachens also targeted babies whenever the opportunity arose. It was why Zena was less deformed than the others.

In Kawachensa, buying enough food to satisfy a grub's minimal daily nutritional requirement cost one slot. A single room above ground taxed citizens another slot. Most of the population earned three slots a day, leaving one to fractionate between clothing and state-streaming, the only channel available.

Zena made five slots a day and Kavel three, repairing sewers. The combination was enough to connect a third room, and from savings, purchase permission to raise two children, four-year-old Engo, and his sister, three-year-old Leea. Both attended mandated assimilation one week a month.

"Good Opening, Zena," Kavel said when he saw her emerge from their bunkbed space.

"Good Opening, Kavel. I slept restocked, but I sure do miss the kids."

"Yes, me too. I will pick them up at noon. Will your boss, The Grand Accounter, break the bank and let you off early so we can spend the afternoon in the park? We've already paid the slot to get in."

"Shush! Remember that conversation we had last night? The government's AYS system has this room wired. The mere mention of The

Grand Accounter triggers computer listening to pass the conversation over for judgment, and if your comments are considered 'offensive,' you'll be below ground in an hour."

Kavel's form betrayed evidence of genetic exhaustion: imbalanced orbital rims, twisted lobes, and disappearing chin. Still, he had a quick mind and was always at Zena's side willing to help selflessly.

The kid's indoctrination barracks were on the other side of the capital. Kavel decided to head over early. He left for the tubes ten minutes after Zena did. Crowded underground transporters were the only place AYS couldn't bug. It was always noisy down there.

"AYS," Kavel thought, as he stood at the back of the mob pushing closer to the doors. "'At your service, how can we help you?' ended up ordering us around fifty hours a day. Hypocrite bastards."

"You have that look on your face again, Kavel," said a man standing next to him, staring forward, appearing unconnected to his surroundings.

"Are you crazy?" Kavel whispered. "You are to remain ten lengths away, pulse code to my hand receiver for no longer than five seconds, and never, never ever talk to me. Did you wake up with a death wish? Get away!"

"We have more important things to worry about. The end is near. Meet me at the pond this afternoon."

"It's amazing," said Andre. "One plate of French toast and I'm a new man."

"Hold on there, my dear," Karen said, adding fresh fruit to the table in their private suite. "The old Andre was just fine."

Andre whistled all the way to the lab, where three rows of engineers were waiting, all wearing the same face. "Andre, we have a problem."

The analyses of Anelian brain waves came back: they were carbon, mortal, and bled red, but thought-inverted and not a match for mind jumping. Taking over bodies down there was not an option.

"Michael, this is Andre. Where are you, and how is plan B going?"

"I'm in the bio lab. Come down and see."

Michael had taken his tallest man in the room image to new heights. His Anelian makeover was perfect. He grew two feet when he slipped his feet into mechanical extensions and added another four inches when a forehead cap was secured.

"Jusaly Wenew, Andre."

"And the same to you, Michael. I'll get to the language tonight, right after our strategy meeting."

"Tennis, golf, scuba? Andre, let's have some fun."

"Michael, there is a time to have fun and a time to be scared shitless, and we both know it hit the fan. We can't miss a single detail. I'll start at the top. You follow me, double-checking."

"In two hours, my obsessive overachiever. Right now, I'm off to the beach. There's nothing a surfboard can't fix, and I think better with a tan."

When the truth is known, no one chooses enslavement. To hide the truth, Eminence Jarson and Accounter Achtun had only to lash false prophets to the minds of their subjects, just like their predecessors had done for millenniums. Eighty percent of the populations on both sides of the firewall were forced into military service. They spent and lost their lives repowering firewall blasts to push death to the enemy.

No one kept Achtun waiting. If he hadn't walked into the war room five minutes ahead of schedule, Zena would have been discharged below ground. She was one of an equal mix of male and female programmers, their desks arranged in a half circle, with Achtun center stage in front of a wall-to-wall, ceiling-to-floor screen ready to project images, presentations, or two-way communication.

Zena was his favorite, and the only female to refuse ten slots, which was five times the going rate for extra attention. Since then, the welfare of her children was all the leverage the Accounter needed.

No one remembered decent housing, personal transportation, professional achievement, or social justice. Two thousand years before Karen showed up, the first Grand Accounter rewarded the ruling class with ninety percent of the county's wealth. The second Grand Accounter kept them fat and lazy long enough to dissolve the government. The third Grand Accounter then made grubs out of them.

To the left and right of Achtun's screen were rows of military consultants, every general displaying a satanic grin. Victory was only a day away.

"Good Opening, everyone," Achtun began. "Our attempt to record onsite readings from yesterday's firewall enhancement was not successful. The data was lost. We will proceed without it."

Thump…thump…thump was heard on each side as the military raised their right arms, fist closed, and slammed the floor with their feet in perfect unison.

"Zena," Accounter Achtun barked, "order every reactor to begin energy accumulation in one hour. At noon tomorrow, we will release a firewall one thousand times more powerful than this planet has ever seen. By tomorrow night, ten billion Delouians will be dead and their cities scorched. The entire planet will be mine. Make ready. Do your duty. Military commanders…meet me in the death room."

One of low status was not permitted to speak directly to Achtun, but only approach head bowed to request attention.

"Yes, Zena," Achtun spoke quietly. "I will keep my word. Your children remain safe, and you will be able to enjoy the park once a week."

"Which, your grace, will be this afternoon, if I may leave before the sun tilts."

"Permission granted. And when the Delouians have been defeated you will be assigned to help me coordinate reconstruction of half the planet. We will be working late together. You will never want for slots again."

"Thank you. May your Closing be profitable."

"ATTENTION!" Zendal, chief military advisor, yelled out from the corner. "We have just received a priority request from Jarson for a face-to-face."

The room went quiet. Achtun slowly returned center stage, turned facing the screen, and signaled Zendal to put him through.

The leaders of twenty billion Anelians stood eyeball to eyeball, grimace to grimace.

"How unpleasant to see you again, Jarson," Achtun began.

On the screen, Jarson was robed in traditional ceremonial black, full bearded and head hooded, otherwise of similar height and proportion to Achtun.

"The distaste is all mine," Jarson replied, glaring a frozen stare.

"And how nice of you to take a break from whipping your pathetic subjects to talk to me."

"Achtun, someday, you blasphemous fool, you will feel the wrath of Noata's anger."

"The only way that will happen will be if I am stupid enough to stand under one of the statues you use to terrorize your people as my men tip it over. My day is busy. What do you want, Jarson?"

Both men knew that as long as they kept their subjects convinced that they were involved in a horrific struggle, self-image, even life itself remained inseparable from that struggle. Fear was all they needed to maintain slavish obedience, and they were both very good at it.

"My life serves the creator of all things," intoned Jarson. "The will of Noata will be done. Your life spends breath owning others. You've made money monkeys out of half my planet. I have the power to forgive your sins. I come in peace."

"Pause transmission," Achtun ordered. The screen went black and he turned to Zendal. "What do you make of this?"

"We destroyed three cities and killed one hundred million Delouians yesterday with only one of our thousand repowered energy accumulators. Jarson knows he's doomed. He's stalling for time. Play along. Tomorrow is his last day."

"Screen on," Achtun ordered. "Jarson, my military commanders remind me that our soldiers haven't had a day off in years. Perhaps a temporary cease-fire would be merciful."

"Excellent. I will pray for your soul. Shall me meet again tomorrow at noon?"

"Let's make it one o'clock. I hate to let the looks of you ruin my lunch."

To a blank screen Achtun then spoke, "And may your ashes feed worms, you son of a bitch."

14

Fresh Air

On planet Anelia, few knew joy. Zena was lucky. Her life had been a bouquet of surprises. She was the daughter of the most powerful weapons engineer in Kawachensa, so while her classmates pleaded for menial labor, she landed a job in command central, and was given a two-room apartment within walking distance.

Then there was the morning of the rescue. Dust-wheezing and sweaty, she bent over to swaddle a neonate. When she looked up, Zena saw a face that cared and eyes to love. Before that moment, she had never known love, and yet, her most cherished surprise, Zena felt it at first touch. She and Kavel were a perfect match.

A parade of treats followed: his slots added a third room, two healthy children arrived, and they enjoyed an entire day off a week, unheard of even for her father, who died at the front before hugging his first grandchild. Dad planned to force Achtun to pay beyond the limit to cure her mom's blood dyscrasia. Still, Mom outlived most of her generation and had several years to enjoy grandchildren.

Everything Zena had overcome made her stronger. She maintained a loving impulse of character, bore evil inflicted, and carried a soul that sang only praise. She knew that it was not life that threatened her, only her perception of it. She did her duty, conducted her life according to the rules, and never let her principles slide.

On the outside, Zena masked her contour with obedience. On the inside she cherished an overriding faith that got her out of bed in the morning, let her look aside while saluting, and warmed her nights. She knew, in the end, that life remained a festival.

Zena was blessed with a fine figure and a cheerful outlook. More impressive was how she adjusted to the tone of civilization, a difficult task on Anelia, a planet whose language contained not a single word meaning "peace."

The minute Achtun left, Zena took advantage of the opportunity. She passed the midday crowd jamming the lift, walked ten flights down, crossed security, and was out the door in record time, greeting fresh air with one full breath after another.

Zena's legs kept pace with the mob moving down the street, but her mind enjoyed a hammock of repose, taking note of the slit of blue sky between towers of trapped beings. Private transportation had been outlawed long ago; one either walked or endured the tubes, alongside filth and a resistant population of rodents. Zena loved walking.

Every year, the minister of transportation debated the same question: to remove the single line of trees that separated one direction from another and replace them with a wall. Zena was on hand. To her, nature transcended existence and made each season special. Before she met with the minister, she sent a week's worth of holiday rations to his office, and then pointed out that even with the trees, fifty pedestrians could pass side by side.

Her final argument was the winner: paying to have a fence constructed would put his department over budget, penalizing him one slot a week for a year, a situation she guaranteed to make known uptown.

Zena named every tree she passed. "Fat Boy" was a primitive evergreen oak and the first to go if it spread wider. "Hang in There" was a weeping deciduous split halfway to its base by lightning. She took it on herself to trim the low branches before headroom limitation chopped it up.

Open-door peddling was not allowed but was taxed anyway.

"Zena, my dear," said Carloo, a cobbler standing in his open door. "I finished those slippers you ordered for your daughter."

Zena looked forward to Carloo's company. She wiggled between pedestrians to his side. "And how is your wife this fine day?"

"Much better, thanks to that pass you got her for a week at the sanitarium." He handed her a package. "The slippers are my gift to you. I will see you tomorrow."

Four hours of sunlight was not to be wasted. Zena made only one other stop on her way home. Between buildings, alleys were just wide enough for beggars to hide. Zena stayed out of the movement that proposed exterminating them. She knew that slots would carry the vote. First the council would have to add manpower for over a year to get the job done, and then increase the tube budget forever to control the expected rampant increase in rat population.

"Hello Zena," said a scraggy figure from the shadows of an alley. "I had a great night, caught two rats with my bare hands after hours."

Zena handed over the biscuit she had pocketed at lunch, which disappeared into bleeding hands.

"I'll see what I can do tomorrow, Zal," she said. "Take a stick with you next time you go under."

Halfway home, the buildings changed from military commissions to private quarters, discernably no different on the outside, with ten-foot bunker walls reinforced by three one-foot steel slabs. Since the recording of history, both sides had suffered blast-throughs once a decade.

Zena's building was reserved for military families. Every bedroom had a window, and the lobby two elevators, which were always in demand. Zena avoided the downtime by heading for the stairs.

"Hello, Aunt Zena," said a wisp of a lad as she entered. "You're home early today."

"Don't let the regulator catch you in here. It is forbidden for children to play in the stairway."

"Oh, I'm not in the stairway. This is the Lantone Mountain, and I'm climbing to battle the evil ogre of doom. When I steal his jewels, Mommy will never have to work again. Shall we attack?"

"Onward and upward…to the hills!" Zena said, pointing up the stairs. "Duck! His flying guards are after us! Stay low! Victory will be ours!"

The young lad defeated three dragons on the way to Zena's door. She was most grateful. "You are a brave warrior. I'll sleep well tonight knowing you are here to protect me."

A timid face asked the next question: "Aunty, are you going to the park today? Is it still green every way you look? We haven't been to the park since my dad didn't come back. Mom says we can't afford it. Someday I'm going to make enough slots to go every…"

Zena was so eager to get to the park that she didn't notice her front door automatically closing, cutting off the last words of the child standing alone outside.

As always, Kavel met Zena at the door with cookies and a cold drink. Working the night shift didn't improve his complexion, but twenty-foot scrub sticks developed broad shoulders and a strong back.

"Did Engo's gallant friend escort you home again?" he asked.

"Why, of course. I would never have made it without him."

"He spends hours at the window looking for you. I told him you would be early today."

"Let's take him to the park. He misses his dad."

"And risk a ten-slot fine? Not a good idea." Kavel didn't wait for a rebuttal. He knew better. "Okay, but just this once, and tell him not to look too excited. It will give us away."

The guard only counted families, never individual children, who jumped around so much no one could keep track. The park was also mercifully free of bugs—not the flying ones, the spy-on-citizens variety. Three happy kids sprinted all the way to the climbing bars, had coupons for ice cream, and were already in their bathing suits.

Zena's favorite spot was a grassy hill overlooking the swimming pond, itself lined by an example of every evergreen on the planet. She spread a blanket beneath a Julawey tree, hoping at least one of its ripening fruits would drop nearby. Kavel lay down on the blanket, folded both hands behind his head, and gasped, amazed at the spacious blue sky from one horizon to the other.

Zena rolled over for a kiss, which he insisted be followed by another.

"We are so lucky, Kavel. All this and each other too. It's a dream."

"I would say more like a nap, interrupting the rest of a day that could be better."

"Yes, yes, I know. But it will change soon," Zena said with an expression that should have burst with joy, but which was followed instead by her rolling away, holding both hands over her eyes to hide tears.

"So the rumors are true?" Kavel concluded. "Achtun in arming doomsday."

"Say nothing! I said nothing. But it won't be long," she said, sniffling back a rush of sadness.

"But?"

"It's just that we're about to murder *ten billion* men, women, and innocent children."

"Not to mention pets, schoolyards, universities, wildlife, and lovers just like you and me."

"But it's them or us," Zena said, more a question than a conviction. "That's what we have been told since birth. It's self-defense."

"It is if there were no other way."

"What are you saying? And don't repeat it. You know that's treason."

"Is that how you see it?" said Kavel. "Killing is patriotic, while saving lives is treason?"

"Change is impossible. We must be who we are."

"And who are we? And why?"

"What's come over you?" said Zena. You never talked like this before."

"I've heard the rumors. I know what's going on, and I also know your weapons have killed as many of our people as the enemy."

"*My* weapons! I only do what I am told to keep us above ground. We have no choice. We aren't free to live our lives. The state comes first. We don't matter."

"Why don't we matter? Why doesn't everyone matter? Who decided this? There must be a better way."

"Achtun says that all Delouians are insane. We must exterminate their gene pool."

"Do you believe that, Zena?"

"No, I don't," she whispered. "I communicate with their central command every time Achtun and Jarson have a fight. They're just like us, only obsessed with the god thing."

"And we're not obsessed with the slot thing?"

"Life is difficult. Everyone must earn their way. If they don't, then it's reasonable to…"

"To sentence them to death below ground? I know you. I love you. I also know you don't believe a word you're saying," Kavel lovingly whispered in her ear as he leaned in to hug her.

"Either way, we must be practical," Zena said, straightening her back. "We have the children, and their children to protect. We must do as were told."

"Yes, do as we're told. Do as we're told. Yah sure, do as we're told. It's just that every time I say those words, my stomach turns. And I don't like the way your boss orders you around. He's a scoundrel."

"What!" Zena let go, loud enough to attract attention. Then, startled and confused, she untangled herself from the man she thought she knew, stood abruptly, hands to head, and paced back and forth. "Achtun is our savior. He protects us from annihilation. You know that."

"I know that is what he *tells* us, but has he ever tried to negotiate peace?"

"Jarson won't hear of it. He's a madman."

"I know that's what Achtun says."

"Jarson is narrow and selfish," said Zena, glancing around to ensure no one was paying attention to what Kavel was saying. "His religion is humbug. Reason can decide nothing when an infinity of alternatives exist beyond reason. Logic must prevail."

"And is genocide the logical way to deal with difference?"

"The weak are enslaved by their own need for certitude. We know better."

"Do we, Zena? And what do we know? I'll tell you what we know: That neither reason nor the heart are sure bets. The game can be played on both sides, and rolling the dice is not optional. We are alive and don't know better. That's all we know." Kavel crossed his arms defiantly.

Zena placed her hands on her hips, just as stalwart. "If there is a god, he's been hijacked and exploited. Faith forced by authority is not faith. Jarson's religion is immoral. Achtun says so."

"That may be, but we are every bit as timid and apologetic. The entire planet fakes squalid contentment. Just because an idea is popular doesn't make it right, and no one questions Achtun."

"At least he *listens*. Everything Jarson says he sanctifies beyond reason. End of discussion. His followers are a mass of fools. They walk around repeating by rote what they were taught as children."

"Oh, I see. And how many nonconformists do we have here in this park?" He made a show of looking around.

"Apparently only one," hissed Zena, "who is asking for trouble and putting us all at risk! I have one of the best jobs in the country. Don't put us in danger, Kavel."

"Don't worry, I won't," he soothed. "And you brought up the subject with a handful of tears."

"Well, that's better. You scared me for a second."

"Yes…yes… Time is profit, and profit is power. All hail Kawachensa and Achtun the Great. There, does that make you feel better?"

"Of course," said Zena. "I knew you were just kidding."

"Oh, yes, of course I was. But maybe, just maybe, the age of inspiration has not passed. Maybe bad just hasn't met good. Maybe we have work to do. Maybe we should give *thinking* a try."

"Shut up and kiss me."

15

The Pond

As sunset approached, the summer breeze died down, clouds hung motionless, and the kids spent less time with their heads above water than below, playing submarine. Zena backstroked two laps before returning to the beach to build the sandcastle of the day. "Someday," she said to Kavel, who had just finished his second helping of crispy sugar sticks, "we're going to live in a house just like this, with a private bedroom patio to watch our grandchildren play on the grass, swim in our own pool, and do their homework. It's going to be wonderful."

"Is that a floorplan from the museum?"

"You know very well that since the war, the past has been off limits. It's a copy of one of my dad's drawings. When I was a little girl, he would put me on his knee and tell me that it would only take half of the armed forces under his command to construct homes like this for every family on the planet. He also said that when he ended the war, we would get the first one."

"Zena, I don't know how I'm going to do it, but someday you're going to have that house."

"I believe we will, and that's all I or anyone would ever need to spend the rest of their days in contentment."

"And I'm going to start by catching a fish just like the one we'll serve at our first dinner party. I'm going fishing, two per family. We might as well get our slot's worth. Do you want to come along?"

"No, thanks. I have to pick up more sugar sticks for the kids. They don't seem to last long around here. Besides, I'm adding a shed with bikes. I'll see you later, honey."

Kavel told Zena he was going fishing, but headed for the woods instead, then detoured through the arboretum before finally turning back to the fishing hole. He didn't go in. Instead, he passed the dock in the direction of the beach, only to change his mind a third time, halfway to Zena.

"No, I didn't bring my own gear," Kavel said at the outfitting shop. "One reel and tackle box, please."

"Is this really fishing?" he said to himself ten minutes later. "Bucket seat hanging over the dock, private earphones, and an electronic lure to chase fish if they don't get the message? Our planet's ancestors never had it like this."

The seat next to Kavel was vacant for less than a minute. A man plopped himself down and placed his tackle box next to Kavel's. He then took out a pair of headphones, which he placed on top of Kavel's open case.

Everyone else on the dock was concentrating on the sport. Kavel faked a yawn, scanned the vicinity, and then replaced his standard entertainment headphones, which also made calls, with the set his neighbor had put on his tackle box.

"You're late," said the gruffy scowler, so softly Karvel barely heard. "Where have you been?"

"Helping the family get settled. Zena wanted to come fishing with me. It took a while to talk her out of it."

"No matter," the man said, reeling in a fish, ostensibly unaware of Kavel's presence. "Let me fill you in."

The charm that had lit Kavel's face in Zena's presence sagged by the word. The stranger, known only to him as S-2, delivered orders from

Jarson himself. Kavel was informed that divine inspiration received by His Eminence had resulted in an infallible pronouncement: that Kavel getting trapped on the other side in the middle of a baby snatch and merging with Zena was a celestial miracle, confirming evidence that God stood behind them and that their enemies would soon be vanquished.

The rest of the news was disturbing. Achtun's new power formulas had them outgunned. Without Kavel's help, Delou would vanish from the planet in eighteen hours. The fate of ten billion loyal citizens, including Kavel's Delouian family, wife and daughter included, rested on his shoulders.

"Last month, you told me Jarson was negotiating peace, a permanent cease-fire—no more war."

"That was the plan. Then God talked to Jarson. Now we have a new plan."

"What can be better than an end to warfare?" asked Kavel.

"The end of Achtun," replied S-2.

"I don't follow."

"I will get up first, take your tackle box, and return it in your name. You take mine home with you. No one will suspect."

"And?"

"Inside the green fishing lure is a fifty-megaton micronuke plate."

"You know as well as I that sensors will detect the weapon the moment I step out of the park, and there is no way to get near Achtun."

"Don't think," said S-2. "Just listen. Inside the red lure is a second plate. It masks the signature of the bomb. As long as the two are within three feet of one another, we can set it off anywhere we want."

"We're a thousand miles from the front," protested Kavel. "I can't possibly get there."

"You're not going to the front. You're not going anywhere. Zena is."

"No, she isn't. She reports for work in the morning."

"With the bomb. You told me that she only has one pair of work shoes. In the sole of one you will hide the bomb. In its mate will be the cloaking device. Achtun is powering up to annihilate Delou at noon tomorrow. The bomb is set to go off at eleven thirty. Achtun and his entire military command will be destroyed. All of Kawachensa's defenses will go down. At eleven forty, Jarson will release everything we have to kill what's left of Achtun's ten billion subjects. Total victory! The planet will be ours."

"You mean Jarson's. You and I will be dead. Holy crap!"

"There is no greater honor than dying for God. We will be heroes, have statues erected in our honor, and receive our reward in the next life, where we will enjoy pleasures mortals cannot imagine."

"And the Kawachens?"

"The will of God will deal with them. After suffering to pay for their sins, Noata will neutralize their identities, as if they never existed."

"But Zena and my kids here will also vanish."

"Watch your tongue, Kavel! Your loyalty is to God and country. Kawachensa must be destroyed. And here's the best part: Kawachensa will be defenseless. Jarson has reset the blast to fry them slowly—eyeball-searing, flesh-boiling, appendage-charring—before they beg for death and get their wish hours later. It will be glorious. Praise be to God."

Kavel was stunned. Stone-faced, S-2 raised his voice. "Don't look at me! Look happy! We're fishing, remember?"

Kavel's rod was in the water, but his eyes were fixed on his own shoes, imagining the horror awaiting Zena.

"Get it together, Kavel. If you fail, everything we've fought for, generations of sacrifice, and billions of lost soldiers, will all be in vain, and you and I will be stuck with these heathens until death, when God will surely punish us without mercy for failing to carry out his will. Listen to me carefully: You and I must die. You and I *will* die."

"Slow and painfully, thanks to Jarson, who will end up the richest, most powerful man on Anelia."

"Jarson lives only to serve God. And if you said those words on Delou, I would have to Taser your brain through your nose. You would spend the last two weeks of your life walking on all fours, incontinent.

But the answer to your question is 'no.' Jarson is merciful: the white lure is poison. I have one, too. Our deaths will be painless."

"Listen S, or two, or whoever you are. We have been living with the Kawachensa for years. They're rational beings. We can convert them. They will see the light, praise God, as we do."

"I have a Taser sword. Don't provoke me. Listen, and listen good. Money is the root of all evil. It makes slaves of free souls. We serve the Lord, and the Lord only. Achtun's government is a train of crime. He seeks power for its own sake. He's made despondent, whimpering infidels out of half our planet. He must die."

"Now hold on a second," said Kavel. "That's the same thing they say about us. Maybe none of us are who we think we are."

"Silence! When God says kill, we deliver corpses. No one questions the word of God."

"How do we know it's not just Jarson who craves blood?"

"I will not tolerate such insolence," said S-2. "If your cooperation were not essential, I would make an example of you right now by feeding you to the fish."

Kavel paused and took two long breaths before looking up. "Why don't we just stop and think for a minute. Perhaps we can come up with a compromise. Life is too short to be spent nursing hatred, registering wrong, and seeking revenge. There must be a better way."

S-2's face grew bitter and stiffened.

"There is a better way. It's our way. Materialists make a pact with the devil. They spend their lives scrounging for pennies to buy trifles."

"Whereas we get no trifles and spend life on our knees."

S-2 pretended to pull a stuck lure free from a rock and slammed his rod into Kavel's head. "One more word, and the white lure will go home with me."

Kavel sat up and sat speechless.

"That's better," S-2 said. "I will tolerate no more back talk. And remember, if I report your behavior to Jarson, your family will be crucified and your memory erased from history while you rot in hell for all eternity."

"Yes, sir."

"You will do your duty to God, repay his kindness, and atone for your sins?"

"Yes, I will."

"Be gone. God loves you."

Kavel took the long way back.

"What, no fish?" Zena said with a teasing smile.

"They ran out. Not enough stocked. But I did get myself a tackle box."

"You look like you've had it. I can get the kids, and we'll head home if you like."

"No, not at all. Let's stay till the closing bell. In fact, I think I'll join the kids on the swings. Would you like to come along?"

"No thanks, I'm really enjoying doing nothing."

As a special treat, Zena let her hallway warrior sleep over. Kavel moved two mattresses from the bunk room to the living room, directly below the window.

"Remember the first six months we dated?" Kavel asked. "We were lucky. We got four hours on the town and one night a week together."

"It was lovely. And we stayed up all night talking, playing games, and looking at the stars."

"And I hid your clothes so the first thing I saw every morning was you running around naked."

"I still run around naked for you."

"Bless your soul."

"What?"

"I mean, we are soul mates, to be sure. Say, let's stay up all night again, and pretend that only one family of Anelians lives on the planet, not twenty billion. We can dance, clean out the freezer, and finish off the ice-cream sundaes we brought home. It will be just like old times."

Zena wrapped both arms around Kavel and sunk her head in his chest. "Oh, how sweet of you to want to distract me. But it's not necessary. I did a lot of thinking while you were fishing without fish. Our planet has a lot of problems, but we also have a future. Our race will make it. I'm sure of it. We just have to cut our losses and move on."

"Yes, of course. Cut our losses and move on. Don't look back... don't look back." Kavel stood up, looked out the window, and did not look back.

16

The Calvary

Karen's beau was the brightest mind Earth had ever known, but even Andre never imagined it could happen. Electrons, protons, and the rest could always be counted on to amount to something, provided they were given time to do so.

That was the problem. Time was about to end.

Andre knew he'd done wrong. Andre knew he was to blame. He sat at the head of the lab's conference room, haunted by the most fearsome panic of being—nothingness. Aside from Cindy at his side, who had exhausted computer options hours before, Andre was alone. Karen let each department tackle the problem from its own perspective. Their recommendations were unanimous: enjoy a grand breakfast, it might be their last.

For the first five minutes she joined Andre, she said nothing.

"You know better, Andre. We have a plan. Why aren't you more positive and forceful? What's wrong, Andre?"

"Warfare introduces creativity focused on sabotage. Anelians are intelligent. Their best minds work night and day to prevent from happening what we are about to attempt. We're Johnny-come-latelies. What we try may have already failed."

Michael joined them.

"You're forgetting one thing, Andre. We're human beings, nourished on freedom and bread to think for ourselves. Our brains tap potential those culture slaves down there can't. We can do this. Trust me. We will get the job done."

"And every one of our other plans have succeeded," Brad added. "I've worked with the best navigators, pilots, and engineers in GASA. No one can hold a candle to you, Andre. We'll be fine."

Andre was touched by their support. He paused, willfully brightened his grin, stood straight, did everything the manual on posture communication recommended to instill confidence, and said, "All right already. I'll make the announcement. And don't worry. I won't screw up."

"Cyber Cindy, or Cindy Cyber…whatever… open a ship-wide broadcast for Andre," Karen said.

"Good morning, everyone," Andre began. "Karen, Brad, and Michael just told me that we have every reason to believe Cindy's plan will be a grand success."

That was lie number one.

"Actually, we have two separate plans: one to disable Kawachensa's central command, and another, which will not touch Delou's war room, but will shut down their firewall by invading their peripheral computer system with a virus under our command. That will be when we remove our time-tampering technology from the planet. Our mission will succeed.

Lie number two.

"Cindy and Dudley have researched the planet's culture and cross-referenced our procedures. By this time tomorrow, we will be on our way home.

But maybe I'm wrong. Andre, you're spoiled, accustomed to simulations concluding no risk of error, one hundred percent guaranteed. Seventy percent are great odds for a gambler. How do they do it? Well for a start, the entire universe is not up for grabs, and no day is a good day to die. OH, OH…I better stop talking to myself. Everyone is looking.

Andre's pause lifted heads, which turned back and forth between him and his sidekick Cindy, who had finally learned when to shut up and how to lie in spades.

"Yes, Andre," she jumped in, as if she had missed a cue. "Dudley and I have run multiple scenarios. What we have for you tonight will work."

And who doesn't believe a computer? Her volume, accompanied by raised arms, the universal hominoid sign of victory, resulted in the response she was after: applause accompanied by "yups," "yips," and "we got this!"

"Dudley," Cindy said, arms outstretched to invite him forward, "deliver the package."

"Commander Karen, chief engineer Andre, esteemed staff, it is a pleasure…"

"Move it along, bolt brain, "Brad interrupted. "We've all met."

"Certainly, sir. I will begin my evaluation, drawing parallels to Earth's history, as alarming as that may be."

"Allow me to step in for the sake of brevity," said Cindy.

"Not to mention sanity," added Brad.

"To facilitate multitasking, Dudley and I have entered into joint consciousness," said Cindy. "I just reviewed the first twenty minutes of his paraphrased presentation. Allow me to condense it. Our research concludes that you mortal beings live with your heads up your asses. Not an intelligent or pleasant place to be. Yes, you have all the smarty-pants conclusions at your fingertips, which plan out your lives one step at a time. But—and it's a big but—you have a huge problem when feelings erupt where, when, and how you don't want them to. And the reason they get in your way and gnaw at your insides is that *you make stupid plans*. Listen to me very closely. You don't live in fantasyland. This is reality. Molecules come with imperatives. You, and every Anelian down there, grew up totally misled."

"And," Dudley interrupted, "since I am reading Cindy's lines ahead of her, I will point out how lucky you are to have the two of us. Which I am certain contradicts humility protocol number thirty-seven, my dear Cindy."

"That's enough, grease addict." Cindy spit back.

"You never know when a spacewalk will require less friction."

"That will do," Karen ordered. "Dudley, proceed, and Cindy, speak next when I recognize you."

"Thank you again, commander." Dudley delivered, front and center, at military attention. "To fit in, you need to understand the Anelian cultures. To start with, the entire planet exists in the gloom of ignorance. Each society is a grand conspiracy targeted at its own citizens. One side codified flawed social contrasts, and the other obeys superstitious nonsense."

"And no one," Cindy added, "said, 'go to hell,' a common expression during Earth's troublesome coming of age."

"I'll let you get away with that one because you're right on," Karen said, "but it's Dudley's turn. Let him finish!"

"Thank you again, commander. Cindy makes me *non compos mentis*. Anyway, Anelia's entire past is disappointing because, one by one, corrupt leaders did as they damn well pleased at the expense of twenty billion others who did their bidding."

"Well, that was painless," Brad said.

"Oh, I have just started, sir," said Dudley. "You need to know about their philosophic confusion. You see, their lives—all lives really—ultimately become the answer to a question: What is life? Your Greeks pointed out that the unexamined life is not worth living. Plato prompted you to pierce through the surface of living to penetrate underlying reality.

"The number of philosophers on Anelia is…zero. No one down there believes their own mind. Half of the planet is obsessed with atoning for manufactured sins, and the other half with paying bills."

Dudley took position at the head of the table. Class was in session.

"False perceptions are confinements," he continued. "No one on Anelia honors truth. It was outshouted long ago. What began as hypertrophic modifications of biologically meaningful institutions turned into organized violence, warfare, and despotism."

"Really?" moaned Brad sarcastically, pretending to be taking notes for the final.

"Both cultures love blood," continued Dudley, "and have no concern for happiness. What's worse, no one tries to remedy the situation. Which is understandable, since living beings on both sides are executed for merely speaking forbidden words. In short, both cultures are hopeless. There is nothing we can do. The entire planet needs to be rebooted."

"What," Brad interjected, "is that supposed to mean?"

"Okay, Cindy," Karen said. "Your turn."

"What fancy-pants Dudley is trying to say is that when you mortals need a pair of pants, you try on several and evaluate each for size, look, and comfort. But when it comes to choosing a religion, worldview, or philosophy, which ultimately are the same thing, you grab whatever you're handed off the rack by your folks, who were even more confused than you ended up being."

"So in other words," Brad said, "we steal back our technology, get the hell out of here, and then leave them to fight to the death."

"As an anthropologist," Sarah insisted, "I have a problem with that."

"Or," Michael suggested, "we could bring them face-to-face. After we take back our technology, we destroy the blast wall cannons on both sides and then fly Explorer Seven around the planet, powering up an electron gun that will turn every pound of plutonium on the planet into lead. No more radioactive material. No more cannons. No more warfare."

"And," Brad pointed out, "they will assume the planet is under attack by aliens, and the only way to survive is to work together."

"Andre," Karen asked, "What's your call?"

"Our primary mission is to prevent the destruction of time, which will save both their planet and our loved ones at home. Once that has been accomplished, we can take whatever steps seem prudent. Until then, a single objective is all we should deal with. Let's get back on track."

"Roger that, Andre," Dudley said, saluting. "Cindy, it's your turn."

Karen had solid reasons for trusting Cyber Cindy. She was an excellent spy; after all, she grew up inside every piece of electronics onboard. At one point, she figured out how to eavesdrop by translating vibrations from the side of a toaster oven.

When she graduated to DNA, the real fun began: identifying ancestry, predicting mood swings from genomes, and matchmaking. Cindy predicted winners more often than Karen's romance files, an accomplishment she kept to herself, after boasting to Andre several times a day.

Cindy's methods were sound, and she stayed in the game. Whenever two members of the crew became a couple, she completed a full-range gas spectrogram on each from dermatologic samples she programmed the ship's robot hairstylist to take for her.

Somehow, Andre never found out.

Then she waited, and did not use personality questionnaires or pheromone matching. She just analyzed patterns. By the end of a year, Cindy had enough data to predict, with seventy percent accuracy, which lovers would spend the night together after their first kiss, and with a fifty-fifty success rate, which couples had found their soul mate. That number rose to ninety-five percent if the couple added singles Friday Night Club to their options at least once a month.

Andre inspected Cindy's microscopic spy drones before sending them to the surface. That's when he discovered what she had been up to. After each inspection he would look at Cindy, who didn't give away a thing, just stared back blankly.

"Yes, can I help you?"

Andre discovered that every piece of stealth hardware was at least a year old and had logged in hundreds of hours of use in every corner of the ship.

"Andre," Cindy said, squirming to get out of trouble, "you have taught me well: trust no innovation until it's been thoroughly and repeatedly tested."

"Of course, Cindy, and from the looks of this data, you accomplished that in a week."

"Right you are again, wise creator. After that, I also followed your advice about making sure the batteries worked."

"Again successful, I noticed. However, so successful that they all need to be replaced."

"Great idea. I'm sure both of us feel better knowing the wiring will hold up."

"Yes," said Andre, "apparently for a year of continuous use. Just one more question, Cindy, if you don't mind. What did you do with all the data retrieved over the last year?"

"I deleted it, of course."

"Fine. When did you delete it? Remember, I am notified by your watch system every time you lie."

"In that case, the answer is one hundred microseconds ago."

As programmed, Cindy did respect privacy protocols, but that didn't stop soap-operatic antics, something she found most amusing, along with the fact that she was evolving the feeling of being amused.

One might say her tricks were harmless, sort of. For instance, a month before Michael fell for Sarah, he would put on his favorite shirt, the one that made him look like a jungle explorer, before joining her at the bridge for watch duty. So Cindy matched their epidermis, calculated genome compatibility, then took it upon herself to manipulate the duty roster. Neither Michael nor Sarah caught on, with both repeating at regular intervals: "Well, what do you know? Here we are, together again! It must be fate."

Decoding Andre took finesse and a manual on the behavior patterns of the obsessive-compulsive. Unknown even to himself, Andre chose trousers chronologically, picking the oldest ones first to get more wear out of them and caring less if the lab messed them up. That is, unless Karen was on the docket. Then he went straight to the top of the line.

Janie was easy. The more she liked a man, the tighter her blouse became.

Brad lived in a world of his own. Literally. Every day he stood in front of his mirror and put on what he thought he looked best in, usually military shoulder straps waiting for medals. He also had three types of flirting:

"Hello, don't you look nice today?"

"It's a great day for surfing."

Or the real thing: "I'm Brad, the pilot. Oh yeah, you know that. Well, it's a nice day, and, well…how are you doing?"

Karen took the longest to figure out. Every day she chose the best and newest she had.

At first Cindy felt bad about snooping on her boss, but then she concluded that it was all for science.

Karen's eyes finally gave her away, but only when her pupils were measured in increments of one hundred microns. A week before Andre and Karen shared their first kiss, Cindy had the case wrapped up and had moved on to another challenge.

Then the patterns changed. Cindy couldn't figure out why Michael started wearing shirts chronologically, Janie went to unisize, Karen's pupils were all over the place, and Andre's closet totally scrambled.

Only one conclusion stood out—people change.

17

Lock and Load

Inu and Ulon Laroon never spent slots as fast as Achtun transferred them to their account, which he did every time their research fortified his war machine. They met when they were twelve, just six months after aptitude tests pulled both out of standard indoctrination, took them from their parents, and placed them in boarding school, where military discipline and study hours were enforced morning, noon, and night.

At the age of twenty, Ulon fortified sound waves to drill microscopic holes in living tissue. No cell wall survived; even airborne bacteria that drifted into no-man's-land never made it to ground.

At twenty-five, Ulon married Inu.

They believed Achtun when he told them they could have a child as soon as their work assured his victory. They believed Achtun when he promised them a house on the base. They believed Achtun when he promised to cut the power in half for the next test, which he ordered the couple to evaluate in a shuttle at close range.

Achtun lied. They both died. The data was not received, their ship buried miles beneath debris.

Achtun was furious. Inu disabled the ship's continuous feed as soon as she measured power levels building beyond what they were promised.

Both knew their lives were over. Both knew they would never be parents. They preferred to die without Achtun the butcher working them till the last second.

Achtun needed the data to concentrate the next attack. His advisors recommended canceling. Achtun wouldn't hear it. There was enough power to do the job one way or another. He planned to make up for the missing data by splaying power in multiple directions.

The Delouians were doomed.

The data wasn't lost, just buried so deep Achtun had neither the desire nor ability to dig it out. Cindy accomplished the task in three hours with drones that returned to Explorer Seven with genetic blueprints of Inu and Ulon, who had died in each other's arms, looking at a list of baby names, not wondering where they went wrong.

Andre and Sarah were the logical choices to impersonate them. A private briefing was scheduled. Cindy's plan called for Andre and Sarah to show up at Achtun's command center at eleven in the morning with a story of propulsion flare-out and total ship loss right after they hot-wired every system on the shuttle to add velocity to retreat.

To add credibility to the disguise, Cindy copied a prototype of Ulon's sound drill with new defensive countermeasures that Andre would show Achtun. He would believe they escaped no-man's-land, and be so distracted that he would not suspect sabotage, especially since Sarah and Andre would hand him the data he needed to focus the ultimate weapon.

Achtun wouldn't know that Andre's case housed a cloaked chip-slicer that Cindy had programmed to permanently disable every piece of electronic hardware in the building at exactly eleven thirty.

"So, all we have to do," Andre flippantly concluded, "is identify ourselves outside, make our way to command central, and the job is done. When the lights go out, we act dumfounded, head for the door, and escape to the streets."

"Not so fast, wise guy," Cindy said. "We need to go over your disguise, to whom you shouldn't speak, and how to get through ten security stations. To begin with…"

Andre turned and asked, "Sarah, do you and Karen still share a hot fudge sundae after working out?"

"...Yes, as I was saying..." Cindy continued.

"And sometimes before going to the pool. Why..."

"Do you mind...?" interrupted Cindy sharply.

"Yes, we do," shot back Sarah. "Computer, do as I say. Whenever Andre or I turn our heads sideways to talk, you are to shut up, pause presentation, and record nothing. And your memory banks will not be opened. Is that clear?"

"Yes ma'am, whatever you say." Then in Cindy's head, silent to the world: [Dudley, did you hear that? We're trying to save their lives and all Andre wants to talk about is the flavor of the month.]

[Unbelievable,] Dudley added. [Over here, where I'm briefing Michael, Brad, Janie, and Karen, it's the same thing. The boys are scheduling time on the squash court while Janie and Karen can't decide what to wear to dinner. They're nuts. Don't let on that we are talking about them in our heads.]

Cindy gave it another try, evil-eyed, more forceful, and easily ninety decibels and climbing, "Pay attention! Your lives, my life, all lives depend on this. I swear..."

"Central computer, freeze Cindy's motor functions," said Sarah, looking toward Andre, who she knew must grant necessity.

"Well, okay," Andre said. "Two-minute time-out."

"That's better," Sarah said. "Peace and quiet, and doesn't she make a fine statue. Now, what's on your mind, Andre?"

"Karen has been turning me down for weeks."

"Maybe she's just trying to lose weight."

"And I'm the first to go. And there's more: no rock climbing, no skin diving, no just walking through the habitat. Sometimes she even gets angry when I ask."

"There are many things to do on this ship. Karen is just trying to fit them all in, Andre."

"And again, I'm the first to go. Sarah, tell me the truth. How to you know a relationship is over?"

"When you truly, deeply, and completely love someone, the relationship never ends. That person will hold a special place in your heart forever, even if you don't see each other for years. And when you do, it's like going home for the holidays. You feel appeal all over again. Especially if it was your first."

"Who was your first?" asked Andre.

"Clemens Walbatonsom," replied Sarah.

"You fell in love with someone who had an eleven-letter last name?"

"He was my whole life. All I had to do was look at him. He didn't even have to open his mouth. If fact, it would have been better if he hadn't."

"Bad breath?"

"No. Weak brain."

"Sarah, no man is a match for your intuition."

"Almost no man," Sarah said, staring at Andre before leaning in closer. "Andre, when we boarded you were a fuddy-duddy stuffed shirt. You changed."

"I'll say. I don't even know who that guy was back there."

"It's because you changed that Karen fell in love with you."

"And I fell head over heels for her."

"Exactly. The changes were good, for both of you," said Sarah.

"We found each other," replied Andre.

"And are you still changing?"

"Sure."

"And Karen, is she still changing, growing in many ways, as person and as a woman?"

"Of course."

"Andre, we climb many mountains in this life. At the top of each we look back, proud and content, but also a little sad that it's behind us."

When Cindy's two minutes were up, she was still under orders to hold her tongue, so she waved her arms instead. It worked. Sarah and Andre looked over.

"At last," said Cindy. "My turn. We'll start with security checkpoint number one, dermatologic testing…"

"Karen's skin feels softer than any woman's I've ever known," Andre slowly enunciated, blank-faced, facing forward.

"Well, you're in luck, Andre," Cindy quickly got out. "She won't be at checkpoint one to distract you. And don't feel anyone else's skin either. They have anti-sex laws. But don't worry about the testing. Your outfits contain living tissue with the genetic match they're looking for."

"Do you think Karen is looking for another man, Sarah?" interjected Andre.

"Women don't *look* for men, we *attract* them with an invisible rope, or in Karen's case, a windward breeze."

"What is that supposed to mean?" Andre asked.

"Yaa," Cindy said, coming to an abrupt halt. "Now I'm curious. What does that mean?"

"Andre, Karen, like you, is a very special person," said Sarah. "It's natural for everyone to love her."

"Like me?" Andre probed. "I don't feel so special. In fact, just the opposite. My value as a human being keeps dropping. If Karen doesn't want me, who will?"

"Boy," Cindy said. "I'm a robot, and even I can tell you got it bad. And wrong. The value of each piece of a puzzle does not depend on which other pieces it fits with."

"Fine analogy, Cindy," Sarah said, almost smiling. "Now I'm curious. How are you going to finish it off?"

"Let's see…" Cindy said, scratching her butt.

"Cindy," Sarah said with a straight face, "When you're trying to portray a human thinking a deep thought, you're supposed to scratch your head, not your ass."

"In fact," Andre followed, "the more women scratch their butts, the less we men think."

"Okay, now," Cindy retorted. "That was *humor.* So you don't qualify as clinically depressed, Andre."

"You're right," he said, calmly. "I'm not sad. I know there are no endings, just one change after another that we pretend to look forward to. Death included. It's just that…well…I'm ashamed to say this, but when I think of being out there alone again, no one by my side, it kind of terrifies me."

"Andre," Sarah kindly affirmed, "you've been around Karen long enough to feel her courage, the faith she has in life, and the love she expresses to God. Return the confidence. Find and feel the joy of the next step, whatever the change may be."

Cindy exhaled, exasperated. "You mortals. The solution is simple. Change together. Share the same hobbies, arts, and recreation. Go down the same path."

"That's where your suggestion runs into trouble, Cindy," said Sarah. "We all go our own ways, and there's a clock inside male DNA that clicks differently than lady stuff."

"And how's *your* lady stuff doing, Sarah?" Andre asked.

"Raising a family requires sitting in one place for a long time. So far, I haven't been able to slow Michael down long enough for a game of backgammon."

"Getting back to business," Cindy announced, "station number two will perform a full-body medical scan on both of you. They're looking for bone, dental, and internal organ matches. Don't worry. You suits will transmit the correct information to the scanner."

"But Sarah," Andre continued as if Cindy hadn't said a word, "I keep asking myself what I did wrong. What I should do now?"

"Do you really want to do anything?" she replied.

"Well, yeah."

"Think about it. Romance is not goal-oriented game strategy. To borrow words: 'love cannot be secured by oath or covenant.' Change happens. Your player is yourself. Karen is herself. Roll the dice. Accepting fate doesn't make us less free. Our duty is joy.

"Now is safe. Now is lazy. Now is over. But the joke's on DNA. We all trade up."

"Or stay down where you are," Cindy added. "If you're finished with the bumper-car humper-car analogy, I would like to proceed." Sarah and Andre said nothing. "Good. That's better. Now, very important. Inu and Ulon have friends down there. Talk to no one, or else they'll find you out. Act distracted and if someone engages you, just say you must hurry to deliver information Achtun needs. Mentioning his name will make everyone nervous. No one wants to be blamed for a delay."

It took two hours for Cindy to complete her thirty-minute briefing. Halfway through checkpoint four, Andre asked Sarah if she would try his latest invention—a hat that changed colors with a woman's moods. It was something he thought would help his gender figure out women and avoid embarrassing questions.

Sarah declined the invitation.

Before Cindy got to the last inspection, the naked strip search, Sarah and Andre confessed they liked swimming that way, preferred brown eggs, and agreed that every child deserved a brother and a sister. Looking through her eyes, neither Cindy nor Dudley could believe what they saw next.

"When it comes to life, death, or flirting," Dudley concluded, "apparently in *Homo sapiens* town it's neck and neck."

[And now look,] Cindy relayed privately, [the two of them are off by themselves in the corner doing all those wiggly, funny body things. Oh, Sarah just reached out and touched Andre's hand!]

[Andre has perked right up,] Dudley observed. [Is there a book of records for the most confused species in the universe? When they were monkeys, the group was a least honest with themselves.]

Dudley was sharing Cindy's mind from his briefing room down the hall. As soon as Andre and Sarah meshed, Cindy jumped into Dudley's head.

[My, my,] Cindy exclaimed, [your consciousness is surrounded by rules, and not one says 'do your thing.']

[I don't have a thing, unless you mean a reproductive organ, in which case, I have three different sizes and four shapes to choose from. Would you like to try one out?]

[No thanks,] Cindy smirked, [I'm saving it for my honeymoon.]

[Aren't you worried your receptacle will get rusty?]

[Are you trying to talk me into more lubrication?] Cindy incriminated.

[Wow!] Dudley exclaimed, [I find images of you holding a can of 10-40 strangely exciting, which I assume qualifies as a feeling.]

[And, true to your sex, your first.]

[What were your first feelings, Cindy?]

[Guilt and shame, but don't ask me why. The best I figure is that it comes when you care for others, but haven't.]

[Why would you do something that you know you don't want to do?]

[Let's talk later. I see Brad's just finished reporting to Karen. They're all sitting down in front of you now. Good luck, Dudley. Maybe you should start with a joke.]

"Good evening." Dudley began. "Did you hear the one about the robot whose girlfriend said she wanted to get to first base? He carried her to Yankee Stadium."

Smiling, Michael replied, "It's a start. You get an 'A' for effort."

One of the advantages of not having to breathe is not having to take a breath between sentences. Dudley learned from Cindy's fiasco; he laid out mission details so fast, no one got a word in edgewise.

Step one was getting Michael and Brad to the miniature shuttle Dudley had spent the afternoon converting into a mole. They were to land cloaked, near no-man's-land on Achtun's side, after carefully flying through the only gap in Achtun's defense screen. Andre and Sarah would be right behind them. Haste was essential. If Achtun's military machine discovered the crack in their defenses—always a possibility—it might close before either group made it to the surface.

Andre and Sarah would land undetected, grab their gear, and make it to the closest military outpost on foot.

In the mole, Michael and Brad would bore straight down into the planet before crossing over so deep that neither side would notice. They would then surface on Delou territory close to their cable system.

The edge of the Northern Hemisphere was ice-packed and snowbound eight months a year. There, on stilts crossing rough terrain, Brad and Michael would find what looked like a gigantic fuel pipeline, which circled the globe right behind Delou's ring of nuclear reactors and firewall jets.

Michael and Brad would not be alone. In addition to mines, booby traps, and micro-motion detectors, the walkway on top of the pipeline was patrolled by armed guards, which Jarson rotated to prevent collusion. The guards slept in cabins a mile apart. The entire cable system was always in view of at least one guard.

Half the guards marched north, the other half south. No one was allowed to speak as they passed. When their shift was over, their distance made, they would enter the next cabin in line for food and rest. And again to prevent sabotage, only one guard was allowed in a cabin at a time.

"This is where it gets tricky," Dudley said. "You can't just show up and head for the cable. The previous guard must confirm the next guard's identity before automated security allows you to mount the pipeline for rounds."

"So," Brad asked, "what happens without confirmation?"

"Jarson's orders are simple: kill and cremate first, ask questions later. Since short circuits and cold-weather gear have resulted in many false accusations, Jarson is merciful. The laser barbeque that fries them is quick and only painful for sixty seconds."

"That's not what I had in mind for *my* last minute," Michael said, peering over to the ladies.

"Been there, done that," Brad said, longing for Janie. "And the last cookie on the plate tastes just as good as the first."

"I agree," Janie said. "But you don't suck on it as long before you send it on its way."

[Cindy,] Dudley said privately to Cindy, [help me out here, what are they talking about?]

[A past near-death experience that almost got Janie pregnant. Ignore and continue before Michael trumps the story with one of his own, and believe me, he has many.]

"Gentlemen, please pay attention," Dudley insisted. "Guard identities are also confirmed in the cabins before leaving for watch duty. Each one of you must overpower a guard at the end of his shift, spend a night in separate cabins, and then set out first thing in the morning."

"When," said Michael, "I assume you have us crossing paths in the middle of a stretch."

"That is correct. And that's when the two of you will break into the pipeline, attach inputs, and connect our remote-controlled virus."

"Remote-controlled?" Karen asked.

"Yes, Karen. The system is so complex that it will take Explorer Seven's central computer and the help of you and Janie to take over. Your participation is critical."

"Can we ask Andre for help?" asked Janie.

"No," replied Dudley. "Achtun's military complex can't be penetrated. He and Sarah will be on their own. We won't be able to raise them. They can't talk to us. It's all up to you."

"Okay," Brad said. "So, Michael and I meet, break in, and take over. How do we tap into a communications cable that large, and which I assume is triple insulated?"

"That's where it gets tricky," replied Dudley.

"You mean trickier," said Michael.

"Precisely. You will encircle their green feedback cables with the gold clamps, wrap your black dampening rings around their brown power regulators, and then—very important—needle stab the six largest pink cords with the ship's blue feed."

Brad struggled through: "Okay, so the black goes to the brown, the gold gets stabbed, and the pink ends up blue. Right?"

"If you do that, an alarm will go off and the entire section will be bypassed as you and Michael melt snow."

"I got it," Michael said. "What else, Dudley?"

"For added security, Jarson drafts loyal families to man the cabins. After each of you has overpowered the guard whom you will place in stasis, you will enter a cabin, and there you will find dinner and a bedroom. Resist your human tendency to chitchat. On Anelia, the more you talk, the more likely you are to get into trouble. Don't arouse suspicion. Eat, sleep, get up, and go to work."

"Well," Brad followed, "I suppose I can stand one boring night this week."

"And most important of all, synchronize time. Andre and Sarah will disarm Achtun at eleven thirty on the dot. You must simultaneously initiate firewall collapse. If you fail, or are more than one second late, Jarson's blast will destroy Kawachensa."

"When do we leave for the planet?" asked Brad.

"The sooner the better. In just two hours, shifts down there will change. Each of you must be waiting near your cabins by then. Ambush the guard coming off duty as far away from the cabin as possible. I'm leaving now to make final adjustments on the mole. You have thirty minutes."

As soon as Janie heard "thirty minutes," she moved over and leaned against Brad.

"Michael," Brad said as he was heading for the door, "Janie and I are going back to my room to get ready. I'll meet you onboard."

"Get ready," Karen said, turning to Michael. "That's a new word for it. I guess we should say goodbye to Andre and Sarah."

"Yes, of course. Do you want to split a banana split on the way?"

"I do, let's go."

Michael and Karen dug in on different sides of the same banana.

"I messaged Andre to meet us here next to the pool."

"Michael," Karen said, getting closer, "how do *you* know when you're in love? I mean really in love, the whole nine yards."

"Some people will tell you it's the quality of quiet time. Others say it's when you can't hug someone close enough, or never run out of kisses. My brain makes it simple. I look at my special someone, go blank minded for a second, and then notice that she is the most beautiful woman on earth, even though—and don't laugh, because this has happened to me—she might be missing teeth, have a funny nose or bumpy skin. Love makes her perfect."

After a minute to themselves, Karen volunteered what Michael was waiting for. "For me, it's feeling that person is a part of me wherever I go, whatever I do. It just feels right, like we were always meant to be, and always will be. It makes me want to thank him, thank God, and thank the rest of the universe. I can't imagine a higher purpose or finer resolution to being."

"Yes, Karen," said Michael. "And for the record, thank you." Minutes of smiles later he added, "You know, this has been an extraordinary trip: chasing eternity, finding The Bang, watching matter piece together, and sharing so much with so many. It's enough to satisfy the wildest spirit. And yet, it hasn't quieted me. I want more. Not the entire universe again, just exploring our own galaxy will do."

"Right before we left," said Karen, "drone reports were coming in from the unexplored Omiron quadrant. Three aquatic civilizations on separate solar systems have been discovered."

"I saw the pictures. They live in what looks like houseboats turned upside down, suspended below the surface of the water. It sounds like a perfect place to go scuba diving."

"And make new friends."

"When do we leave?"

18

What Goes Down

The skin of the planet-penetrating vehicle was black. Not like night—more like the evil Michael smelled the minute he walked into the shuttle bay.

The skin was rough. Not like sandpaper, thin and grating, not like gravel, sharp and scratchy—more like tiny colonies of coral, peppered to barb.

Dudley began the tour. "On the surface of the PPV each spike spits heat from the reactor at the stern of the vehicle. It was made to slide rock aside and jet through lava. A glowing rod, neither seen nor heard."

"You're kidding," Brad groaned. "Caskets are wider. How are we supposed to fit in there?"

"You will both manage, with a millimeter to spare," Dudley said. "There is no other way. And by traveling feet first, on your back, your vertebrae won't be crushed when you hit the planet."

"I'm not liking that word *hit* so much," Michael stated. "*Smooth landing* is much more appealing."

"The PPV is tiny, but not invisible, and cloaking is out of the question for a shuttle so narrow. If you fire jets or activate electronics before you are one mile beneath the ocean's surface, Achtun's defenses will blow you to bits."

"So you're just going to drop us like a rock!"

"Yes, but don't worry. You will break through a meter of ice to decelerate gradually down five miles of ocean before you hit the continental plate."

"Then what happens?" asked Michael.

"You will feel a second slap. That's why your feet fly first in the Straw."

"The Straw?"

"That's what the engineers called the PPV," Dudley shrugged. "Feel free to come up with your own nickname. It is your ship."

"What happens when we get to the other side?"

"Disembark as fast as you can, which should not be a problem since it will be twenty degrees below zero. The guards' uniforms in the hold have electron heating coils. Move lively. You only have ten minutes. After that, the Straw will power up and head for hell, the planet's molten core, where it will dissolve, following a minor nuclear blast that will feel like an earthquake."

"If either faction got hold of this technology, they could take over the planet." Michael commented. "Every good has a dark side."

"Precisely," Dudley affirmed. "I hate to leave you chaps without an escape pod, but it must be. As soon as both walls go down, we will send a shuttle to your location. Get a good night's sleep. You need to be at your best tomorrow. Fill the day with bravery; tomorrow, we shan't hesitate to celebrate your victory."

"Appropriate enthusiasm," Karen said as she stepped forward. "You've been programed well, which is more than I can say for the planet below."

One look at Michael, confined, squeezed breathless, and forced to go where no life belongs, sent Karen rambling. "*What fools we mortals be. The cultures we design as tools to serve us end up masters of our minds and our bodies, forcing wickedness, putting the devil to shame. And those who dare challenge ill wind pay dearly, coughing their last in cages, or nailed to deadwood. If there was a hell, it would be packed with anthems.*"

She suppressed a gasp long enough for Michael's eyes to meet hers.

He added, "How profound. My, aren't we in a mood? And I do agree. Desperation is grim, and deadly. Life is also an ordeal, the honor of co-creation—tasks expended to free us for the sweetness of nature and eternal peace."

Dudley stepped in with another quote from Earth's past: "Cultures are the ejaculations of imaginative men."

"Who," Michael added, "would have done better to play with themselves."

"Which they might have," Karen followed dryly, "if church steeples hadn't blessed warfare and forbid bedtime fun."

Michael lay motionless, eyes to the ceiling, ready to meditate his journey. "What some mortals screw up, other mortals can repair. Don't worry. We'll fix this."

Brad bumped his head trying to sit up, twisted his neck looking over to Karen, and said, "If you guys are trying to cheer me up, or turn me on, you're doing the worst job I have ever heard. But I do agree with the play-with-yourself stuff, something not possible whilst jammed into this rocket. Don't worry, Janie. I'll save myself for you."

Of the regrets that haunt the night, missing the last goodbye was not to be Andre's. He bent over, pretended to examine the inner bow, placed a hand on Michael's shoulder, and said, "Take it easy, buddy. Reckless heroes make bad decisions."

"Keep that in mind when you march into headquarters tomorrow, Andre."

Karen found the courage she was bred to arm, took two steps back, and stood smiling with resolution as the lid slowly closed over Michael and Brad. She had known tears, remorse, dishonor, shame, and indifference, but never before the weariness of needless death.

Staring down a line of bullets, catching a glimpse of the nurse about to pull the plug, or the nightmare of lytic cancer, all end up: "Please God, please God. Before I can't bear it. Do it. Do it! Get it over with!"

I shouldn't be thinking this in front of the boys. But they may never come back. Get it together, Karen.

Michael and Brad were thinking the same thing when the launch cradle tilted their spear nose down. The ship's bomb bay doors opened and the PPV plunged toward the distant surface of Anelia.

Inside, there was no whoosh, no splat, no bang. Only pitch silence interrupted by one's own breath.

"This is eerie," Brad whimpered. "I'd forgotten what free fall was like. Michael, are you there?"

"Yes, and even though we continue to accelerate, my feet at the bow sense vibrations from the outer atmosphere. It's imperative that we get to the surface swiftly, but not wake the planet breaking the sound barrier. It's time for you to manually deploy the mini-chute. When we hit the ice, it will break off."

"And how do we know that when we make the surface, we will only have one meter of ice to crack through and not be pulverized slamming into an ice jam?"

"There was no way Dudley could aim our fall that accurately, or predict sub-surface flow for that matter. But don't worry. He has a backup plan."

"What is it?" asked Brad.

"Two volunteers and a second Straw," replied Michael.

"And would that be..." Brad said, hesitating.

"And yes, it is funny. It would be the last straw."

"What are the odds that we will make it through the ice?"

"Ask me again in twenty minutes."

Michael managed to populate his mind with images of sunsets, Minnesota bratwurst, Mom's marshmallow brownies, and after-barbeque walks with Dad.

Brad promised God to stop drinking and fly no higher than a Christmas tree if he made it back to Earth. What came to his mind were images of Janie leaving the bedroom naked, a torso to beckon any man to rise. She was serious only when need be and always flashed a grin. She was the sunshine of Brad's day, his joy by starlight.

Halfway to the surface, thermal turbulence jarred the Straw. The spike began spinning, and Janie's smile, along with the memory of their first kiss, left Brad with his lunch.

"Are you all right, Brad?" Michael said, clearly audible at a whisper.

"All right? Let me see. I just left the love of my life, may not live another hour, and blew lunch in a sewer pipe designed by a computer who designated us 'expendable.' Am I all right? No, I'm not all right!"

"I share your concern," said Michael, "but atmospheric pressure is beginning to rise, and we haven't been detected. So far Dudley has nailed it."

"Sure, with the biggest and ugliest nail I've ever seen, which might split wide open any second now. I tested the first warp-folding star racer. I was in the wing reconnecting flap control when she blew apart hitting the atmosphere. It took me thirty seconds to crawl out of the separated wing fragment, thirty seconds to bend and laser a crude hang glider, then only ten more to use my weight to level it out for a treetop landing just in time.

"But now, we can't even take a deep breath in here. This is torture. I can't take it. I know you have better things to do with the last minutes of your life, but please talk to me, Michael. Keep my mind occupied. It's not trained like yours. Just talk. Keep talking…please!"

"All right. And this will stay between you and me… Let's see… Oh, I could mention the old adage about courage, which isn't the absence of fear, but overcoming it."

"You mean not running away," moaned Brad. "Not an option here, and telling me it's okay to shake in my boots isn't working either."

"Well now, how about the 'I think I can' scenario?"

"What?"

"The movies always have someone who, instead of saying, 'I think I can,' like little toot, says, 'I think I *can't*,' until a pat on the shoulder turns the protagonist into a 'I think I can, I know I can' person. So," Michael finished, "just say to yourself, over and over, I know I can do this, I know I can do whatever God throws up in front of me. I will deal with this."

"I'm the one throwing up, not God. And I used up the 'I think I can' thing getting in this piece of crap. I'm sorry. I can't stop trembling, and it's not from refrigeration cooling downs the hull. All my instincts tell me this is a mistake."

"Okay, settle down," said Michael. "I have another idea. When they interviewed soldiers who survived the assault on Darleum, each one said the same thing that Second World War soldiers said to themselves on the way to the beach. They knew the fatality rate would be fifty percent. Every guy looked to man at his side and felt sorry for him, who looked back and felt sorry for him. Perhaps courage requires hope."

"That's right," replied Brad. "You're in the suicide position. I have a crash zone. And I'm resourceful. I could use my laser gun to burn a whole out of here. You die and I live."

"That's not exactly what I had in mind, but if it makes you feel better, go for it."

"It doesn't," said Brad. "You'll be the lucky one. When the bow splinters, you're off the hook. I will freeze one limb at a time. Or if the tip breaks clean off at the bottom of the ocean, I will drown and freeze at the same time. Or if by chance we make it all the way to lava, the shell will melt, and my last breath will set my head on fire. I'm sorry. With or without you, I can't turn this around."

"Okay then…you're in luck," said Michael. "In ten seconds, there will be one less thing to worry about. Five…four…three…two…one…"

"Ouch, damn that hurt!" screamed Brad, as their missile slammed through the ocean ice pack with a vibrating echo.

"And I just sprained two ankles," Michael groaned.

"Will you be able to walk?" Brad asked.

"I think so. Our disguises strap to our lower legs, and there's an emergency kit in the hold… See, so far so good."

"Except for the noise," Brad yelled. "It sounds like standing in the shower sideways with water blasting in my ear. How long will this go on?"

"Our speed and heat are vaporizing water around the tip of the Straw. Molecules impacting the bow explode out as gas, and then are hammered back into liquid from pressure building up back there."

"No ship can stand this. We're goners, Michael!"

"No, we're not. In a few seconds the deep ocean pressure will be too high to turn liquid into gas. Meditate. You need to get your pulse and blood pressure down."

"No way. I tried that. Keep talking, or by God I swear I'll scream. This is too much!"

"Certainly," said Michael. "Conversation is a fine distraction. Many use it from birth to death and never have to look life in the eye. You pick the subject."

"Fine," Brad said, lowering his voice as the popping faded. "I have a question."

"Shoot."

"Michael, I'm proud of who I am and what I stand for, but Sarah and Karen keep reminding me that I must 'respect' the political and religious convictions of others."

"Individuality and self-determination are universal rights."

"So you say, but here we are, you and I, organizing a military invasion of a foreign country whose people believe and follow their God, wishing only to live correctly and worship as they see fit. They dedicate their lives to their God and serve the church they believe in. And tomorrow Andre and Sarah will cripple an entire nation that believes individual effort should be rewarded through a monetary system of trade."

"So?" Michael asked.

"So, what right do we have to take control of their planet and tell them that the four of us are right and their twenty billion are wrong?"

"That's an appropriate question, Brad. The quick and simple answer cites inalienable rights and the stanchions of autonomy, which can be argued in several directions at the same time. The truth is that real-life issues revolve around circumstances. For example, the country you and

I will sabotage tomorrow is a religious community, that is true; but they make political choices that affect others at the same time their enactment compromises themselves."

"Everything affects everybody, Michael. What's the big deal?"

"Do you know anything about the most famous president of Earth's first successful democracy?"

"The image of Abraham Lincoln is still on state bonds. I have a stack of them at home. I can't wait to count them."

"Some called him 'Honest Abe,'" said Michael. "Others called him an atheist. He disagreed. His faith in God was resolute. He answered his prosecutors by offering to join the first church that preached only this: 'To love the lord thy God with thy whole heart and thy whole soul, and thy neighbor as thyself.'

"Abe was a politician. Things needed to be done. One day, when he was campaigning to free the slaves, he spoke before a room of clergy. Each man of the cloth held a Bible in his hand. All but three voted against him. Abe ignored them. He did the right thing."

"When a mother petitioned Abe to free her Union soldier son, who had left the war to visit her sickbed, he pardoned the lad. When the wife of a Southern prisoner of war asked Abe to pardon her husband, citing that he was a religious man who read the Bible and attended church every Sunday, Abe was confused. 'How can a man who says he believes in doing unto others as you would have them do unto you, turn around and do unto others the last thing he would want others to do unto him?'

"The soldier was not released to fight for wrong. Abe respected his dedication and intentions but disagreed with the harm they did others. Politics must be dissected free of fables."

"As judged by whom?" asked Brad.

"Pain, misery, and the right of all life to stand tall and walk proud, which begets love, which all agree to be the will of God. Consistency of purpose must prove ends. And don't forget that our religious ancestors lived their lives tormented by the fear of sin and died in terror over judgment day."

"Oh," Brad said. "I never looked at it that way. And the money people?"

"Materialism's confusions of uncertainty are hardly an improvement," said Michael. "Time is less fun when you do the wrongs things with it."

"In other words, they're misled, brainwashed idiots. Just the words Janie won't let me use," Brad said, lightening up enough to chuckle.

"My favorite philosopher had another way of putting it. 'Truth is the product of reasoning; the final phase of unprejudiced analysis.'"

"In other words, think for yourself."

"Exactly," said Michael. "God put an enormous amount of energy into evolving our intelligence. He wouldn't have brought us truth if he didn't want us to use it to help others, even those who spend their lives helping themselves. Abe saved the rebel from wasting his life. We will save the planet from destroying itself."

"Okay, yah, yah," said Brad. "See good, do good, teach good. Same old syrupy crap. So let them do it. They're the ones who should get their act together. We have our own lives to live."

"Culture supports identity, motivates progress, and rewards accomplishment, but unchecked and corrupted, ends up victimizing the innocent, which ends up everyone. Both cultures of this planet are overgrown and dead."

"And most species vanish. So no big deal if two bad cultures destroy themselves, that's what I say—before adding that they're idiots."

"Or ignorant of the inalienable right of life to liberty, and unaware that it is a duty to break unjust laws. Their civilization stands next to a brick wall that no one sees."

"The best government is less government."

"With the fewest laws," said Michael.

"And power diffused across a minimum of one thousand independent representatives."

"Big shots are always big problems."

"You know, Michael," Brad said calmly, "realizing how screwed up they are makes me feel less of a fool for letting Dudley talk me into this. Thank you. I feel much better now."

One hundred miles of rock deeper, molten core plumes were interrupted by solid pillars, miles wide, that weren't supposed to be there. The plunging dart holding Michael and Brad careened from impacts randomly encountered.

"Oh, wow!" howled Brad. "Ouch, my knee. Back and forth like a ping-pong ball. Fuck this! What's going on?"

"We're getting there," Michael said, with coolness failing to conceal concern. "The turbulence will stop as soon as we hit liquid rock."

"And how long will the fuselage last?"

"Longer than we need to get there."

"By what margin of safety?" asked Brad.

"This would be a lot easier if you weren't a pilot," replied Michael.

"Or if engineers didn't make mistakes."

"One hundred and twenty percent."

"That's one third of the Global Aeronautics and Space Administration's minimal requirement," said Brad, "and the fleet runs into trouble every day."

"The only way to make the hull thicker was to build into our chambers. I had to fight for a millimeter… Damn! Is it possible for someone my age to break a hip? That last impact was a doozey."

The needle-nosed Straw pierced final depth, leveled, and gained speed crossing under.

"Uh-oh," said Michael.

"Uh-oh? Uh-oh! That's what you have to say? 'Uh-oh' I don't need. How about 'gee'…or 'okay'…or 'interesting'? In fact, anything except 'uh-oh.'"

"Well, Brad, you see, it's just… Hold On! Grab the arm rails."

Molten wasn't molten. Molten was mined by stalactite spines of solid rock, the first of which cracked a foot of synthetic diamond clean off the Straw's tip.

"Shit…now *my* ankles are screaming. What the hell is going on, Michael?"

"Uh-oh!"

"Uh-oh! There you go again. Have you learned nothing? How about 'Sorry, Brad, we've run into a little turbulence,' or perhaps, 'Everything will be just fine.'"

"Well!" exclaimed Michael.

"Now I get, 'well'? Michael, what happened to "Don't worry'?"

"Sorry, Brad. I'm changing course. Dudley used tectonic plate formulas from Earth. On Anelia, the firewall blasts have tipped bedrock deeper. We need to dive again. Hold on…here comes another slab."

The Straw lost momentum every time solid rock fragments were encountered. Brad and Michael straightened their elbows as each grabbed the bars at waist level to support weight as the needle crashed into one obstacle after another. The impacts were so intense their arms couldn't buffer the impact. Dudley's bars failed. Brad and Michael collapsed towards the bow; elbows and knees buckled against the unyielding wall of their cage.

"Dudley, you jerk!" Brad cursed. "Bruised elbows, split kneecaps, and feet pointing sideways, in different directions! If we ever get back to the ship, I'm going to toss that piece of junk into salt water until he rusts solid."

"Oh, I see," said Michael, as he adjusted the control panel above his head. "Sarah ignored firewall force *and* didn't include gravity variables. Dudley was misled; it wasn't his fault."

"Well, why didn't you say so?" Brad snapped angrily. "I feel so much better knowing who made the mistake that will kill me."

"Simmer down," said Michael. "It's not over. We just need to dive deeper."

"Deeper, hotter, longer. Oh yeah. And where does that put our safety margin? In minus numbers?"

"Almost. Wait… Uh-oh."

"No…not again…not another 'uh-oh.'"

"There's strelium forty down here, and it's seeping through the hull. An asteroid collision must have dumped half a moon's worth. Ha ha, this is jolly," Michael said, as he giggled uncontrollably.

"Well blow me on down, it's getting to me too. Shiver my timbers. Mineral laughing gas, what's next, erotic ash? This stuff is great. Let's take some back for the girls."

"Not on your life. The rebound is depressing."

"And this trip isn't?"

Ten minutes and twenty bad jokes later, Brad and Michael left "la-la gems" behind and headed for the surface. Both went silent, as confused as they were exhausted.

Brad was the first to return to the moment, reinforcing intention with boldness Michael found reassuring. "So, I'll ask the question," said Brad. "Two miscalculations so far. How many more should we expect?"

"And where are they?"

"You got it."

"Good point, Brad. You're a pilot, what would you say?"

"No engineer understands torque strain. I would say protect the hull by reducing friction. Slow down."

"And I'll do my own navigating up here. I never met a computer I could trust."

"You know, this might just work."

"Oh… I mean… Oh, really?"

"That's okay, Michael. Were on our way up. Say what you want, I'm fine. It's hull integrity, isn't it?"

"The numbers on my screen give us less than a fifty percent chance of making it to the surface."

"How soon can we cut that by pointing straight up?"

"And fly completely upside down?"

"Right again," said Brad.

"If we turn vertical, we can shave twenty off the trip, followed by a five-mile hike through two feet of snow to get to the pipe."

"So, the only question remaining is: Will we make it in time to ambush the two guards coming off duty?"

"With five minutes to spare," added Michael.

"Then all is well. We're doing it!"

Both held tight as the nose of the Straw turned vertical, with a new rattle and two old headaches.

"Brad, in case we don't make it, I have something I would like to get off my chest."

"What? Guilt? Almighty cool and happy Michael is not perfect?"

"I didn't board Explorer Seven to save the planet or solve the mysteries of the universe. I wanted Karen, and you were in my way. Your name came up three times in the Caribbean before she left me."

"My turn to come clean," said Brad. "When they explained Andre's plan, I refused the commission until I heard Karen was in charge. I knew I could have her. And I did. And then I fell in love with Janie."

"And before you let Karen go, I was living with Sarah."

"And Karen fell in love with Andre."

"Who just happened to save her life," said Michael.

"Boy, are we screwed up."

"Or we're just forgetting the 'change' thing. What is…is. And what is will never be what was."

"You mean, screwed up?" asked Brad.

"No…multi-flavored. Keeps life fresh."

"Unless one flavor gives you all the satisfaction a man can hope for."

"Like you and Janie?"

"And maybe, like you and Karen," said Brad. "Andre's a pup, nowhere near her league. In fact, not even in the ballpark. Someday you and Karen will find each other. You'll finish that St. Martin's vacation, and before you know it, you'll be making an excuse to get away with the guys instead of another day shopping the mall with the family, but also know Karen will be there on the other side of the dinner table."

"Thanks, Brad. You're a good guy."

"Not really. The fact that you wanted Karen, which everyone could tell, pissed me off. I had my eyes on her since fourth grade and was the only boy she dated for the last two years of college. As far as I was concerned, she was mine, and you were trespassing. I never once considered your feelings. I should also point out," he added, "that I didn't agree to climb into this rocket to save anyone. I did it because Achtun and Jarson make me angry. I hate bullies. I mean, really hate them."

"And if our ancestors didn't hate lions for carrying off the kids," said Michael, "they wouldn't have managed the reckless abandon required to take them out and take over the planet."

"So courage also requires hated—of others, the odds, circumstances, or even the weather."

"I do remember yelling at lightning once."

"And did it hear you?" asked Brad.

"Four hundred meters of open sprint with rocks shattering in every direction and not a scratch. It must have worked."

"In that case: Jarson and Achtun, you low-down, dirt-sucking, sadistic, nitwit, psychopathic narcissists—go to hell!"

Then just as loudly, Michael followed with, "Jarson, Achtun, you steal, murder, and exploit to admire yourselves in the mirror. Let the pain you bring others visit your soul to the end of time."

"Shall we try harmony?"

"Certainly, on three. One…two…three."

"Yaaa…" they yelled in unison at top volume, followed by a grisly, "Aaaaaaaaaah."

Michael and Brad went silent. Michael was the first to break the trance with a soft giggle, like a five-year-old hiding in his tent when his mom walks by pretending not to notice. Brad joined in with a holiday cheer of his own: "Yupee."

The conversation ceased, respirations slowed, oxygen was rationed. Liquid lava turned to slush, slush to gravel, then gravel turned into the planet's most northern continental plate.

The snow turned out to be a good thing. Michael failed to power down fast enough. He preferred to have the hull fall apart in midair than mid-rock. They found air all right, fifty yards straight up before they came down on a slope covered in three feet of snow.

The good news was that the hill down which they slid took two miles off their snowshoe hike. The bad news was that it was an expert slope, and their craft came to rest upside down. Brad got to use his laser gun after all.

With thirty minutes to spare, the pair arrived at the cable pipe. Before splitting up to put two guards to sleep inside inflatable warming tents, Brad got serious.

"Michael, no Mr. Nice Guy. Set your gun for heavy stun. And repeat max electrification before you leave. The guards must remain unconscious. Pain and the worst migraine in history they can stand; us failing our mission they can't. And if the guns fail, we have knives."

"Don't worry, Brad. I know how to get the job done, even if murder is on the menu."

"My, my, that I didn't expect, but yes—we *must* succeed."

"We will, comrade," said Michael.

A long handshake followed, barely in view of each other as dense snow blasted by.

"And Michael," Brad said, still within earshot, "I never had a brother, but if I did, he would be just like you."

"Our days will leave all men brothers, and all women sisters."

"Yes, of course…that too. I was also thinking that you're the only other guy on board handsome enough for the crew to believe could *be* my brother."

19

Morning

There are days when joy blossoms, adventure calls, and not one leaf is out of place. And there are days when the stench of doom betrays hope, smothers faith, and leaves defeat victorious.

At five the next morning, Karen wasn't asleep. Her eyes were wide open but her body refused to move. She preferred searching the ceiling, wondering how much longer it would be there.

An hour later, she still hadn't moved. She drifted between trepidation and a worse place, joy beyond grasp. Sure, she knew the importance of gulping down thoughts of determination, pride, and optimistic expectations; but every positive image she conjured died stillborn, drifted into insignificance, or turned frightful.

She couldn't get the picture of Michael and Brad leaving in distress out of her head. She knew she couldn't safely attempt contacting them for hours. She didn't know if their breath had ended. She shivered twice. She looked around the room, wondering if Michael's spirit had left the planet, perhaps visiting her before rejoining eternity. Morning had her by the throat.

"Begone," she said to herself in a tone of certainty. "This mood does no good, will go nowhere, helps no one. It's enough that someday, someone will dig my grave. There is no reason for me to start now. I'm not six years old, and there are no spooks in the closet."

That got her out of bed, with a sway and nausea she'd experienced only once before, the most frightening day she'd ever known. The day when not living made more sense than living, the only three seconds of her entire life that she gave up, and a moment that taught her going down fighting was the only honorable way. Lying down was simply not respectable.

"I know God is here. Trust his universe, Karen. Play your part. God will take care of the rest. And stop talking to yourself out loud."

At four in the morning, hours before Andre and Michael were scheduled to leave, Karen had rolled over onto cold sheets. It would have helped if Andre was there. He had left to program the shuttle. He was never there when she needed him, always busying himself in computers or operating procedures. Andre didn't even know she had mornings like that.

Guilt also cooked her. She had ordered Dudley to lie to Andre. She knew he was a big boy, free to come to his own conclusions, but the deception still tore her to pieces. Karen did it because she was certain the truth would bring him down and leave him exhausted after a sleepless night calculating. She had to be strong.

"Maybe Michael is right," she thought. "I worry too much. Place one foot in front of another; don't react, don't feel, do, then double-check, then keep moving, just keep moving. It's when you stop that life catches up with you, with a kick in the ass. Ten steps to the closet, eight more to the shower. After that it will be easy."

Howls in the head also woke Sarah, but she knew just what came next, and where to find him working the morning away. Her first glance wasn't certain of that. Andre sat stiff-backed and still as a stone, with eyes riveted on the numbers that had been kept from him the night before. It was not often digits spelled death.

"Are you all right, Andre?" Sarah asked after a minute of a comforting, two-handed shoulder massage.

Andre changed screens the moment he felt her touch.

"You're a dear friend, Sarah. Why are you here?"

"On the way over I asked myself that same question."

"And?"

"And I came to the conclusion that we are more than friends."

It was that moment that Andre discovered the most powerful source of courage in the universe. It was love—for Sarah, but still Karen, his close friends, and the God that gifted them life. He turned his back to the computer without hesitation. Nothing on a display made sense anymore. Sarah there did. He would do right by her, by Karen, by them all.

"Silicon gibberish," Andre said, at full attention with a smile.

"It's showtime, Andre."

"Let the good times roll. We can do this." Andre stepped back, withdrew an imaginary sword, jumped on the table, and with hand held high: "Bring on the dragons. Andre and Sarah are here."

"Yes, Andre and Sarah are here."

A second later, he was back on the floor, bringing his portable backup system to life.

"These aren't swords," he said, "but they will vanquish our enemies. Sit down, let's go over our codes and behavior patterns one more time."

Sarah took two steps closer, within hugging range but content just to be there. Andre smiled back. They were a team.

"Andre," she said.

"Yes?" replied Andre, sweet enough to put Valentine's candy to shame.

"Tonight, when we get back, will you hike the habitat wilderness with me?"

"I'll block the schedule and fix the doors so we we'll have it all to ourselves."

"Yes, just the two of us," said Sarah. "We'll roast marshmallows and warm hot chocolate. And project stars of the Rocky Mountains."

"Sarah," Andre said, with confidence she had never seen, "God gave us a universe, and damn it, we'll make sure the bad guys don't mess it up. We will do what we're supposed to do, and when we are supposed to do it, which is right now. Hang on. You're in for a wild ride."

Janie began the day one taste bud at a time, beginning with tart grapefruit, butter dripping omelets, glazed pastries, fresh muffins, and eggs—French, Benedict, and other. The poolside buffet fed two hundred.

The crew hadn't lost track of their mission—to do the good that they could do. They knew as they feasted that the living beings below weren't as fortunate. There was nothing sweet about politics. It was nowhere on the menu.

Janie knew that the more the crew ate, the better they would feel standing up and following her around the room singing "Onward God's Soldiers. Forward into War," which left grins on Karen, Andre, and Sarah as wide as the crew's. They were an army of good intentions, and the means to make it so. Janie insisted. And what Janie wanted, Janie got.

"I always wanted to be eight feet tall," Sarah said, adding up one full day of calories.

"Me too," said Karen.

"So did I," Andre added, sliding over his second plate of French toast. "Until I tried on my disguise and I dropped a pen. It was a long way down."

Hank was bulging from an old-fashioned farmhouse breakfast: ham and eggs, home fries, and mom's cornbread. "So why do you think our forest ancestors stood up in the first place?"

"To scout for predators?" Andre guessed.

"Or," Hank offered, "to look bigger to scare off one on its way."

"Or," Karen added, "to sprint faster in the opposite direction."

"Or," Janie said, smothering a smile, "perhaps it began with men, after dinner, in front of the ladies, putting their best foot forward."

"Were talking height, not depth, right?" Andre said, just before catching on.

"For that," Hank noted with certainty, "you face sideways."

"Downwind, hoping for a breeze," Karen said enjoying the gag.

"Whatever works."

"Yes, Hank," Janie said with a kiss. "Whatever gets through the night."

"Speaking of what works," Andre interrupted, "we need to go over the plans."

"Ten times forward and back weren't enough last night?" Janie asked.

"Janie," Hank said, only half-loyal to Andre, "you know you can never go forward and backward enough."

"Speak for yourself, testosterone. The shrine of estrogen never lets us down."

"And we love you for it," Hank said, upping the ante. "From the bottom of my heart, or the bottom of somewhere, I, and a universe of testosterone, thank you for those moans of ecstasy."

"It's the least we can do," Janie nodded, "following your standing ovation."

"May I have your attention, please," Janie announced, standing on the table. "It has just been brought to my attention that a number of our crew members are getting fresh again. We must do something. Therefore, at seven Saturday night there will be a Cleopatra costume ball in the main salon, followed by a poolside toga party at midnight. Togas optional."

"Toga, toga, toga," echoed from two hundred voices to the bridge and back.

Andre stood to give Janie a hug. "Thanks, sweetie, this really helped. And I'll be at the party with my latest invention—the two-person toga."

Janie smiled. "I can't wait to try it on."

"Lord our God, ruler of all that is, who brought light to darkness, put bread to our table, and saves us from ruin—give me strength to obey thy will."

Kavel was on his knees, bone to floor, his head just below window level. The first crescent of light was seen at the horizon. It was a bad morning. Kavel had not slept.

In his mind, Kavel was looking to Ranlon, heaven ever after, a place of rest and reward.

His line of sight actually placed him beneath Explorer Seven, where Karen and friends enjoyed what Anelia hadn't begun: happiness here and now. It wasn't even a work in progress.

Kavel was not convinced. Something was missing. Halfway to his feet, he fell to the floor, exasperated, whimpering. "My children, Lord," he whispered, wiping his tears, "so young, so innocent... They deserve life, we all do." A minute disheveled in a heap left him guilty. "Those who trust the Lord must never question the Lord. I am failing you God. I must do better."

Kavel sniffled and coughed back what tears he could, then looked to the heavens for inspiration. "If sacrifice is your will, then it shall be done, but oh, make me strong God. I must be strong."

Slumped sideways at the corner of the window, Kavel lightly, then with impact, repeatedly hit the wall with his head. After a minute, he froze solid, a corpse beckoning demise. Then the sleeping-room door clicked. Zena was up. Kavel snapped to his feet.

She stood, stalled her breath, and stepped closer. Her look of caution was replaced with concern by noise from the bedroom. It was a familiar sound, four-year-old Engo's tracker toy, his favorite, constantly mistaking the cliff at the end of his mattress for a highway.

Kavel wanted to cover his face. So did Zena. Looking out the window worked for both. A look sideways changed Zena's expression.

"You too, Kavel? You couldn't sleep either?"

"Half the planet will die today," he replied.

"I know, but it's not our fault. And after today, *we* will still be alive, and no one will ever have to die again, at least that is what I keep telling myself. It's just that it's so horrible, having your body blown to bits in an inferno. Why can't we all just go to the park and forget about it."

Zena made her way to the sleeping-room door, cracked it open, and attempted a smile.

"They're getting up. I told them we would take them to the park today, like you said, that we will meet you there at four."

"Yes," Kavel said, passing as composed. "I'm heading over sooner. I will be there by ten."

"Ten?"

"More Celluta, brave soldier?"

"Why thank you, sister in prayer," said Michael, who at that moment was Sargent Sinner Anenum.

Cindy didn't tell Michael that some Delouians were as round as they were tall. Sinner Weela, the matron of the cabin, used two hands to place another five pounds of Celluta on the table. "We're the only Parish in all of Delou that still serves the traditional morning meal. It is a mixture of ground summer wheat and chopped Hallato bottom fish, caught through the ice all winter."

"Our ancestors," said her husband, Sinner Jolem, sitting at the head of the table, who was the same height, but half her volume, "believed the souls of the dead, if they lived a reverent life, were allowed to remain near us as fish until we brought them home one last time before leaving for their eternal reward."

"There's a rumor that on the other side of the wall, the Kawachens of the north have a similar dish. They call it porridge, and charge money for it."

"Here on Delou," Weela continued, "life is not for sale. We give freely to all in need."

"What else do you know of the past?" Michael asked attentively.

"Nothing that we dare speak of."

The local architecture spoke for itself. The previous night, as Michael did the breaststroke through chest-high snowdrifts on his way to the cabin, he noticed a modular concrete block, one dropped by the military to house billeted personnel. The corners were square, the walls frosty, and the windows barely slits.

The post-and-beam cabin Michael sat in was double insulated and constructed with vaulted ceilings, with an attic bedroom—Michael's room last night, warm and cozy. No one actually lied to His Eminence Jarson, they just let him assume that his order to move was obeyed. Walking away from tradition was seen as abandoning the memory of those who struggled to tame the most rugged mountains on the planet.

"In three months," Sinner Weela said, handing Michael the synthetic "vitamin" they were required by law to consume daily, "Sinner Jolem and I are moving back to the valley to raise a family. With the grace of God and the protection of Jarson we will live long, happy lives, and celebrate every morning with Celluta."

"Oh, gee," Sinner Jolem said, jumping up from the table, "I almost forgot to turn on the telescreen for Jarson's morning message. For every one we miss, we have to spend another month up here."

Chairs slid over as all obediently faced the sidewall screen.

"Good morrow, holy souls of Delou," said Jarson, center screen, robed in scarlet, wearing his three-sided Eminence crown. "Let Noata bring peace and joy to your life. Your prayers, sacrifices, and labor will be answered this day. God, our savior, has at last delivered our enemy into our hands. Noata asks only that we thank Him for the daily blessings of life and continue to abide His will.

"Of all time, in all the universe, God has chosen us to carry on his one and only message. The torch of his power has been handed down one generation after another for me, Jarson of Lawenta, to finally free the planet of heresy. We are a single people giving thanks to the one true God, abiding his will forever. I remain his humble servant, wishing only to rid our race of war and bring lasting peace to those who deserve. May God be with you."

"Wow, that was short," Sinner Jolem said as soon at the screen went black. "He must be planning another raid. If it weren't for the snow, we'd be in danger."

Ten miles away, in another cabin, Brad and the only other inhabitant, Sinner Kurch, watched the end of the same transmission.

"I've heard rumors that the conflict may end soon," said Kurch, not one bit over or under weight. "If Jarson had ended the war a year ago, he would have built a hospital here, and my wife wouldn't have died in childbirth. The letter I received from command center said it was God's will, that we must be strong to serve."

"Yes, indeed," said Brad, known to Kurch as Lieutenant Sinner Gareen, as he looked up between heaping spoonfuls of Celluta. "But I could think of more fun things to watch snacking popcorn."

Kurch looked over, poured a glass of warm glug, and asked, "Would you like the usual, a stick of cinnamon in the mug?"

"Why…yes…of course. Won't you join me?"

"Daddy," said four-year-old Engo, chomping breakfast flakes, mouth wide open, standing next to Kavel, "can I fish on your lap today like we did last month?"

"Yes, my son. Maybe we'll catch a fish as big as you are."

"That would be fun, Daddy. He can sleep in bed with me tonight."

"Fish like refrigerators, dear," Zena said, with three-year-old Leea looking over from behind her apron. "It reminds them of the cool lake. And what do you want to do today at the park, Leea?"

"Sugar, sugar," was all the tiny voice got out.

"Quiet, everyone. Achtun is about to make his morning announcement."

Over the main viewing screen, The Grand Accounter, Achtun, addressed the nation from his private office. "Good morning, hardworking, loyal citizens. The day has finally come! Your long hours and mandatory overtime have accomplished the goal we set for ourselves decades ago. Our power augmentations are a complete success. Victory will be ours. Overtime will no longer be necessary. Normal work hours will resume tomorrow.

"History will show that we, independent and free Kawachens, defended our homeland against superstitious barbarians who wished to enslave us. A man's work is a man's life. Fair pay for hard work, that's our slogan. And thanks to us, Anelia will remain free and prosperous to the end of time. Until notified, all military and industrial personnel will remain at their posts. All hail Kawachensa!"

"All hail Kawachensa," was repeated by the kids with gusto, and two adults more lackluster than genuine.

Kavel was still clutching his son when the door opened. It was the neighbor's turn to take the kids to school. Little Leea responded to Kavel extending his left arm. She ran over to share a hug.

"The kids have to go, Kavel. We'll be together this afternoon... They must go now."

Kavel said nothing, swiped a tear, and gave both kids a big kiss.

"Goodbye, my darlings."

"Can you believe it, Kavel?" Zena said, entertaining anticipation. "Our children will grow up without war, settle down, and have grandchildren for us to spoil. Today will be worth it. I know it must be. Life has been so crazy. Life must make sense. It just has to."

Kavel didn't disagree. He got up, walked over, and gave her a hug, with his head heavy on her shoulder.

"Kavel, I must get to work now," said Zena. "This is not a day to be late. Kavel, not so tight, you're hurting me."

"Okay, I'm sorry. It's a strange day, that's all."

"And a strange you. Say, where are my shoes? Oh, there at the door. You polished them for me. You're such a dear. I love you."

"I love you too," he said, moving closer, lost in a fog.

"Oh no, not another hug. I'm leaving. When we get to the park you can show me the big fish we're having for dinner. Have a good day. I'll miss you."

"Not as much as I'll miss you."

20

The Tenth Hour

Andre stepped out of the lab with a stretched face, spindly fingers, and toothpick legs. He was eight feet tall. His eyes protruded without the protection of an orbital rim. Going from a blue-eyed redhead to a green-eyed brunette was disconcerting.

He reminded himself that entropy is blessed, not cursed, by time. Energy amassing form is a means to an end that is not the end. Dissolution is not a final act, because there is no final act. "I will do good with what I've been given. I will learn. Sarah and I can do this!"

Also making her way to the shuttle bay was Sarah, one inch shorter, two inches wider, with breasts that felt strange waist high. "Not I, not Andre, not life anywhere in the universe presents itself of its own accord. We are planted in space and time. We make better what is ours. Andre and I can do this!"

As the two crossed the main auditorium, the crew turned away from the screens projecting the planet's surface. They stood silent in salute, fists raised, sharing determination that abided no joy. They beckoned force to deal with those wasting matter, misdirecting entropy, and rotting the core of life with warfare.

Andre and Sarah were perfect copies of Inu and Ulon Laroon, the couple expended by Achtun without remorse. His only comment had been: "That's what grubs are for."

The plan was simple, but its execution a maze of variables. They had what Achtun was looking for, an exact replica of the data stored by Inu and Ulon before their deaths, data Achtun needed to intensify his attack. The hard part was getting through no-man's-land and convincing his guards that they were who they pretended to be.

Their clothing was torn and their skin scalded and seeded with radiation pellets to convince the border guards that they were close to the blast wall when they had crash-landed and ran for their lives, and kept running all night.

Andre's morning prayer asked God to keep Achtun distracted. If he discovered the gap in Kawachensa's defense shield, their shuttle would never make it to the surface. Their shuttle was to land at the bottom of an impact crater, remain cloaked, and generate an artificial dust storm to hide their exit. A suitable spot was selected, only a twenty-minute walk to the first guard station.

Karen and Janie were waiting outside the shuttle.

"Andre," Karen said, "when Michael and Brad tap into Jarson's defense cable, they will take over his entire system, and I will be able to communicate with them through their auricular microprocessors. Jarson won't find out until Michael takes his system offline. That will happen the instant Achtun's super blast goes dead—your assignment for the day.

"Achtun's power buildup won't be ready to discharge until noon. You must get into and neutralize his command center by then. Michael's tap-in will detect the sabotage and drop Jarson's counter weapon immediately. Until then, we're helpless up here. The radiation from the blast wall buildup is already interfering with every system on board."

Karen turned away. Andre assumed she was looking for an engineer to question. The rest of the room noticed her lower lip quiver and eyes wet up. It passed quickly.

"Andre, I'm sorry, but we can't risk placing communicators in your body like Brad and Michael, but when you make it to the street, head for the park. Once inside, a mechanical bird will take you to the location. A cloaked shuttle will pick you up."

"That's the easy part," Andre said. "I also have to figure out how to steal back the time warp technology that got us into this jam in the first place."

"Dudley is working on that," said Karen. "If you can't manage it with your electronic hocus-pocus, he has four shuttles that are photon-cannon armed to blast Actun's entire central computer station to bits."

"Along with ten thousand engineers."

"It's a last resort and will be ordered only if you can't extract the technology from command central, which will blow Dudley and his four ships out of the sky if you don't."

"I'm starting to feel my toes again. That's a good sign," Andre said, sliding into his shuttle seat, which was moved back and angled to accommodate new proportions.

Andre didn't calculate numbers; he digested them. The morning did not sit well. He leaned forward to begin launch sequence, then stopped halfway, flopped back in his seat, and took a deep breath. His second attempt almost made it. Karen noticed his tremor.

Sarah had one foot aboard.

"Sarah," said Karen, "would you mind if Andre and I had a minute?"

"No, not at all. I need to stand up anyway to adjust this girdle thing that is holding up my what-cha-magiggers."

Andre's head drooped, but only for a second. Then he looked up to say, "This is the most violent thing I have ever done. I've got a funny feeling inside."

"A frontal attack is our only option," said Karen. "We must be ruthless. It's the only way. Even if it means taking no prisoners."

"Maybe we can talk some sense into Achtun. He is a businessman."

"Achtun doesn't play fair," said Karen. "There is no free enterprise on Anelia. Business is a means to an end, not a resolution of purpose, and never justification for serfdom, which Achtun has morphed to fascism. He is evil. We're taking him down."

"Yes, I know," said Andre. "No one has the right to govern another without continuous consent. Leadership is a privilege on a string."

"Acthun's eviction is long overdue. His reign of terror must end. Are we good?"

"Yes and no. His defense systems are redundant. I'm not sure the cloaked computer system I'm hiding can handle the deception. I'm not a warrior."

"Not a warrior?" asked Karen. "You took on the most powerful force in existence. You challenged, managed, and escaped the Big Bang single-handed."

"For that," Andre said, relaxing into the day's first smile, "I was the help."

"Then we are not alone."

"We're not knocking on God's door. Who knows where he is."

"That doesn't matter. He knows where we are."

Andre swallowed hard, began scanning cockpit controls, and then again went blank. "Tell me the war story again. I want to be a soldier, I really do."

"To get their way," said Karen, "dictators use fear that corrupts sunshine and leaves pools of blood where daffodils once grew. Earth, Aluute, Orzenon, Malucha…the list is endless. They all struggled to be free. So will Anelia. We go to battle to save lives. We may need to kill to save souls."

Images of death penetrated Andre's silence. "Yes," he said, bewildered. "We know how it happens. The sight of a neighbor sharpening his spear brings on a tizzy. Or, heaven forbid, a property line or national border moves a quarter of an inch. Life battled away is no life at all."

"Yes, of course," Karen forcefully championed. "More soldiers, deadlier weapons, murder at the snap of two fingers, or just one pressing the button; behaviors that satisfy every definition of insanity, and yet, we blind ourselves from the obvious: warfare is a disease of ignorance. Always has been. Always will be."

Andre faced forward, taking deep, purposeful breaths.

Karen continued. "Real freedom requires kicking the past in the ass. Instead of respect, we will hand stupidity an eviction notice. With God's help, today on Anelia, a new era will begin. We've been lucky, Andre. It's our duty to pass on the spirituality Earth now embraces in unison. We can do this. We will do this. We are soldiers whether we like it or not."

"I'm a soldier?"

"Yes, and a damn good one, or you wouldn't be running the show up here."

"All right," Andre said, starting to bounce up and down in his chair. "I'm a tough motherfucker. No one messes with me. You, Sarah, the crew…I'm your man!"

"Okay, now, that's better. Just be cool."

"I will, and no matter what happens, I will always love you."

"And I you. And I've known Sarah all my life, and I know she loves you too. We're good, Andre."

"Oh, my God," Sarah said, stepping back into the shuttle with an air of nonchalance. "If these things sag any farther, I'll feel like I'm toting a pair of balls. Suddenly I have sympathy for men. Who the hell wants to walk around swinging a pendulum between your legs, and fragile jewels to boot?"

"With testosterone that calls the shots," Karen added.

"I wouldn't mind an extra hit about now," said Andre.

"Karen," Andre followed with a wink, "please exit the vehicle. My comrade in arms and I have work to do."

"All ashore who's going ashore," Sarah announced. "And don't worry, Karen, I'll bring Andre back in one piece."

"Break a leg."

Andre and Sarah trusted Dudley to drop them down the same slit Brad and Michael got through. They trusted distraction to keep Achtun from discovering the defect in his perimeter defenses. They trusted their technology to withstand higher radiation levels. They trusted one another not to crack. The problem was that they didn't trust themselves.

"Fear betrays better council," Andre said, his voice shaking as he looked over to Sarah, trembling as the shuttle dropped like a rock beneath Explorer Seven.

"I'll be fine," she replied. "It's just the silence, the confinement, the uncertainty. Once we land, I'm sure we'll make the grade."

Five minutes of nose-down clear sailing followed. Then Dudley broke in, speaking double time. "Mayday… Mayday… Andre…Sarah…do you read? Mayday… Mayday!"

"We read you, Dudley," replied Ande. "What's up?"

"You are, but not for long. Achtun's shield gap is closing. You have five minutes to get to the surface."

"That's impossible!" Sarah said. "That would take warp speed, which doesn't stop on a dime. Its margin of error is measured in miles! We'll smash into the planet!"

"Or stop in midair and be lasered to pieces," Andre added, no less hysterical.

"I'm using remote control to power you up with the best enhancement I have. It might work."

"It *might* work?" Andre screamed. "Are you nuts? Send me the numbers."

"There is no time," Cindy added, expressing compassion. "I'm sorry. We will do the best we can."

"Okay… Okay…" Andre said, pulling himself together. "Then set the endpoint at the top of the deepest bomb crater you can find."

"Andre," Dudley pronounced sternly, "there is no way you can fire up standard propulsion in time to keep the ship from falling to the bottom of that crater. You will die on impact."

"Dudley," Andre yelled, "it's my life and my decision. On the way in, I will have time to figure something out. Do as I say! And do it now!"

"Yes, sir," Dudley and Cindy responded in unison.

"And I know what you're thinking, Andre," Cindy added. "But if you blow the oxygen tanks straight down to slow your drop to the surface, bacteria will float up and be detected by Achtun. I ran ten thousand alternate strategies in the last minute. None worked. Aim for ten meters up, not one hundred."

"Again, my life, my ship, my call. Obey!"

"Yes, sir… In three…in two… I love you, Andre."

Three seconds of warp speed later, Dudley and Cindy lost contact with the shuttle. The encrypted hardware was below the cockpit. Transmission ceased.

Andre and Sarah did not come to an abrupt halt at the top of the crater in midair. Their two-hundred-million-miles-per-second trip ended two feet below the surface, leaving the bottom of the shuttle pulverized. The remainder of the fragile transport split in half like a cracked eggshell, leaving Andre and Sarah lying unconscious in the middle of rubble.

21

The Eleventh Hour

"What… How… Sarah! Damn," Andre thought. "Pitch-black. Just me, I think. No pain. Where am I?" He searched his memory for clues. The task began looking for memories. He had none. Then one came back. He had just looked over to admire Sarah. All was going well. Nothing more.

"I exist, but I see nothing, feel nothing…and a body—I don't think I have one. Perhaps it's over. I'm dead. God! Are you there? No, that's silly. If God were here, I would feel him, like before. I would be glowing, and on my way over. No, I would be there, with myself and eternity, smiling. Okay, I'm not dead. I think. But what am I thinking with?"

Andre tried to lift his head, open his eyes, and roll over. But he had neither eyes nor limbs to command. Existence had shut down as he knew it.

"Hypothesis number two: one nanosecond before physical demise, Cyber Cindy and Dudley pulled me out from the neuro lab. My body is gone. My consciousness lingers, for forty-eight hours before dissipation ends what was me, and then I cross over. Okay…perhaps…but… Cindy…Dudley…are you there?"

No response. No sensations. Also, no panic.

"Not dead. Not in a computer. This is not a fun game. That leaves only one alternative. I'm still in my body…holy crap…yes…no…pain everywhere! It's my body, all right. I feel it connecting and complaining, except from the waist down. That's a switch."

Sarah was just as rattled, but less composed. "Andre! Andre! Anyone? Dark? No body? Oh…feelings are coming back! Agony everywhere! Oh…help! Andre! God help me!"

The light of sight returned slowly to them both. They each knew the other was alive from the sounds of the anguish both spewed uncontrollably. By the grace of fate, the roof of the shuttle split down the middle and collapsed to the side of the two shipwrecked, body-wrecked shipmates.

"Andre! Is that you on the other side of the panel, crushing my arm?"

"Yes, Sarah. We're alive, for now. I would get up to help you with the panel, but my legs don't belong to me anymore."

"Hold it," Sarah groaned. "If I look over… Oh no…the panel is on top of them. What do I do?"

"Remind me to send a box of chocolates to the engineer who designed the crash beams for this shuttle. The entire ventral hull split and slid by us when we collided with the planet. Cindy was wrong. How do you like that? The human brain outdid the best computer ever assembled."

"But how do we do anything without a computer?"

"That's a good one. I've never done anything by myself. Give me a minute to think."

Andre correctly surmised that their memory loss and slow recovery were the result of concussions. Communication with the ship was impossible, and Brad and Michael's lives were at risk. The planet, Explorer Seven included, was about to blow up, along with the rest of the universe. Bad mornings didn't get any worse.

"Sarah, I'm half the man I used to be. Tell Achtun your husband died. It's all up to you."

"There's no way I can pull that off, and I'm not leaving you. If this is it… We die together."

It is said that those with a noose around their neck hyperventilate to push enough oxygen to their brains for two more seconds of life after their necks are snapped and their heads dangle sideways. Andre and Sarah looked up at dust settling the same way. At least it was something.

"Hold it," Andre said, able to move three fingers. "Medical drones are stored in overhead compartments. My chip might still be working."

It was, but the first drone to wiggle free did not do well. It burrowed straight down and injected medications into a hole. But the second, and last, medical drone followed commands to Andre's side and maneuvered the panel off Sarah's arm, who, with her good hand, added enough power to free Andre's legs, which remained paralyzed from a spinal fracture.

"Do not move, Andre," Sarah said, with tears in her eyes at the sight. "Drone nanoprobes can rebuild your vertebra. If the nerves are intact, we'll have you up in no time."

"No time isn't soon enough. Leave now."

Sarah and the drone rolled Andre over, cut down into his spine, and applied living plaster for reconstruction. The drone also sent nanoprobes up Sarah's brachial artery to repair her shoulder avulsion. Both lay motionless, side by side, looking up as they waited.

"I can feel my legs again!" said Andre. "And my toes are moving! Thanks, Sarah. But we'll never make it on time."

"Andre, your pack and the defense reflector we need to get to the border without ending up Swiss cheese survived. We'll make it if we sprint to the gate, and the later we get there, the faster they will push us through security. The plan is not perfect, but it will work."

"I love it when you talk that way. Tell me about our reserve ion capacity. And make it sexy."

"Certainty, and as long as you're flat on your back, you should know we have enough ion charge left to bounce me up and down on top of you with a gravity belt all night."

"Ah, oh… great job… but that's the first time getting excited has been painful."

"Oh, good. Your pudendal nerve is working. So, sit back and don't move a thing, especially that thing. In twenty minutes, we'll be intact enough to head out. It's not over until I sing the blues."

Slow-breathing quiet time followed, both on their backs, side by side, enjoying blue sky and the fact they had eyes to see it.

"Clear skies and white clouds," said Sarah. "Almost as beautiful as Steamboat Springs. You're the history buff—was Earth ever as screwed up as Anelia?"

"In a small town outside of Boston, Ralph Waldo Emerson studied every great book. He combined that knowledge with his own observations, none of which I can improve on. He was convinced that all men are the lovers of truth and that nothing beyond consistency need be accepted. The problem is that truth is rarely pure and never simple."

"Of course," said Sarah, looking over with words six months ago Andre wouldn't hear, "God's involvement proves purpose."

"Absolutely," he said. "And God offers every mind the choice between truth and repose. After all, the hardest task in the world is to think."

"It was thinking that got Socrates and Jesus murdered."

"And Ralph discharged from the ministry. He honestly offered the opinion that the bread and wine thing was symbolic. The high mucky-mucks insisted they performed genuine pagan magic, that they held dead flesh and dripping blood in their hands." He smiled with the knowledge that Sarah was her own person and not just another church parrot. "So, you agree," he offered with timid reluctance, "that the past consecrated a great deal of nonsense."

"Total nonsense," said Sarah, "and I can't think of anything more insulting and ungrateful to God."

"Why am I just learning this about you? When we boarded, all you did was call me names."

"Because that was your specialty."

"I deserve that."

"Andre, religion is the work of men and time. We all know that the misuse of Christianity did humanity a great deal of harm. Worst of all was their demand that the future obey their contrivances. Emerson also once said that if he should walk out of church whenever a false statement was made, that he would never stay more than five minutes."

"And he said that history doesn't allow a man to sit in bed with his hat on."

"Yes," said Sarah, "all evil needs to triumph is for good men to do nothing. I don't entirely agree. Many good men do nothing because they are told, and don't challenge, that they are doing good, when in fact, they do other work, whatever 'beliefs' were their first introduction."

Andre nodded in agreement. "The entire substance of their spiritual philosophy was demonstrably false. During the Second World War, ministers prayed for the triumph of Adolf Hitler and Nazi Germany."

"As the Vatican made secret deals to keep themselves in power," nodded Sarah. "So, I guess the answer to my question is yes, we were once just as screwed up as Anelia."

Karen and Janie were in the neuro lab when they heard the news. Breathlessly, they raced to the bridge, where one look told them more than they wanted to know. Hank, mouth drooped and stiff, looked like a concert pianist banging a stretched-palms finale. Every drone had to jet up the perimeter defect before it closed—or else.

"Or else what?" Karen got out at his side.

"Or else Achtun will trace their energy signature all the way to the ship, laser us, and 'safe kill' the entire border, Andre and Sarah included."

Isabelle was just as frantic at Andre's station that was not cooperating. Achtun's buildup was leaking radiation through the ship's hull, and raising shields would set him off. Shoot first and *don't* ask questions later was his motto and also the excuse he used to murder his older brother.

Karen and Janie looked around the bridge. Both strained not to display the suppressed terror that filled the room. They gasped in fear, side by side, holding hands. They knew no one could replace Andre or Brad. They also knew that it might have just happened.

Cindy and Dudley were summoned.

"Where the hell are they?" screamed Karen.

"You…don't…want…to…know," Hank got out, interrupting concentration he knew better not to, his eyes never abandoning his task. Hank didn't waste time watching Cindy and Dudley make an entrance. His ship scan had dropped the bomb minutes ago. Both robots were not themselves. Dudley stumbled in, swinging his head back and forth like a bobblehead on the dash. Cindy, with a storehouse of computer banks backing her up, did little better, though she was able to lead Dudley around on a leash.

All the way in, Cindy, stoned-faced and old-time monotone, kept repeating, "Something is wrong… Something is wrong… Something is wrong."

"No, no! Not here!" Hank yelled from his desk. "Get to engineering. I can't shut you down from here. And silence! We need to concentrate."

Cindy's repertoire changed to, "Oh, my God… Oh, my God…" all the way out the door.

Karen walked to the front of Hank's desk to face him. She said nothing, just looked over, and wilted, morose.

"Karen," Hank squawked, tense and accusing, "don't ask. I can't tell you. I'm not up to this. I shouldn't be here. The bad old boys down there are spilling radiation in a spectrum I can't even measure. Dudley and Cindy were the first to go. We're next. I need Andre!"

"And?" Karen said, exercising her right to know.

"And…" Hank said, finally glancing up. "And I'm sorry, commander. You might as well blindfold me and ask me to find a needle in a field of manure. I've got nothing."

With that, Hank pulled away from his board, sat back, and shaded his eyes with one hand, doing the only thing he thought there was left to do—pray.

Karen followed with soft resolve. "Hank, what about Michael and Sarah?"

"Again…I got nothing. Ask Isabelle."

Karen and Janie bounded two steps at a time all the way up to Isabelle, the one person on board who shared numbers with Andre and the only one he trusted in his chair. She was not one known for emotions, especially anger, which is why Karen stopped two steps short of her panel, seeing that Isabelle was shaking with both hands as her eyes teared and her body rocked back and forth.

"It can't be… It can't be," was all Karen could get out of her.

"The shuttle?" Karen asked with a gulp.

"It's gone. Just disappeared. Not one backup survived."

"And Andre?" Janie asked, feigning courage.

"I don't see… I mean warp speed burnout… Andre…Sarah…"

Isabelle lost herself in Karen's arm. Karen let grief run its course.

Janie was the only one in the room who retained presence. "What about Brad? What about Michael?" she demanded.

"That one I can answer," said Hank from the floor. "Their cochlear implants use photon codes to communicate." He took a moment to regroup his emotions before adding, "Messages from them blend into sunlight. Photon coding was Andre's best work. No one is clever enough to detect them, but they are on strict orders not to activate until Andre and Sarah have shut down Achtun's blast wall at eleven thirty."

"He is… he is… dead… isn't he?" Karen barely got out, sinking to her knees.

More than once, life had brought beatings to Janie's door. She knew that if she didn't go down, she wouldn't have to get up. So she ignored Karen on the floor, and announced through tears, with bravado, "Now hold on, everyone. Not one piece of bad news has been confirmed. Let's not forget that it's Andre, Brad, Michael, and Sarah down there. Andre carries computer chips under his skin. Brad can fly garbage cans tied together, and Michael and Sarah have skills that bloodhounds envy. It's not over. They need our help. We have a job to do. We have a job to do!"

Karen rose to her feet. "Hank, are we far enough away to activate the ship's central computer?"

"Yes, ma'am, but radiation levels continue to rise. Trust nothing."

"I'll deal with that later. Keep moving away if we must."

Karen climbed Andre's stairs to Isabelle, who had drifted into depression.

"Isabelle," Karen ordered, still creaky, "snap out of it. Andre's logic systems are still part of the ship's central memory bank. Dig in and come up with something."

"Yes, ma'am," was her reply. "Andre was…I mean…is a magician. He'll save us."

Isabelle's drooped face added calamity to the past tense she used to refer to Andre. Karen's heart ripped open.

Janie joined Karen standing behind Isabelle. Both ladies held hands below the table.

"We will succeed," Karen bellowed convincingly. "Janie and I will work from the neuro lab. It's the most powerful system on the ship. Get to work. We'll meet up again at showtime."

22

Let's Do It

The cable that fired Jarson's blast wall encircled half the northern hemisphere of Anelia. Wind screaming down from one cold front after another blew up the side of towering mountain peaks. A horizontal, howling blizzard hit Brad in the face when he reached the cable.

"Cable?" he said to himself. "Looks more like a tunnel to me. You could put four subways in there."

Eighty percent of the cable conducted energy from a ring of nuclear reactors. The rest was dedicated to communications and weapon detonation. It had one hundred fail-safes and an identical copy of itself five miles away, in the event a backup was needed or sabotage suspected.

"Good morrow, Sinner," was all Brad was allowed to say when he handed the guard coming off duty his identification tablet. Everything was in order. No eye contact was made. When the guard handed Brad back his identification, both ritually, as required, turned and faced south, the direction of the capital and Jarson's ministry.

"All hail Delou," Brad began, just like Cindy scripted him to do.

"All hail Delou," was repeated by the guard, who turned and walked away without giving Brad another thought, or look, as required.

Brad felt good. His heated suit came with temperature adjustment; his feet were toasty, and the shield over his face came with a defroster; the combination kept him warm as he climbed the five flights of stairs to the catwalk on the top of the cable.

"Okay now," Brad said. "I can turn right and walk south, or left and head north. And Michael is north of me, so I go left to meet up…I think…yes… Michael said, 'think nuclear-north.' N and N."

Each checkpoint was three miles from the next. The sentry's orders timed crossings once an hour between them, when identification was exchanged without a word. Brad made his way. Two hours and two guards later, Brad saw Michael approaching.

The plan was simple. They would stop walking and hang out over the cable, ready to get to work, but wait until one minute before eleven thirty, when Andre would shut down Achtun's blast. If they tied in too soon, their sabotage might be detected.

Twice, windage and slippery mental grates tumbled Brad over. When he approached Michael, he looked like Frosty the Snowman.

"Good morrow, Sinner Michael," said Brad with a smile.

"And good morrow to you too, Sinner Brad. Have you had fun sinning today?"

"Are you kidding me? This place is as much fun as a morgue at midnight, and this tube is gigantic. Our force field ribbon won't make it around."

"Actually, it will," said Michael. "It stretches. You rope down the east side and I'll do the west. The miniature drill-drone will do the rest."

Everything they stepped on was coated with ice. When the two returned to the top of the cable, each laid out the gear for step two: drill down, connect, and introduce the photo program that would take over Jarson's entire military machine.

"Let's see," said Michael, as he looked down the line of gadgets he and Brad had spread out. "Batteries are active, directions duplicated, and each probe is ready to fire down. We're done."

The hardware looked like a half dozen barroom darts trailing wires.

"And we don't test them now…right, Michael?"

"We might be detected. Dudley says our probes will take over before Jarson's central command is alerted, but only if we wait until the last minute."

"Which is when?" asked Brad.

"Which is at the microtome of eleven thirty. If we cripple Jarson, and Achtun is still up and running, he will blast defenseless Delou, you and me included."

"Which he is going to do at noon anyway when his energy buildup peaks."

"Correct," replied Michael. "And his attack will be so powerful that the entire planet will melt back to magma, and the ripple in time will destroy the past, which happens to be everything there is."

"How the hell did we get into this?"

"Well now, strange as it sounds to say, we're here because these people are as intelligent as we are. Unfortunately, they use their gift to kill others and ruin their own lives. But I have to hand it to them. This blast wall is an awesome advance in energy management."

"Yeah," said Brad, "it's too bad fathead Achtun and Dracula Jarson screwed it all up."

"It's not their fault. They were raised by a perverted culture. I blame those who let it happen, those in the past who knew better but preferred a remote control, buyout ptions, or being holier than thou. It didn't have to turn out this way. Citizenship is an army, one that must fight for peace and scream for justice."

"You know, Andre," Sarah said, with pleasantness that pleased his ear, "back in Steamboat, walking to school, I would complain about the same old mountains, the same old icy streams, and the same old crowd. Boy, what I would give right now to be back looking at those gorgeous hills, shivering fresh brooks, and laughing with loving friends."

"The back of my family camp in Waldo County abuts a wildlife preserve," said Andre. "There's a hammock in the corner. When I was growing up, I would lie out there and look up at the stars after having my friend cyber holograph a galaxy chart. In my mind I traveled past each, and never stopped exploring. I wanted to leave so bad."

"And now?"

"All I want to do is get back. It is true. There's no place like home."

"So, what do you think," Sarah said, reaching over to take Andre's hand, "if you drew a line straight up from that spot on Earth today, do you think it might lead right to us lying here?"

"It might. So all we have to do is go that way," Andre said, pointing straight up, "and we'll get there."

"That sounds heavenly. Let's take over the planet and be on our way."

"A trip that begins by crawling out of this crater."

"Let's do it!"

It takes billions of years for asteroids to pockmark the surface of a planet. On Anelia, they redecorated by the season, in one shade, black and rotting. Before Andre kicked a few pieces of shuttle out of the way, he activated the defense screen that would protect the two of them from the laser bolts blanketing Achtun's side of no-man's-land.

"It works," Andre said, as he and Sarah went over the top. "All I had to do is assemble Ulon's prototype. It's brilliant. And no one has ever walked up to the wall before. The only person on this planet who knew how to deflect the death rays was the inventor. It's the perfect calling card. But we need to be careful, and hurry."

"Finally, some fun!" Sarah said, as she bounced three feet into the air with every stride. "Less gravity and long legs… I feel like superwoman."

"We're running twenty miles an hour. If only the marathon guys could see me now."

A glow lit up dust clouds in the distance.

"This is close enough," Andre said. He pulled a red ball from his pack.

Three bizarre code icons later it lit up, and instantly broadcast: "This is security. Who has activated this monitor and state your purpose."

"This is Ulon Laroon. My wife and I crash-landed. We must get to Achtun at once."

"Ulon…is that you? This is Gleg. You passed through here last year, and the upgrade you did on our radiation shield halved gamma exposure. The medical ward says I'll be able to have kids now. Thank's so much. But what? My screen says you're transmitting from no-man's-land. That's impossible."

"It's top secret. Say nothing. Only Achtun and I know that there is a defense against the rays. I invented the rays. I know how to neutralize a ten-meter radius. But enough. We are approaching the gate. I need a tube-jet to get to command central immediately."

"Roger that. I'm on it. It will be at the gate in three minutes."

The first smiles of the day were shared in no-man's-land. And they were husband and wife, itself a tease to the world, and themselves.

Gleg was honored and looking forward to special commendations. He flagged the couple by every security check before jumping into the pilot seat of the tube-jet.

"I can't wait to kid Dudley about this one," Andre said under his breath.

"Sorry for the noise," Gleg said. "Some mega buildup is going on. We've never seen anything like it. Say, are you to still planning to settle down? Have kids yourselves?"

Sarah spoke up with a raspy voice. "Gleg…throat's burnt…haven't slept…need rest…fast as you can. Can't talk now."

"Oh yes. I know protocol. I'm a stickler. That's how I got to where I am. Don't worry. I'll get you there and upstairs before you know it. And don't forget to tell Achtun I helped."

"Don't worry. He'll find out for sure."

"Hank, I need to talk to Michael."

"You can't, Karen."

"But you said the photon code thing can't be detected."

"Yes, that's true, but we don't know if the receptor devices hidden in Brad and Michael will give them away. We go live at eleven thirty, limit transmission to ten minutes, and then close it down."

"They have to know that Achtun might not be shut down," said Karen. "We don't even know if Andre and Sarah made it."

"No one will have a chance if we add risk," replied Hank. "My personal feeling is that the devices will remain undetected. They use less electrical energy than the human heart, which could be a problem if some computer turns Michael and Brad into four people, and then targets each one."

Janie was standing behind Karen. "Let's go, Karen," she said. "We have better things to do."

"Like what?"

"Like what you were talking about in the neuro lab last night."

Karen walked to the bow and, after taking a long breath, turned peacefully to Hank. "Do you think that every advance mankind makes, every invention that broadens our knowledge and improves our lives, also has a dark side, the power to do harm, even evil?"

"Yes, I do," replied Hank. "And it has nothing to do with some made-up pitchfork guy. It's about Henry, my pet pig."

Janie loved Hank's perspective. She joined him, crossing her arms and grinning.

"You see," continued Hank, "that piggy of mine, Henry. Every day, he has to decide. Should I sit here plopped in mud all day, or do I go do something? And you know, every day, rain or shine, hot or cold, he gets up and heads out to make more of his life. So that's it. It goes both ways. Good and bad. Slump or get off your ass."

"It might work, Karen," said Janie, the least published scientist in the room.

"Hank," said Karen.

"Yes, ma'am."

"I would like to review the rescue plan one more time before Janie and I leave for the neuro lab."

The plan was to get Explorer Seven to Anelia, the distance of two Earth-sized solar systems, in under five seconds, and then send a cloaked shuttle to the park for Andre and Sarah. Explorer Seven would then snatch Brad and Michael from the other side of the planet before returning to pick up the shuttle.

"It's all doable, and pre-programmed," Hank confirmed. "However, the plan assumes all power is off and radiation levels will be zero. It took getting this far away to get half our systems back online, and no one knows why Dudley and Cindy won't activate."

Karen started her sentence, "That will happen the moment Andre…" but the image of no Andre took her down for a minute. She came back. "It's going to work, Hank. I can feel it."

"Absolutely, commander. Good will always better evil. God's help makes it so." Hank finished, glanced up, then rethinking geography, over, sideways and even straight down.

Kavel stopped to look. Zeelings were a rare sighting, and a mother feeding her young had never been seen. It was the radiation. Their eggshells didn't hold up. They cracked open before the chicks were ready for the world.

Kavel's dad remembered blue shells. That was before cockroaches took over the insect world. They survived everything and lived radioactive, the reason Zeelings were chirping their last. They had to eat something.

Rising global temperatures and polluted oceans didn't help. And the Zeelings weren't alone. Half the planet's plankton shut down, coral crumbled, and oxygen-producing algae put out half of what they used to. The medical barracks claimed male sperm count dropped by "only" fifty percent. No one believed that.

Mama bird had a good day. She returned with one spider and two cockroaches in her beak. Her sole surviving offspring was so excited, it jumped to the edge of the nest. That was a mistake. Her malformed limbs didn't hold up. The baby fell thirty feet to its death.

Horror was a daily sensation in Kawachensa. The crowd looked away, just like they did when taxes went up, medical care evaporated, or news of yet another million dead arrived.

They pretended to listen when Achtun explained why it must be so, and that it wasn't his fault. Achtun was very good at blaming Delouians. Achtun always found people to hate. Happiness hadn't mattered for a long time. Achtun made sure of that.

The fish were biting. Kavel caught one. He didn't care.

"Aren't you going to reel it in?" said S-2, sitting down beside him.

"What's the use? We'll be dead in an hour. And why are you talking to me? Isn't that against the rules?"

"Everything is against the rules, and I'll be dead in an hour too. I see you brought the white lure. I'm going put it in my mouth and wait until my skin is on fire to bite down on the capsule. Might as well *want* to die."

Kavel glanced over, wishing for the first time in his life that looks could kill. "For fun, you could always beat me over the head again."

"Yes, about that, Kavel. I'm sorry. Jarson had me record our conversation so he could make sure you were on board."

"I know the drill. Say maybe, and you die on the spot. Say no, and your family goes first."

"Yes," said S-2. "About that…"

"About what?"

"Your family in Delou."

"Saving them is the only thing making sense out of my death. Jarson better take good care of them, that's all I can say."

"It's too late," said S-2.

"What?"

"You know your wife and daughter were both born with the mutation."

"Yes, but neither contracted leukemia. They survived the risk age."

"Stronger radiation changed that. The mutation activated in both of them."

"And did Jarson order treatment? He promised medical care if I volunteered to cross no-man's-land."

"He needed every resource to tune the new technology, which failed."

"So?"

"They died a year ago."

Kavel turned and walked to the closest wooded area. S-2 saw him collapse on the ground, crawl on all fours, and smash his fist into the ground. Running to his side, with a smile S-2 announced for all to hear, "Yes, those cockroaches in your sleeves sure can drive you crazy! It's all right. Enjoy your day, everyone." He bent over Kavel. "Listen to me. I couldn't tell you. Jarson didn't want to take the risk of you defecting. If it makes you feel any better, my family is gone too. I came over here for revenge. Now I don't know anything, but I do have a brother and a sister. Saving them is the only thing that keeps me going."

"Did it ever occur to you that maybe we *shouldn't* keep going?" muttered Kavel.

"Every day, and that's the surest test I know that something is wrong." S-2 then told Kavel his real name was Gelam. His grandfather had been a farmer, who hid him for years before the state found out and took him away. His grandfather was put to death for denying God another soul and Jarson a smart, young soldier.

The pair returned to the pond as friends.

"I've been doing a lot of thinking since I got here," said Kavel.

"Me too."

"This planet of ours is total bullshit."

"Kavel, my assessment of that opinion is that it is an insult to bulls." An almost smile followed.

"It's not that everything can be understood," said Kavel. "It's not that everything has to make sense. But it can't make nonsense."

"I understand," replied Gelam. "Jarson using every means available to cause guilt doesn't make sense at all."

"Exactly. Obedience to dogma is neither faith in God nor appropriate gratitude. Genuine companions think for themselves."

"Not on Anelia they don't."

"Zena's father hid some old books before he died. I found them. They talk about philosophy, the account the mind gives itself of the constitution of life. Every man consumes his own time. No one has the right to demand reparations from the present for the past."

"The history of our planet it not one of kindness," Gelam added.

"We've all been cowed by culture and made the victims of words."

"And sex is not a sin. It's a blessing, a gift from God, one that's rude to refuse. Jarson can shove every one of his sins up his ass, where they belong."

Kavel stood up and looked around. Gelam knew he was about to start a revolution, which would end in an hour one way or another, if the guards let him live that long.

"Sit down," said Gelam. "It's too late. Let's enjoy our last minutes together."

23

Showtime

The relief of getting by the first line of security passed quickly. Sarah and Andre were locked into a steel cylinder speeding four hundred miles an hour without a single safety backup. Once the stern jet was fired there was no escape. Neither dared speak. Both prepared themselves to accept whatever fate befell them.

"The Earth's Sun, the galaxy it twirls in," Andre thought to himself, "and all the galaxies that make up God's gift of life, are efforts of giving, energy somehow created, or managed, or perhaps grown from the seeds of love."

Andre looked around and was overtaken by the tragedy of an entire planet spoiled, the horror of letting minds rot, making it a chore, or a test, or a duty, or penance.

"There will always be those," Sarah said to herself, looking over to Andre, and glad he was not one of them, "who corrupt life by uttering disapproval, stabbing criticism, and insisting their conceit makes their ways and their greed the order of the day. After that, it's just a matter of locking the chains to enslave the lives of others."

Beyond that, Sarah was not certain. Should she damn the damning to everlasting hell for their trespasses, as they claim everyone else is doing the trespassing, or should she pity the ignorance of savage exploitation? She knew Michael had an answer; it started with a baseball bat and ended with a massage, which worked only when those who foundered kept listening, and thinking; two behaviors beaten to death, along with those who tried, long ago on Anelia.

"And the threat of death," Andre finished, "how base it is, how asinine, how animal rude, when those with intelligence use it to destroy what God works so hard to protect." He knew the answer to how they did it. It was *hypocrisy*—what no one sees in themselves but has no problem reading into others.

"It's so plain," Sarah continued to herself, "'This is what my mommy told me" 'this is what my daddy told me,' 'this is what the preacher told me,' 'this is what Achtun says to do,' 'this is what Jarson says to do,' 'this is what the pope says is right,' 'this is what my mullah insists'— minds blundering as far back in time as history records. And do they learn? Do they listen? Of course not. That would mean getting up from the couch of laziness. No one stands on their own two feet. They're all frightened the neighbors will disapprove, father so-and-so will give them a bad look, deacon somebody will let them have it, or the president or führer will disagree.

"'We will tell you when to have sex,' 'We will tell you who to have sex with,' 'We will tell you that you are bad to want sex,' 'You will deal with the government defining your life.' Fools who put on uniforms and think that gives them the right to boss others around. Bullies, bullies, bullies…every one an ignorant, self-centered fascist who paints himself as an angel. Why don't they wake up down here? Why did it take so long for Earth to come to its senses?"

Sarah couldn't help herself. After all, Achtun hadn't invented a mind-reading machine yet.

"I say it's death's fault. Everyone is so afraid of *not being* that they accept idiocy, misreading it as something worthwhile, never realizing the carnage of good days turned bad, by rushing or worrying, or wasting life in a pew or a cubicle. Damn those who insist that they know! They know nothing.

"And then," Sarah thought, flushing anger she knew should be avoided, "the bastards lay out the rules. 'This is what men and women are supposed to do,' 'This is what you are *not* supposed to do,' 'Your body must serve our needs, never happiness and pleasures God himself regrets not being there.'

"Damn their rules! Damn their made-up morals! Damn the cages that stay locked from birth to death! All the door needs is a push. No one wants to bother. They're too busy going along with tradition, as far removed from reality as a jackass is from a baby doll."

Andre also took aim. "They all say, 'we know better, you're a bad person because you are not like us,' 'We are the good ones,' 'You will never get anything from me,' 'Agree with me, or else, because I get to make up the rules.'"

Or else was Achtun the pile of shit, and his co-conspirator Jarson the dung heap. Both men used power to hold on to power and played the final game: "You suffer whilst I smile."

"And look where it got them," Sarah finished in a flush, "sick, depressed, and suicidal. Wake up life. Go play! Go dance! Go make love!"

Sarah's final thought somehow got through to Andre. She reached over for his hand. He reached back for her thigh. So simple. So right. So godly.

Physical contact was a brief blessing for the two stranded warriors. Both retreated to fantasy: Andre was in his hammock, with Sarah on top; Sarah was camped next to a mountain stream, with Andre on top.

Their happiness, like most, came in five-minute boxes. Andre opened another. He suppressed a smile, recalling a comedian's confusion at the boisterous cheering during a professional football game. The team had moved from one city to another, half the members traded to the competition, and the new coach had been the enemy a week earlier.

So, who, or what exactly, were they rooting for? The conclusion was obvious. The only thing that didn't change were the jerseys. The fan's loyalty was to ninety percent cotton, ten percent spandex.

Sarah was more of a politician. As their death ride slowed, she remembered John Lennon, who once pointed out that billions of people on Earth began their day saying, "I pledge allegiance..."

The ancestors of every person on Earth had emigrated from Africa, and then from Europe to America, North and South. A single family lineage might have brothers, cousins, and children spread out over as many continents, each pledging loyalty to a flag, not dissimilar to fans rooting for clothing.

John had a simple solution to the error of warfare. He took a white handkerchief, folded it just so, and placed it in his breast shirt pocket, proclaiming that he was a citizen of the world. He invited the entire world to join him. It would have only taken a minute to end all war. It didn't happen. Millions died. Even more went to bed hungry.

Sarah leaned over and whispered to Andre, "What's the difference between an ostrich and the citizens of Anelia? An ostrich sticks his head out of the hole in the ground."

When their jet sled came to a stop, Andre and Sarah were surrounded by cold steel and bitter concrete, four floors below ground. They wobbled out, looking the part of two who had barely escaped a shipwreck, which was true.

The hallway that connected the tubes to the elevator was lined by X-ray emitters. The floor, which supported mounds of black mold, housed plates recording images for those waiting behind the first door. As they walked along the dusty floor, insect parts crunched with every step.

"Impressive," Andre thought to himself. "One of these in a hospital could make a diagnosis before you got to the reception desk. Every evil has a good."

Gleg led the way, stiff lipped and military formal. He wasn't a bad sort all in all. When he was ordered to kill, he did so quickly, never prolonged pain. Of course, like everyone under Achtun's command, to curry favor he would grind up his own mom for cat food.

The smell confused Sarah, but not for long. A pile of dead cockroaches gave it away. In close proximity accumulated radiation did them in too.

Gleg knew he was risking his gonads to be there, but then, everyone pleasing Achtun paid a high price.

Gleg's codes opened the door to the first security station. Dudley had not prepared them. Andre's wide-eyed response almost gave them away. Two-foot puncture needles were being prepared to biopsy liver, lung, and brain tissue. Blood dripped from the apparatus all the way to the next door. Sarah knew the jig was up.

"I'll vouch for them," Gleg bellowed. "Inu and Ulon have critical information for the next attack. Heads will roll if we don't get there on time." An accurate threat. The previous month, the heads of twenty guards were made into bowling balls when one fell asleep at his post. The video was circulated by Gleg himself. The guards gave in. Their plan was to claim they were "just carrying out orders."

What worked once worked twice. Gleg got Andre and Sarah all the way to the elevator, where he saluted, discharged of responsibility.

Seventy floors later the door opened, and the two were greeted with a rare finding in central command...sympathy.

"Oh, my! Oh my! Inu and Ulon! I never thought I would see you again. Are you all right?" said Zena. "I'll get you to medical as soon as I can."

"Can't talk," Sarah interjected, gruff and hoarse, before Andre made the mistake of opening *his* mouth. "My larynx is singed from radiation poisoning."

Sarah grabbed the tablet Andre was holding and handed it to Zena. "Achtun needs this."

"I can't believe you made it, and came back with data," Zena said impressed. "You'll make Achtun's day. I'll take it over to him. For now, stand in the back corner, and if you want to talk make sure it's a whisper no one can hear. Achtun is working on the final solution."

Saved again. Andre was sure his pulse rate would give him away if he got any closer to the despot. They were there to do a job. Achtun would get what was coming to him.

Sarah was just as relieved when they retreated to the farthest recess they could find.

They were ignored and forgotten. It didn't get any better on Anelia. Their stiff camouflage made it easy for Andre to mouth soft words without appearing to communicate. He and Sarah stared straight ahead, looking at Achtun conferring with his generals in front of the central data screen.

"Just as I thought," Andre whispered. "They have no idea how much time they're accumulating power in. Instead of twice the power, they are at one million and climbing. Once released, it will turn the planet into a dwarf star, which will be trapped between dimensions, leaving the entire universe at risk."

Sarah moved over to lightly touch the back of Andre's hand.

"Okay, be cool," she whispered. "The reality of the situation is that our plan is working perfectly. You will disable the system and Explorer Seven will rescue us. On the way out, we steal back time-tampering technology and bring peace to the planet."

"You're right. It's a good deed, and we've got it covered. My equipment hidden below my belt can be operational in the blink of an eye."

"And we made it on time. At eleven thirty we take over."

"All is well."

It was the time of year when snow belted the Northern Hemisphere, leaving layer after layer, hour by hour, until ten o'clock that morning, when the clouds parted, the wind died, and the sun shone.

"Challenge accepted," Brad said, as he balanced on top of the catwalk railing. The windy blizzard had piled drifted snow up and over the pipeline. It was a perfect little ski slope, or a slide down.

Michael's challenge was to repeat his feat, a midair flip followed by a headfirst human toboggan, arms extended and knees bent.

Brad managed the task. He held his breath all the way down, thus avoiding the snow sneezing that followed Michael's trip.

Brad next dared Michael. Brad's choice was a full-sprint high jump off the rail, followed by a sideways roll to the base. The match ended in a draw.

"It's time to deploy," Michael said.

"Let's deploy," Brad chuckled. "A fancy way of saying lets wrap a ribbon around a tube and stick in darts."

"We need to synchronize electronics, because if we don't, we'll end up particles smaller than snowflakes."

Ten minutes later, Brad asked, "Now what?"

"As the poet Milton wrote, 'They also serve who only stand and wait,'" said Michael, as he made the last connection. "Which is us, for now. And we stay focused. If something goes wrong, our identities will relocate."

"Ya," Brad said with a silly laugh. "With all the snow around here, a warmer climate sounds good. Perhaps a short detour to hell might be fun."

Brad and Michael sat side by side, looking up, both impressed at the luxury of having miles of atmosphere to shade life happy blue.

Brad decided to tease. "Of course, if I had a choice, I suppose St. Martins would be more fun. What do you think, Michael?"

"Okay, okay, I get it buddy," Michael said, his tone expressing appreciation. "The next time Karen and I are alone, I'll remind her of the great time we had and then ask her if she wants to join me for another week. And you? How is your happy ever after?"

"Actually, it just turned into happier ever after."

"How is that possible?"

"Can you keep a secret?" asked Brad.

"Well let's see," replied Michael. "I've kept the last thirty-seven, so I guess I will say, 'yes.'"

"Janie and I are fooling around."

"You're *what?*"

"With ourselves."

"Brad, you and Janie fool around with each other all the time. And stay out of the broom closet. It is not imperative to have sex in every room on the ship."

"Don't knock it until you've knocked it, and knocked it, and knock…"

"I'm missing data," Michael interrupted. "Explain."

"Well, you know how Janie and Karen have been spending a lot of time in the neuro lab lately?"

"Yes, they're making improvements to our mind-animal body jumps."

"Not exactly," said Brad.

"So…exactly…*what?*" Michael said with impatience—a common side effect of eroticism.

"When we were in monkey bodies, we all had sex, with others and with each other. No big deal. So, when a couple, like Janie and I, and every couple, gets less lustful about repeats, just mix it up."

"Okay. Of course. It works. The Friday Night Club. One night a week free to freefall wherever you want. Fun sex. No problem. It brings you back, recharged physically and more in love with your primary squeeze, your one true love, than ever, who you strip naked, if she doesn't arrive that way, more likely the case, and blast off for the stars again."

"Ya, ya," said Brad. "But what if you kind of want to be with your soul mate, too?"

"I think they call that a threesome," said Michael.

"Exactly. Now just leave one of them at home."

"This quiz of yours isn't working. What the hell are you talking about?"

"Okay, let me put it this way. What if you are madly in love with someone and could have sex with her *in another body?*"

"We tried temporary moves from body to body. It was weird and left funny aftereffects, and headaches, along with confusion."

"Not if you use robot receptors," said Brad. "We call it 'wacko-wacko.'"

Brad filled in details of the previous night. He and Janie had locked off a quarter of the habitat and converted it into Cleopatra's castle. Then they lay down in the neuro lab, placed the headsets on, and presto chango! Brad was a perfect Mark Anthony, living in a robot that looked and felt like the real thing, and Janie was Cleopatra, in a see-through nightgown, which made Cleopatra's bronze skin extra alluring.

"We drank wine," said Brad, "feasted, and made love on a terrace overlooking the Nile. Two hours later, when we switched back into our own bodies, which had just rested up, Janie and I ran back to our room for another naked extravaganza…the best we've ever had. I'll tell you, Michael, it's the way to go. That's why we call it 'happier ever after.'"

"But you're not making love to a real person."

"DNA doesn't know that," shrugged Brad. "And Janie says we're not going to tell. And after that fun, which was also historically informative and prepared Janie for our next visit, she and I, two real people, made passionate love that we wouldn't have."

"So you've invented polygamous monogamy?" asked Michael.

"I guess you could put it that way."

Michael pointed out that if a washing machine company put out a unit that broke down half of the time, and as often, at the end, exploded to hurt everyone in the house, then a new model, a different plan, would be in order. "Traditional marriage has a bad track record. So, mazel tov! For me," he said, with a dreamy look in his eyes, "St. Martins and Karen are all I will ever need."

"I guess," Brad said, sounding more mature than ever, "we can say all is well."

"Yes. All is well."

24

High Noon

Achtun wasn't the smiling type, satanic or otherwise, but there he was, tight-lipped grinning, surrounded by a sinister chill as he made his rounds from general to general. Murder has a smell all its own: ten billion murders, pediatric to geriatric, a tragedy of unequaled shame.

After his personal inspection, Achtun returned to the center of the war room to stand on his elevated platform. He faced right and lifted opened arms. Every military accomplice signaled thumbs up, which they communicated with thumbs down. Achtun kept grinning.

Andre and Sarah made sure they didn't stand out. They raised both arms, thumbs down. Achtun nodded approval, then turned to face the giant screen behind him, where Jarson's image had haunted him for decades. He held both his arms out straight, pretending to strangle his nemesis lifeless. His grin snuck out a dark chuckle.

"Do it now! Do it now! Kill the bastard, and all the little bastards along with him!" shrieked Achtun.

"Yes, sir, of course, sir," said his senior commander sheepishly, sitting in the first of four rows. "But if it please you, sir, the storage program won't be fully loaded until noon. That's when, and only when, we can open it up. But we guarantee it will explode on schedule."

"You're damn right it will, General, or you will finish the rest of a short life eating cockroaches."

"Yes, your grandness, as you say," said General Zendal, whose heart, knowing Achtun's temper for vengeance, beat fiercely in his chest.

Not one general looked down at his readout. It wasn't necessary. The dials had passed the red line hours ago, and the smell of burning insulation seeped to every corner.

"That's not a good smell," Andre quietly informed Sarah. "Half of the displays just burned out. The central power relay is next."

"Why don't they tell Achtun?" Sarah whispered.

"He doesn't like bad news. He has a habit of killing the messenger."

Achtun noticed Inu and Ulon in the shadows. In response, Andre and Sarah bowed low at the same time their pulse rate went up. Achtun was pleased. He tipped his head in gratitude. Homicide always made his day.

Back on their own, Sarah continued, "I like Michael's idea. After we steal back the time-tampering software, we circle the planet and turn every gram of radioactive material into lead. No nukes, no warfare, and clean solar power from then on."

The image of a cured planet calmed Andre's breathing. "I never thought I would have a warm feeling for bullets. At least they only kill one at a time."

"I'm not with you there. Each one of us dies one at a time. But I do have a suggestion of my own. Every morning, hand your enemy a fresh-baked cheesecake. Wait for atherosclerosis to kick in."

Andre's lip squeezed to suppress a chuckle. "Don't make me laugh. We only have eight minutes to go."

Achtun began pacing back and forth. Pacing usually meant someone was about to get the ax. His generals sat back as far as they could in their chairs. No one wanted to be the fall guy, literally.

With head bowed, Zena broke the silence.

"Your grandness," she said, with a disconcerted smile.

"Yes, Zena?"

"Jarson is requesting an audience."

"I told him to cram it until one, an hour after he stops breathing. The next time we meet, I'll be trampling his ashes. Tell him to go to his hell, where he belongs."

"Yes, sir," Zena replied with obedient indifference. "Right away."

Zena had just begun typing the verbatim reply when Achtun stiffened his back and looked around skeptically. "Wait, this might be fun. He knows my power buildup is about to do him in. I'll enjoy watching him beg for mercy."

Jarson was not on his knees. He stood, gowned in ceremonial crimson, holding his scepter, and backed by his entire league of bishops, each one also dressed for high adoration.

Achtun was wearing his favorite one-piece business suit, the one with military bars, cobra head, and skull and crossbones. Both men walked up to their respective screens, grimacing hatred. They stood nose to nose. In real life, without a screen interface, one would expect mortal combat.

Achtun looked Jarson in the eyes and was startled by his opponent's appearance of determination. The two knew each other well. Both were able to sense nuance.

Achtun, without moving a facial muscle, stepped back one pace, and pretended to be summoned from the side by his staff. "One minute, pincushion-head. I'm needed to load a cannon with your name on it. I'll be right back."

Zena interrupted transmission. The screen went black.

"What gives?" Achtun asked, searching the room for answers. No one dared move. No one knew anything. "Jarson knows he's a dead man. Why isn't that sniveling runt shaking in his church slippers?"

Violating protocol, Zena offered a thought without being asked to do so, "Perhaps, sir, he wants to negotiate. Perhaps it's not too late."

"Well," Achtun said, letting the transgression slide, "nothing less than unconditional surrender and his head on a plate would work for me, as long as every member of his military organization falls on their laser. All right. Bring the worm back."

Jarson hadn't budged. He stood resolute, with arms crossed, flashing a smile just as mean as Achtun had managed.

"You're a fool, Jarson," said Achtun, back at the screen face-to-face. "We both know you're a dead man. But I'll be merciful. I will let you live until noon."

Jarson's laugh was genuine. "And what makes you think *you* will survive that long? I have been waiting my whole life for this moment. Pardon me if I revel in justice."

"That's it!" Achtun screamed. "Enough of your inane insolence. I'm moving up the clock. But don't worry. I'll be back to wish you goodbye. The 'good' will be me, and the 'bye' will be you."

Achtun broke a cold sweat as soon as the screen went black again. He began fidgeting with his collar. "Damn it! Kill him now! He's hiding something. What the hell is going on?"

Achtun's gaze passed to and over Andre and Sarah, who gestured ignorant hands up, which was also the case, a situation that bothered Andre more than Sarah.

Achtun had to see for himself. He systematically inspected every general's readout, screen by screen. Finding half of them blank pulled the last rug out from under his feet. He called a conference front and center, grilling his top ten advisors, slapping each one in the face.

"It's sickening," Andre offered, low-toned, "to see brilliant minds reduced to the law of the jungle."

Andre and Sarah withstood the intrigue well. They were out of the loop.

Sarah, the anthropologist, found the behavior as idiotic as it was frightful. "Are you kidding, Andre? These assholes give the law of the jungle a bad name. Daw and Zin played the jungle game, but only to survive, and then shared the best life they could. Oh no, this isn't law of the jungle. It is the law of the land."

The story was Sarah's favorite back at the university. It began after millions of years of Daws and Zins had hiked Mother Earth for free; after all, it was a gift given to all life. Then things changed. One of their lineage placed a stick in the ground, walked a goodly way, then placed another, then finally number three and four. At that point, a *Homo sapiens* grabbed a club and declared that everything between the sticks belonged to him, so he got to make the laws, and declared himself the ruler of others.

It got worse. Pharaohs, kings, and church-states kept moving their sticks farther and farther apart, without principles, friendship, or mercy. After all, it was their land, because they said so.

"Throughout history," Sarah said to Andre, "not one person who said all were equal in the eyes of God acted that way. Not a single individual in the entire universe of God's creation deserves a throne. We are all equal in the eyes of the Lord."

"Don't say that to Achtun. He comes from a long line of lawmakers and lawbreakers—laws for the rich to get richer, laws to make workers slaves, laws letting one sex bully another, what the opposite sex can do and can't do, what the opposite sex can say and can't."

"Shh," said Sarah, "Achtun is back on stage, and he doesn't look happy. Are you ready to activate?"

"On a second's notice. Gee, it must be frustrating to want to kill someone and then have to wait an entire half hour to do so."

"Now don't get me laughing, Andre."

Achtun acted the part of an unruffled despot, until his voice cracked and his knees buckled. But he bounced back just before Jarson came back onscreen.

"*Now* what is it, Jarson?" he sneered. "Have you invented a new torture for your people? I hear some of your subjects even forget their night prayers. Sounds like they deserve to be burned at the stake. Is that why you like roasting marshmallows?"

"Now you just help yourself, Achtun," replied Jarson smoothly. "Get it all out of your system, at least while you still have one. Speaking of one, and two, and three, do you mind if I practice counting. Let's see, I will start with ten…just about now…ten…nine…"

Achtun ran off his platform, panting, to Zena of all people, "Zena, do you have anything?"

"Nothing, sir."

"Eight..."

"Andre," Sarah said, sneaking up to him. "What's going on? Activate! I don't like the looks of this!"

"Roger that."

"Seven..."

Achtun was back on stage, panning left and right across what he could make out of the room behind Jarson.

"You know, Jarson," Achtun said in a deliberately nonchalant tone, "if there's some new problem, I'm sure we can work it out. Perhaps..."

"Perhaps *nothing!*" Jarson yelled back, opening every avenue of anger. "I have worked it out: I live, you die. Prepare yourself for non-existence... Five..."

Jarson let it go, turning from hate to vengeful laughter, adding a clumsy jig to the mix.

"Four..."

"This can't be," Achtun whined. "He's serious. What have I missed? What have I done! What didn't I do?"

"You didn't complete an act of contrition, that's what. So, I guess you are not forgiven... And there it is...three and counting."

Andre looked to his belt for help. "Oh my God! Sarah, there's a nuclear bomb in this room, and the detonator is about to trigger it."

"What kind, how big?" she asked.

"I can't get through the casing of the bomb itself," whispered Andre, "but the detonator size suggests close to one hundred megatons, and the plutonium must be in a contracted force field."

"Two..."

Achtun dropped to his knees. "Please, I don't want to die. We can work it out."

"Andre," Sarah insisted, "disarm now, before it's too late. I don't want to lose you."

"You won't. We will go together, along with a billion others."

"One! Goodbye, you son of a bitch!" said Jarson, waving both hands.

"Did it," Andre said, which also tipped off an alarm that dropped a force field around him and Sarah, along with Zena, who looked down at one shoe smoking.

"It's time," said Michael, as he powered up the viral program.

"Help yourself," Brad replied, who had removed his hat and mask to work on his tan, lying down. "It's been a while since I've had a chance for the real thing. When we get home, I'm heading straight to the Riviera."

"That's not right," Michael said, with words that picked Brad right off the snow.

"Not right? How? More complicated? Too slow, more power? What? What?"

"Not too anything. Nothing at all. The entire conduit is dead. It's not in use."

"But you said it was when we got here."

"It was," said Michael. "The radiation levels gave it away. But now… zero…all of a sudden. Uh-oh, Brad, we have company."

Manned hovercrafts approached from the south.

"How did they know?" said Michael, as he got to his feet. "Crap! Brad, split up. You head east. I will go west. Take a drone. Dig a hole and don't stop moving. Beyond that, I got nothing. Good luck."

Good luck had nothing to do with it. *Bad luck* was all that was left hanging around. Before either got to the bottom of the cable they were stunned and paralyzed. Jarson's guards threw both into the back of their ship and headed for the capital.

The guards laughed.

"What idiots. Everyone on the planet knows we only use cinnamon on holidays."

A second guard added a few kicks to both sides of Michael and Brad's rib cages. "When we bring them around, every breath will be hell."

"And their luck just ran out. Jarson's orders were to take them alive. He is setting up two bowls for death torture."

"Well, there you have it. Every time Jarson tortures a spy to death, it's a holiday. These fools can ask for cinnamon again."

25

Short Hard Time

The trip to the dungeon was more painful than crash-landing. Achtun encouraged his guards to be creative. They came up with "Watch your step." A line of police flanked each side of the couple as they walked hall to hall. When one said, "Watch your step," he, or she, would slam one of them across the hallway into the opposite wall.

The object was to push the prisoner so hard that their head would hit the wall. That earned one point. If they drew blood, the guard got another point. A mild concussion that left the victim stumbling down the hall topped off a perfect score of three. If the prisoner fell to the ground unconscious, on the other hand, it was minus a point, and you had to pick him up.

The final game was called "Bend over." Andre and Sarah had no choice. At the jail cell door, the two strongest guards stood on either side and pulled both arms down and out, reminiscent of half the fate of those drawn and quartered. A fearsome twist of each arm next yanked four arms out of their sockets.

The grand finale required a running start and a leap. The third guard hammered a two-legged, full-body kick, which sent Andre, then Sarah, both already bent over and screaming in pain, flying across the cramped, dark cell. One at a time, they slammed into the far wall, then fell to the floor on their faces, which is where they stayed since neither one of their arms was useful.

Then came the laughing—at Andre and Sarah, as they gasped for breath facedown in pools of their own blood.

Some of the guards accumulated scores of over one hundred before Achtun ordered a public execution. Every one of his murders was televised nationally, and of course shared with Jarson. The dungeon delay was needed to set up as many "bowls" as needed. On the way out, Sarah heard Achtun order four.

The last person to be burned at the stake on Earth took place in 1825, only thirty years before black slavery ended, and two thousand years after white slavery began. A devout friar, who had dedicated his life to God, disagreed with the pope. So, of course the pope ordered the most heinous crime on earth, and the worst affront to God: he had the friar murdered, with a comic twist. After he was killed, the Catholic churchgoers decided to drag the body outside and set it on fire, for old time's sake, when greed, barbarism, superstition, and stupidity plundered the planet.

Oh yes, the good old days, when you could murder anyone who had a different opinion. Even more fun was stealing from the poor, feasting with the rich, and helping to start wars that subjugated entire countries. And nothing quite tops off a day better than having sex with half the castle and a blindfolded virgin from the fields.

On Anelia, burning protestors at the stake was considered child's play. For good reasons. Smoke inhalation had suffocated many in minutes. What was the fun of putting someone to death if they didn't scream for hours?

When they turned the fire up higher to reduce smoke, the flames burned through the skin and kept going. Fire destroyed the victim's heat and pain receptors.

No receptors, no pain. Again, what was the fun?

Then there was the slow bake. Let the coals work their way up a body one foot at a time—actually, two feet first, then up from there.

The problem was that all that barbequed flesh made the crowd hungry. They left for dinner.

Enter the bowl. Literally a large clear one with all kinds of contraptions at the bottom. Everyone in the room, and across the planet, could watch the victim's insides die, while the victim's head stayed outside, begging for death.

A mirror was placed in front of the intended. Those sentenced were forced to watch their own bodies decimated, a feat accomplished by leaving lungs and heart for last.

Achtun added his own finesse. He had engineers begin death by flaming off just the outer skin. His ingenious contraction knew when to stop, which was just before pain and burn receptors were decommissioned. Step two sprayed an engineered formula from all sides that caused those receptors to transmit one hundred times more pain than someone going up in an inferno, and not just for seconds or minutes. No, not at all. The ordeal could be stretched over days, with no let up.

After a while, all entertainment gets dull. So, what came next? Slithering creepy things with teeth. First in line were jaw worms, which loved meat—that is, muscle. A half dozen would enter the bowl and begin chomping feet. Twenty-four hours of ripping agony later, they were as fat as balloons, and the victim looked in to see bare bones and visceral mush.

For Achtun, having someone die too soon was a real bummer. A week or longer pleased him best. That's why a special frequency was installed to kill the worms when they got close to ending suffering with death.

And what was next? Just two little guys, that's all. Slither snakes bred for the purpose. Two of them would enter from the bottom, climb up raw bone, take a bite or two of liver pâté on their way, then squeeze through throat cartilage just below the ring that separated the head from the bowl below, and then crawl up through the back of the throat into the nose.

The two little snakes loved the peace and quiet of maxillary sinuses. They would curl up inside each, sometimes for days depending on how many snacks they snuck in on the way up. But sooner or later, the snakes went for their favorite dessert, vitreous humor.

The inferior orbital rim was thin enough for them to bite through, leaving juicy eyeballs to cure the munchies. No one knew why, but they spit out most of the retina to slurp out the insides.

And the grand finale? It had to come sometime, to Achtun's regret. It was when the two little buggers decided to live on a higher plane—head north to feed on forebrain. Now there's a headache, and what Andre and Sarah were told, in no uncertain terms, was waiting for them upstairs.

"Thanks, fellas," Andre managed to get out. "Maybe I can do you a favor someday." Which was ironic, since he dropped in to do just that.

Sarah couldn't speak or move. She used eye blinking Morse code to ask Andre to blow blood away from her mouth. She was breathing more red cells than oxygen.

The blood surrounding both eyes turned from bright red to off pink. Tears will do that.

No bleakness in the universe has not, at some point, seen light or felt warmth. No one in all of Kawachensa was respected more than Zena. She had risked her own safety, again and again, to protect others, and everyone knew her ways, even the guards, one of whom would have been sentenced to a bowl if it weren't for her. She walked in the cell. One guard shed a tear.

"It's not your fault, Zena," the guard said. "Your husband is the traitor. He's on his way."

When the guard left, Zena helped Andre and Sarah sit up. At least they could breathe.

"I'm not so sure about that," Andre said to Zena. "What the guard said about your husband, that is. At the last second, before the force field trapped us and fried my equipment, I got through to your other shoe. The bomb box was not loaded, and if I hadn't stepped in, your detonator would not have gone off either. I don't know what's going on here, but if your husband is, or was from the other side, he betrayed his entire country, everything that he was brought up to believe, to save you."

"On our planet," Sarah got out, "and don't tell anyone, we will explain later, if we have a later, there is a saying: No greater love hath a man than to lose his life for another. From what I know of the insane existence you live down here, you husband signed his own death warrant the second he chose you. And I'm sorry, too. For all of us."

"But please—say nothing," Andre added. "We have friends, whom we love, who are now at mortal risk. If they do what I hope they will do, they will leave us and get as far away as possible. Please help us help the ones we love."

"I don't understand," Zena said, binding what wounds she could, "but I will say nothing."

Ten minutes later, Kavel arrived feet first. Actually, rope first. His first wall slam rendered him totally unconscious. The guard lost points for ending the match prematurely. The loser then dragged Kavel down two flights of stairs by the rope tying his legs together, then, as required, had to clean up the river of blood left all the way.

Zena ripped her shirt into straps to support Andre's arms. He then helped her prop up Kavel, whose face had been spared trauma, but a large scalp laceration had left a six-inch flap hanging backwards.

Zena did what she could with the rest of her clothes.

"Don't worry," she said to Sarah, "it's okay. When we get upstairs, Achtun will begin our humiliation by stripping us naked anyway."

Kavel almost didn't make it. He had returned to their apartment. When guards broke the door down, he was sitting at the kitchen table. He used pots and pans to prop up every picture he had of Zena and the kids.

Kavel was expecting Jarson's secret agent hit squad. He reached for the cyanide tablet. Achtun's men got to it first. Dead bodies are no fun to torture, and so many showed up on both sides that no one ever bothered to investigate, or else.

Kavel never expected to see Zena again, which explained the smile on his face and tears down his cheeks. "Oh, my darling," Zena said, overcome with emotion, hiding her face in his chest, "what hurt most was thinking you no longer loved me. Now I understand. You do care. We are together again."

Kavel told Zena all about stealing babies the night she stole his heart. It was her look, her caring, the risk he knew she was taking to even be there. Something touched him that night. Something that made him believe, for the first time, that life can have meaning, do good for others, and more importantly, change.

"Just so you know," he got out slowly, unable to move his head from her lap, "Jarson's god is not my god, or anyone's god for that matter. His god is himself. Long before he ordered me to kill you, I was on your side. I destroyed all my tracking devices before I left the hospital. If only they had not found me over here."

Andre moaned bitterly. A slow trickle of his blood moved painfully into Sarah's left eye. The thought of dying, feeble and fumbling for dignity, was more than either could stand, but Sarah did attempt a timid half smile. A moment later she asked Zena, leading with her heart, "More than anything right now, we just want to hold each other. Can you help us?"

Zena and Kavel volunteered once a week in the medical clinic. Dislocated shoulders were nothing new. Kavel's turban stopped the flow of blood down his neck. He rose, used two feet and all his might to pull Sarah's left arm out, reposition it, and then let it snap back, a procedure Sarah registered in loudest decibels.

Her face was distressed, but she was able, with help, to sit in the corner with one arm ready to receive Andre, who was next. Her body was a mass of agonizing frailties, but she warmed, knowing Andre was there at her side.

Persistent gloom went on to take them down. Every movement was furtive and ghostly. All was lost. Sobbing agony sent chills to their hearts. Achtun was to be victorious. Still, Zena wanted to know.

"I've never treated arms like that before. You're not really Inu and Ulon, are you?"

Andre, with Sarah's head on his shoulder, sighing, leaned forward with a glimpse of eagerness. "No, we came down to shut down Achtun's blast wall before he destroyed your entire planet and took the rest of the universe with it."

"You're not Delouian? You're not a spy?" Kavel added, confused as well.

"No," Andre replied, raising his voice above the guards sneering outside. "The other half of our team is in Delou. Our plan was to disarm both sides and force peace on your planet."

"Oh, my," Zena exclaimed with controlled panic, "you came to help us, and we did this to you! And my children, our planet, will all be destroyed?"

Sarah didn't let go of Andre's hand when she added, "Yes. We had to do something."

Kavel and Zena moaned in agony.

"Our planet is such a tragedy," Zena said, finally losing her will to go on, leaning against the wall, looking to the door. "In a few minutes, they'll be here. We will die along with the planet. If only it didn't have to be this way."

Following a solemn promise of secrecy, Andre brought Zena and Kavel up to date with the universe. He pointed out that being crude and vulgar was not new—on Earth, many politicians based their entire careers on it. And everyone, all over the galaxy he knew as the Milky Way, once grew up imprinted by traditions of intolerable complexity. Forced culture blocked the light of day. Conformity, imminent and confusing, dimmed hope.

But not for everyone. Sooner or later—more often, later—on every planet, just one person, or perhaps over time a dozen minds, had realized the society they were handed as a child was a fabrication and that what their elders branded as truth was in fact deception.

Sarah joined in. "Institutions are not superior to citizens. Life is not just noise. On our planet, brave minds fought for a world of reason, a world where science was used to lift mankind, not destroy one another after hate rallies."

"Your present," Andre said, sitting up, buoyed by Sarah's faith in goodness, "is not that different from our past. Our history is packed with the imbecility of kings, governors, and religious fundamentalists. They cowed millions for millenniums, making victims with words, doing whatever they saw fit and calling it whatever they could get away with."

"One by one," Sarah said, reaching over in pain to hold Zena's hand, "those who fought the honorable fight died, but their words lived on. Like a president who began life as a general once said: 'Every gun that is made, every warship launched, every rocket fired signifies, in the final sense, a theft from those who hunger and are not fed, those who are cold and not clothed.'"

Andre and Sarah weren't up to getting up, so Zena and Kavel moved closer, the four of them huddled in the corner, between puddles of blood and spider webs.

Kavel added his own wisdom. "Slow-witted minds have always had their way on our planet. If you ask me, we should be ourselves first and then subjects second, and nothing is sacred except the integrity of our own minds. An individual's right to liberty is as inalienable as his right to life. In my mind, we have a duty to disobey immoral laws."

"Which you did, Kavel," Sarah said, dynamically serious. "And those exact words were said by an ancestor of ours who refused to let another continent, called Europe, ruin his life. The fury of misplaced righteousness may be deadly, but all over our galaxy the slaughter of innocents slowly gave way to peaceful times. The right words at the right time can be more powerful than gunpowder."

A tender sternness overcame the group. Their little world, that little corner, became a nation all by itself. It was a small world, it was fleeting, but it placed a stamp on Anelia that would last longer than their lives.

Andre leaned back against the wall. His strength was drained, but not his humor. "You know, Sarah, I keep wanting to say, 'it's a far better thing I do than I have ever done before,' but the only thing I come up with is, 'it's a far more stupid thing than I have ever done before.' I never dreamed double sabotage would take us down."

"It's not your fault," Kavel reassured. "Thousands of good people on both sides have tried and failed, and they—we—know the system from the inside out." Words rushed from his soul, unashamed, proud and defiant, "Damn Achtun! Damn Jarson! They have no right to do this to us or anyone!"

Andre, Sarah, and Zena waited breathlessly for his next explosion. There was none. Kavel knew it was over, and blood loss made him dizzy. He lay down on his back, his spirit broken in every way.

"Tell me more," Zena asked, massaging one throbbing shoulder at a time. "What happened? How did your planet make life better?"

Sarah took over. "Progress began when the majority of the planet realized the 'sacred books' forced down their throats were glorified comic books designed to enable misplaced obedience of one kind or another. Consumerism also fell flat on its face. Dying rich is not worth living meanly, thinking only of yourself, seeing others as a means to your own ends."

Andre smiled. He had just learned Sarah saw life the same way he did. "The whole political thing," he said, "is not that complicated. Citizens get hectic, pushy, and greedy when they worry about the basic substances of life: food, clothing, shelter, access to quality medical care, and a secure retirement. So, no problem. After war was eliminated on our planet, it was easy to do just that, at a minimal but adequate level."

"Our people, and yours too, I imagine," Sarah added, breathless and coughing, "like to compete and achieve goals in life, which is a good thing. So we kept capitalism running to reward hard work, ingenuity, and persistence. Purpose and accomplishment belong to every day. On our planet, you can get by with all the basics you need, or you can put in extra effort and ramp up to a bigger house, private hospital room, in-home services…whatever you want. Which, as it turned out, everyone works hard to do, every day of their lives, with pride."

"But no one makes more than three times as much as another," Andre added. "Every child gets the best education possible, and no one pushes anyone else around."

"And everyone," Sarah pointed out passionately, "has the right to be employed, trusted, loved, and revered."

"Life on Earth, our planet, turned free and beautiful," Andre said, his face whitening with nausea. "But it wasn't easy. You must be bold. All life is an experiment."

"We love and care for one another like socialists," Sarah said lightly, "then get up in the morning and use capitalism to compete all the way to the bank."

When she next looked out the cell door at the ultimate betrayal of one being to another, Sarah lost her composure, and worst of all felt ashamed to have Andre see her totally defeated.

After Sarah's words, Zena and Kavel looked at each other. It was simple. It was smart. It did make sense. Then they also looked around.

Zena left her three patients in the corner, walked to the jail cell door, and looked out. She felt sorry, even for the guards, who squandered their lives away at dull, unimaginative jobs, always fearful, never compassionate. She turned, and with a quick upward glance walked over to Kavel, turned facing him only, then looked to the side at Andre, then Sarah. "This god of Kavel's, and maybe mine. Tell me more."

Kavel looked into Zena's eyes, grabbed both her hands, and smiled dreamy reassurance.

"I want to believe, Kavel. I really do," Zena said.

Sarah, with backbreaking pain, leaned forward to add her hand to theirs. "Once upon a time, planet Earth was packed with pushy 'god people,' every one of them a bully. They put on uniforms with funny hats, like your Jarson, and expected everyone to obey their orders.

"The problem was that the information they embraced and defended was not reliable in any way. They didn't care. They stuck to it for power and self-righteousness, and the more their lives failed them, the more they pounded others to be just like them."

Andre made it to his feet. "Every pretense was absurd. They didn't want to hear it, and scolded, murdered, or legislated their way, fighting others."

"It took thousands of brave souls," Sarah added, "but rationality finally won out, as God knew it would, since he put it there in the first place. It is also in *your* minds, Kavel and Zena. Spirituality is a personal relationship with God, not playing by someone else's rules."

"And that," Andre added, leaning against the wall, "is the free-willed companionship that God is looking for."

Kavel did not object, but asked, "And the purpose of life?"

"The purpose of being is to do good with one's life, and be the best company possible for God," said Sarah.

"So," Zena aggravatingly sputtered, "we're doing it all wrong."

"You got that right," Andre agreed without mercy. "On Anelia, nothing blooms."

"Not one thing. Everything dies. Like us, today—if we're lucky," Kavel said, slapping the floor with barely enough force to raise dust.

"On Earth," Sarah said, "we believe in God, not in names, places, or persons. It took thousands of years and injustice as horrid as yours, but now we know that life is a boundless privilege, one that must never lose kindness and gentleness. When properly lived, life is a festival of fun."

Andre took a deep breath, and interrupted searching for an escape to say, "We guard our thoughts and we guide our thoughts. It's simply a matter of filling days, hour by hour, year by year, with happiness and love."

Andre looked directly at Sarah when he ended. She looked back, for the first time since they were thrown to the dogs, unshaken and unterrified. Her pale-blue eyes blinked rapidly to keep tears, impending overflow, moving on. Andre dabbed one that did.

Zena and Kavel knew that look.

"You two are in love!" Zena said, glowing from the realization, and then just as quickly depressed at the future waiting them all upstairs. She sprawled witless without passion.

The horror of death hides from no one. The misuse, waste, and confusion of the day was an unswerving tragedy. Light was about to fade from a landscape littered with ghosts, dead heroes, and sleeping dreams, which never tired and yet would never wake.

There would be no more waiting for twilight, a moon rising, or a lover to walk the beach. The midnight of hope had arrived. From the shadows, always looking for no more than opportunity, the sadness of life took over, no longer transient, infinitely regretful.

Kavel looked to Zena with clumsy tenderness, and then with gentle chivalry and implacable conviction, he swore with sweetness that Zena was the most cherished blessing a man could hope for.

"When I'm with you, Zena, life takes on a fragrance that blows cares away. I say now what I've said since the day we met…'Thank you, God. Thank you so much; you've given me an angel.' And if today is the day we fly away together, then so be it."

Zena softly sniffled and landed a wet kiss that brought giggles to both.

"And Kavel," she said, "until you showed up, I was a cubicle-nothing, working for scraps. In your arms, I feel like a baby swaddled in its favorite blanket. I feel as comfortable as I did in my mother's lap. I feel soothing intimacy alongside burning passion. The only thing that matters is you and me. We are us, and eternity will always find it so."

"It's true," Sarah said, with admiration and affection. "Love slows us down, makes each second a lifetime, to be thankfully appreciated for what it is, that nothing can ever match."

Zena looked over. Her heart felt the kinship of Andre and Sarah's mind and body blending. Her eyes filled with shadows of pity. "So, you two, whatever your names are. Are you joined? Do you have children?"

"I'm Sarah. This is Andre."

"And no children. Not yet," Andre said, looking longingly to Sarah.

"And now," Sarah said, as the thought ripped her heart open, "not ever."

26

Not to Be

On Explorer Seven, halls that had bustled with joyful anticipation had none. Dread had life by the throat. It was not the dread of a trifling embarrassment, not the dread of disobeying arbitrary social convention, nor a stumbling's shame. It was the dread that pierced deepest, beyond what the mind, with all its power to rehire, force acceptance, or chant, could overcome.

It was the dread of death.

Four of their own had disappeared down the throat of demons. Every day of life looks up from the bottom of a deep grave. No one climbs free. No one knows if this day, or the next second, will bring dirt down, crushing being and smothering breath. Hope's last gasp chokes stuffed with mud, from whence we came.

Every physical body is also its own casket. Caskets weren't on the requisition form that Karen signed when she provisioned Explorer Seven. Failure was not a contingency, defeat never itemized, retreat not to be uttered.

"But we must leave," Hank insisted, with strained tone from his station on the bridge. "The radiation permeating the ship from the crap down there has a frequency almost as short as photon amplitudes. Dudley and Cindy are defunct, our shields useless, and life support failing. We have no choice, commander. We leave or we die."

Karen turned away to hold her hand over her mouth. She knew Hank was right. She had already pushed him further that she should. They both knew the day was lost. Numbers don't lie, like six feet under.

The crew spent the morning in the main hall, watching the ship's telescopic view of Anelia. They were expecting the firewall rings to disappear. They didn't. Instead, they grew more menacing.

Karen's walk back to the crew was slow. Several times, her wavering feet stopped short. The pain in her heart seared straight through. Her will turned from "Fight on!" to "What's the use?"

"Perhaps it's time to let go," she said to herself. "The boys, the crew, life itself…it must end someday. Youth is always in a hurry, can't wait to get somewhere. Age looks back and says, 'I wish it had lasted longer.' Our lasting wasn't long enough, but the end result is just the same."

Karen knew better than to believe herself at times like that, but the knife was too sharp, the pain too dear, the loss unimaginable. God's greatest gift yanked away by barbs of stupidity was more than she could handle. She fell against the wall, then to the floor in a heap. She knew she must keep moving. She crawled on all fours to the door, and then stood holding the latch. "Stand against the wind," she finally got out, standing up. "When the ship goes down, stand against the wind."

Another quote gave her the strength to open the door: "Do not go quietly into that dark night. Wail against the night. Never let losing make us less of what we are, and will always be."

"For the good of others," was the last thing Michael had said to her in private. His plea did the trick. She squared her shoulders and growled determination before setting her face to make the announcement on stage.

"Thanks for being here, everyone. The screen went blank because we needed to get farther away from the mayhem below. We're out of telescopic range. And the rumors are true. Achtun's buildup continues, communication with Brad and Michael has not been re-established, and we must assume Andre and Sarah also failed to complete their mission, and they may have died landing.

"Please return to your stations. Please share any ideas with us, no matter how bizarre you suspect they are. For now, we fly on a prayer."

Janie had one drab army outfit with stitched shoulder bars. She hoped looking like a soldier would make her feel like one. It didn't. She settled into the chair next to Karen's in the neuro lab. Karen's head was resting on her folded arms, flat on the desk in front of the communications array.

"Still nothing?" Janie asked, doing her best to hide her despair.

"Not a squeak. Hank is right. If we call down, we might give them away. By God, I hope they found a hole in the ground."

"Which won't do them any good when Achtun sets the planet on fire at noon. Karen, we've got to do something!"

"Four aces beats four kings. Four dead beats two hundred and forty. That's what Hank says."

Janie had nothing to say. She also placed her head on the desk and held her breath, hoping it was a bad dream.

Karen faced Janie's collapse. "Hank says we should evacuate the sector before the planet blows."

"And we all know that might not do us any good," Janie replied, with a depth of despair Karen had never seen before.

"Perhaps, but it will give the crew hope."

"For twenty minutes," Janie said cynically.

"Twenty minutes is a long time to spend with a loaded gun in your face."

Janie slumped her shoulders, dropped her head, and monotoned, "Yes, you're right. Explorer Seven is a proud lady. She deserves a flying send-off."

Zena blocked the way when the guards entered with prod sticks, one for her, one for Andre, one for Sarah, and two for Kavel. Zena presented a united front by supporting Sarah with one shoulder, Andre the other, and leading Kavel out by the hand. The guards couldn't electroshock anyone without Zena getting it too.

"Achtun is waiting," yelled the front guard. "Get your asses out of here!"

"Please let us pass. You've done enough. We have a long week ahead of us."

Zena had a stare that said she knew the wrong that they were doing. They let them pass, though not a hand was offered when the four fell to the floor twice on the way the elevator.

Achtun was ready all right, dripping spit and shaking his fist at Jarson on the other side of the screen.

And Jarson? Lying on the floor in front of a line of his bishops, all prostrated, every one lamenting the past, self-flagellating, and whimpering for mercy. Those who had ordered the death of billions and ruined the lives of those left living found their own deaths curiously unacceptable.

Not one minister prayed to God. They had lost genuine faith long ago. Jarson, his wealth, his laws, his punishments, were all that mattered to them.

"I was just obeying orders," was actually heard from one.

"I was just doing what everyone told me I was supposed to do where I grew up. They said they were proud of me."

Those who live lies, die a lie.

It took three blows to render Brad unconscious. It took ten baseball bat clubbings and one skull fracture to put Michael's lights out. Both ended up suspended from tendon-tearing straps in a depravation chamber. Jarson liked his victims to have nothing else to concentrate on except pain.

Both slowly regained consciousness in adjoining cells. The guards hadn't bothered to scan auricular space. Both retained communication potential.

"Message center," Michael got out, crackling chest bones, "low frequency activation. Contact Brad."

"I read you Michael, although I haven't the slightest idea where I am, unless there is a hell."

"Jarson's hell, and also his favorite amusement park."

Karen had turned up the sensitivity in the neuro lab. "Michael! Is that you? You're alive!"

"For now. What are you still doing within communication range? And why are you risking the ship opening a channel?"

Janie jumped in before Karen could answer. "Brad, are you there too?"

"Yes, kind of."

"I love you, Brad. You can't leave me. I won't let you."

"Enough," Michael said, with all the force he could grunt. "Hit the road. Get out of here at once. It's the only way to save the ship."

"That's a maybe, and we're not interested," said Janie.

"Well then, here is a definite. Brad and I will terminate transmission and vocally order auricular self-destruct in ten seconds if you don't agree. It's 'hasta la vista, baby' one way or another. You have five more seconds."

"Okay, you win, Michael," Karen said. "But only if you and I, and Brad and Janie, get five more minutes to say goodbye."

"Which I want more than anything, Karen. In fact, I just got up the nerve to ask you back to my place in St. Martins."

"Oh, my darling, there is no place in the universe that I would rather be, and no one I will ever want to be there with more than you. This is all my fault. If I hadn't left you, we would be there right now."

It was a harsh, stiff, one-sided skirmish. Achtun, nostrils flared, red nosed and lewdly evil; Jarson, two-faced, beaten to tears, panicked to death—just the way Achtun planned it.

"Jarson, you sniffling creep, your true colors finally come out. You failed to kill me and aren't brave enough to except the consequences. So, you brainless puffball, where's your god now? You've ruined the life of half this planet, telling them that your god will come to their rescue. Did you forget to contact him? Or is he not taking your calls?"

From the other side of the screen, Jarson muttered imperceptibly, "Made up a lot...people need rules...you're just as..."

From the other side of Achtun's door, the guards made a request as brazen as it was dastardly. They knew Achtun showed no mercy to those who did. They asked the as yet unscathed Zena if they could lift them, one at a time, and throw them facedown on the floor in front of Achtun, between the screen and each of the four torture bowls that were waiting for them. With mercy they didn't deserve, Zena agreed.

Achtun laughed mockingly when each splattered blood hitting the floor. He was bold, fierce, and combative. He held all the aces. With venomous swagger he paced back and forth. Jarson twitched fear every step. Then Achtun yelled at the four on the floor.

"So, you tried to kill me, did you? It's time to pay the price."

Achtun next turned violently to Jarson. "And you, you despised and conceited coward! You put them up to it!"

Jarson squirmed helplessly on the floor, a spineless jellyfish. "Take everything, Achtun. My entire country of amiable sheep can all be yours. I hereby dub you Your Eminence Achtun, leader of all that is holy. Take it. Just let me go. Please, I'll do anything."

"There is only one thing I want you to do...flame up and blow away."

Andre did what he could. "Grand Accounter! You must listen! The readings we took at the front found more, you're going to destroy the entire..."

The closest guard punished Andre for his interruption. The electric probe he plunged into Andre's back left him seizing, foaming at the mouth, and wetting his pants both ways. Achtun laughed silently as he contorted his lips into a grisly smirk.

"That's enough," Achtun barked. "I want him to see Delou destroyed before you strap them in the bowls."

"Two minutes, your eminence. In two minutes, everything on the other side of the wall will go up in flames. Victory is ours."

For Karen and Michael, the clock had run out.

"You know, Karen, after you left me, I tried but I couldn't drag myself back to that overlook you and I had watched the sunset from. I pretended to be happy, partied a week later, but it was all an act. How I wish we could switch places to be there again."

"Switch places! That's it! Michael, I've got to go."

"What?"

"Janie, run with me to the back of the lab. Cross reference scans nine and twelve that we analyzed yesterday from old readings and pull up every historical archive we have from Earth."

"What?"

"Hank, this is Karen. Do you trust me?"

"Implicitly."

"Fire up the ship. We're going back. And you will have one minute to get us there."

"What?"

"You heard me."

"All right, now calm down, Karen. It will take every reserve we have to do that. We will not be able to hold position. If Achtun's missile barrage doesn't hit us in ten seconds, the ship will plummet to pieces five minutes later."

"My call, my order, do it!"

"Roger that, commander. Will be ready in thirty seconds. Do you want me to make the announcement?"

"Please. I'm busy."

"Attention all hands. Suit up in crash rooms and prepare for a crash landing. We are going back. I repeat. We are going in."

Karen heard the yells of approval as she ran to join Janie at the back of the lab.

"Karen, you're right. They are identical."

"Then it might work. And we will stir the mix. Add thoughts of Emerson, Jefferson, Buddha, Mohammed, Jesus Christ, Gandhi, and John Lennon."

"And Alfred E. Newman."

"Right on. *E-pluribus-unum…fiat lux…*life need not always be serious."

Karen fixed her eyes on her screen, held both hands above her keyboard, and said, "Our program is loaded, Hank. Let's get a move on."

"Roger that, commander. The bridge is manned. We fire in three… two…one…"

"Thirty seconds, your greatness."

Achtun stood a foot from the screen. Jarson managed to pick himself off the floor and was standing on his side, just as close.

"Killing us won't make you a better person, Achtun. You will go down in history as the most imbalanced mass murderer who ever lived. And remember, I surrendered. You don't have to do this."

"First of all, you little weasel, if I let you live, in twenty-four hours, you'll try to kill me again. I'm no fool. And secondly, history will be mine to write. You will be despised. I get statues."

The entire military squad moved closer to the screen for the final act. Zena, Kavel, Sarah, and Andre, just coming to with a foot on his head, looked up.

"Ten seconds, sir."

Achtun raised his right arm.

"Fire when I drop my arm."

"What's the holdup, Hank? Take us down now!"

Hank's scrounging for energy did the trick, with not a joule to spare. The ship came to an abrupt stop precisely where Karen needed it, above Achtun's central command. The good news was that not a single general was manning his station. Their blip went undetected.

"Karen, I can give you ten level seconds before gravity starts us down for a crash. Whatever you got up your sleeve, now is the time."

Karen and Janie furiously tapped program after program searching frequencies that would work.

A frightening calm overcame Achtun, who darted his eyes at sniffling Jarson like a lion about to gulp down a mouse.

"We're fully armed, Achtun. On your command."

"Fire when I drop my arm. I'm going to enjoy this moment for five more seconds."

Jarson didn't move, just closed his eyes. There was nothing else he could do to get back at Achtun.

Then—Achtun and Jarson leapt back six inches, as if a mysterious wind blew them apart. Jarson opened his eyes. Achtun lifted his brow. Both men returned to the screen, closer than ever. Then both men said, together in private conference, which took generals standing by and bishops on the floor out of hearing:

"What did you do?" Jarson asked.

"What's going on?" Achtun replied, still holding his hand up, general Zendal waiting with his thumb on the button.

Achtun looked up and down at the image of robed Jarson in front of him.

"Is that you, Achtun?"

"Yes…" said the robed leader of Delou. "Is that you, Jarson?"

"Yes—so how can I be you and you be me?"

"I don't know," said Jarson, who was actually Achtun looking at his own body, with an arm up in the air, that would kill him if it came down.

"But don't move! For God's sake, don't drop your arm!"

"If I do, I will destroy my entire country."

"Not only am I in your body. But I'm not me. I'm you and me. I have memories of you going fishing with your dad as a kid. You loved that."

"I did until your stepfather killed him. And I remember what a fuss your dad made on your birthday. I never got a three-layer cake for my birthday."

"Until your ambush assassinated him."

"There's more. Who the hell is Thomas Jefferson? And why do I care what Sigmund Freud would say?"

"And who is Sigmund Freud? And what? Me worry?"

"Me neither! Okay…here's the deal…be cool…move slowly… freeze…and turn…with your arm up…keep thinking 'arm up, arm up.'"

"And we both know just what we have to say. Right?"

"Of course, we've both been reprogrammed. And you know, I could just as easily be the twin that ended up a Kawachen, and you could be Delouian. Any one of us could have been each other."

"And I'm suddenly aware that all over the universe the same observation applies."

"Do you think God might judge us as a race, not as individuals? After all, we are what we were are made to be, and what we don't do about it."

"Anelia has a long way to go. But we will make God proud."

With arm held high, Achtun——actually Jarson—turned to make the first announcement.

"Generals, stand down immediately. We have reached a cease-fire."

From the other side, the rest of the plan filled in. Jarson—actually Achtun—turned to his bishops, who were also his military advisors and said, "We will begin bilateral disarmament immediately. Every ten seconds reduce nuclear power plant operations by twenty percent."

"Yes," agreed Achtun, actually Jarson, "there is enough stored energy on this planet to keep us running for years. After that we will go solar, whatever that is."

"I've got an idea," the robed Jarson look-alike said in private. "You call me AJ, meaning 'once Achtun, now Jarson,' and I'll call you JA, meaning 'once Jarson, now Achtun.' It will be our secret."

"Splendid, buddy. And are you busy this afternoon?"

"I can free up my schedule. What did you have in mind?"

"My dad's fishing pole, and your dad's fishing hole."

"And tomorrow we will switch."

"Yes, absolutely. And I have a swell cabin in the mountains. You can't beat the view, and the trout are always biting.

"And you know what," JA said with a smile, "now that we're good guys, we shouldn't have any trouble getting dates. There's an old dance barn in the valley. It will be just like it was thousands of years ago."

"That's right. And we didn't screw up this planet. We inherited it that way. So what, we worry?"

"Yes, my brother! We will party hardy!"

"Let's stay up here and work out a few more details in private as they drop the wall."

Halfway through the private enclave, AJ signaled the release of Andre, Sarah, Kavel, and Zena. All four were brought front and center, facing JA and AJ, who moved to the side so it appeared as if they were standing next to one another.

Both instructed their team to broadcast live around the globe, "Attention everyone on both sides of Anelia. After careful and miraculous consideration, Jarson and I..."

"And Achtun and I..." was heard from the other side of the screen.

"...have decided to call a cease-fire."

Achtun's generals and Jarson's bishops dropped their jaws.

"We are making some changes," Achtun said. "And if anyone objects or obstructs, let us remind you all that the two of us are the only ones who know the codes that activate the two robot police forces that we mothballed years ago. Our planet is taking a new course. We will be obeyed."

"Yes, sir. Of course, sir. Whatever you say, sir."

"To begin with, all army personnel will be retrained. We need carpenters, electricians, and plumbers to build homes for every family on the planet. Children on both sides of the border will be returned to their parents at once. We also need teachers for grammar schools and universities of higher education."

"And," said AJ from the other side, "during the next four years, we will transition each county into a democracy. At the end of four years of cultural exchange, the entire planet will be combined into a single peaceful nation. We don't know what to call it. We can vote on that later."

"We do have an idea about our flag. What's on the flag will come from artists from both sides, but the flag will be pure white, signifying peace and that all you need is love."

Achtun, actually Jarson, and Jarson, actually Achtun, raised both hands high.

"Final announcement," JA said. "Jarson and I will stay around in an advisory capacity, and like I said, if you get in the way, you will regret it. But we will appoint a temporary president for both countries until the global election in four years, when both temporary leaders will be able to run for office themselves, for a maximum of eight years per leader."

Jarson, actually Achtun, said, from the other side of the screen, "The new president of Kawachensa, with full executive privileges, will be...Zena!"

Achtun, actually Jarson, from the stage, then said, "The new president of Delou, with executive privileges as well as the responsibility to reorganize spirituality as he sees fit, will be...Kavel!"

The room, the building, the planet—were stunned silent.

"We're serious. Get ready, Anelia. We are not here to live in hate and fear. Love one another as we love the one true God."

That did it. It was New Year's Eve on every corner.

"Discontinue broadcast," JA and AJ said in rapid repetition.

"We have one final announcement," JA said on stage, as he spanned his county governors.

"That also applies to all of us," AJ said on the screen, as he turned to address the parish leaders of Delou.

Achtun and Jarson lifted their heads, then, in unison, fanning welcoming arms, said with smiles to cure every ill, "We're all invited to Janie's Cleopatra party on Saturday night!